the perfect mistress

(a jessie hunt psychological suspense—book 15)

blake pierce

Blake Pierce

Blake Pierce is the USA Today bestselling author of the RILEY PAGE mystery series, which includes seventeen books. Blake Pierce is also the author of the MACKENZIE WHITE mystery series, comprising fourteen books; of the AVERY BLACK mystery series, comprising six books; of the KERI LOCKE mystery series, comprising five books; of the MAKING OF RILEY PAIGE mystery series, comprising six books; of the KATE WISE mystery series, comprising seven books; of the CHLOE FINE psychological suspense mystery, comprising six books; of the JESSE HUNT psychological suspense thriller series, comprising nineteen books; of the AU PAIR psychological suspense thriller series, comprising three books; of the ZOE PRIME mystery series, comprising six books; of the ADELE SHARP mystery series, comprising thirteen books, of the EUROPEAN VOYAGE cozy mystery series, comprising six books (and counting); of the new LAURA FROST FBI suspense thriller, comprising four books (and counting); of the new ELLA DARK FBI suspense thriller, comprising six books (and counting); of the A YEAR IN EUROPE cozy mystery series, comprising nine books, of the AVA GOLD mystery series, comprising three books (and counting); and of the RACHEL GIFT mystery series, comprising three books (and counting).

An avid reader and lifelong fan of the mystery and thriller genres, Blake loves to hear from you, so please feel free to visit www.blakepierceauthor.com to learn more and stay in touch.

DEATH (AND APPLE STRUDEL) (Book #2)
CRIME (AND LAGER) (Book #3)
MISFORTUNE (AND GOUDA) (Book #4)
CALAMITY (AND A DANISH) (Book #5)
MAYHEM (AND HERRING) (Book #6)

ADELE SHARP MYSTERY SERIES
LEFT TO DIE (Book #1)
LEFT TO RUN (Book #2)
LEFT TO HIDE (Book #3)
LEFT TO KILL (Book #4)
LEFT TO MURDER (Book #5)
LEFT TO ENVY (Book #6)
LEFT TO LAPSE (Book #7)
LEFT TO VANISH (Book #8)
LEFT TO HUNT (Book #9)
LEFT TO FEAR (Book #10)
LEFT TO PREY (Book #11)
LEFT TO LURE (Book #12)
LEFT TO CRAVE (Book #13)

THE AU PAIR SERIES
ALMOST GONE (Book#1)
ALMOST LOST (Book #2)
ALMOST DEAD (Book #3)

ZOE PRIME MYSTERY SERIES
FACE OF DEATH (Book#1)
FACE OF MURDER (Book #2)
FACE OF FEAR (Book #3)
FACE OF MADNESS (Book #4)
FACE OF FURY (Book #5)
FACE OF DARKNESS (Book #6)

A JESSIE HUNT PSYCHOLOGICAL SUSPENSE SERIES
THE PERFECT WIFE (Book #1)
THE PERFECT BLOCK (Book #2)
THE PERFECT HOUSE (Book #3)
THE PERFECT SMILE (Book #4)
THE PERFECT LIE (Book #5)
THE PERFECT LOOK (Book #6)

KERI LOCKE MYSTERY SERIES
A TRACE OF DEATH (Book #1)
A TRACE OF MURDER (Book #2)
A TRACE OF VICE (Book #3)
A TRACE OF CRIME (Book #4)
A TRACE OF HOPE (Book #5)

PROLOGUE

The snow crunched beneath her feet.

In the bright moonlight, Sarah Ripley could clearly see the exact spot where the snow gave way to the slicker, far more dangerous ice at the edge of the road. She made sure to steer clear of it as she walked up the last stretch of the hill to the cabin.

She could have taken a rideshare home. Even in the small mountain town of Wildpines, there was always a driver available. In fact, that's how she'd gotten to the bar earlier in the evening.

But her face was flushed and she felt warm from the drinks and the heat of the crowd at the Wild Things bar. The walk would cool her off and clear her head. It needed clearing and even a night out with the girls hadn't helped.

She glanced at her phone. It was 9:41p.m. That was more than enough time to get back before her visitor arrived at ten. Even though this was hardly new to her, Sarah's stomach was a bubbling cauldron of nervousness and anticipation.

She had almost crested the hill. The top of the cabin, or as her friends called it, Chalet Ripley, was in sight. Smoke billowed from the fireplace, obscuring the moon slightly and giving the night a ghostly vibe.

Her husband had warned her repeatedly not to leave the fireplace roaring when there was no one in the house. But she liked how toasty it made the place when she returned. Besides, he barely came up here anymore so he wasn't in a position to dictate how things should operate. By contrast, Sarah came up here at least once a month, more often in the winter. While Dwayne considered the Wildpines cabin an investment, to Sarah it was much more: a respite from the noise and crowds of L.A.

There was plenty of time for the Beverly Hills soirees, elaborate beachfront parties, and dinners at the restaurants of James Beard Award winners. This place offered something far more valuable: solitude.

And if things went as planned, it would also be the second location of her store, SEE, which specialized in funky gifts and collectibles. The

1

small town was popular with hipster tourists and she was pretty sure her wares would be catnip to them.

When she finally got to the top of the hill, she stopped and allowed herself a moment to catch her breath. Bending over and resting her hands on her knees, she watched as her exhalations rose into the air like the smoke from her chimney. The walk had been close to a mile long—almost all uphill—and after a period where she'd felt pleasantly cool, she was warm again despite the 30 degree temperature.

She allowed herself a moment to take in the beauty of her surroundings. The town was encircled by multiple peaks. The combination of snow and intermittent exposed rock made the mountains gleam like diamonds in the night sky.

She carefully made her way up the wooden steps to the front door. They too could get icy, which her left hip had learned the hard way a few years ago. She dug her key out and opened the door. Immediately, she was hit with a wave of warm air and hurried to take off her coat and beanie before she got sweaty. She hung them on the rack and locked the door behind her. The house was quiet.

She was about to get a glass of water to soothe her cold-parched throat when her phone buzzed. She looked down to see an alert. She immediately went to the affiliated site and logged in, where she found a message from the person she'd hurried back to meet. It read: *Have to cancel. Can't get away. Sorry for being so last second. Another time.*

Sarah sighed. She was disappointed, as she'd been looking forward to this for days. But it was hardly the first time it had happened and it wouldn't be the last. Glancing in the foyer mirror, she briefly wondered if the cancellation was related to her. Had her appeal faded? She didn't think so.

She studied her features. Maybe she wasn't as fresh-faced at thirty-four as she'd been at twenty-five, but she thought that she still looked good. Her workouts had paid off to the point where she could still wear those twenty-five-year-old's clothes. Her skin still had a golden glow. Her dark hair framed her face nicely. There was nothing obviously objectionable about her appearance. The cancellation had to be on his end.

She was just starting toward the kitchen again for the water when she heard a noise outside. It sounded like a cry for help. Checking the peephole, she saw what looked like a smallish woman sitting on her butt at the edge of where the driveway met the road.

Sarah could guess what had happened. The woman was likely doing the same thing: either walking to or from town, when she lost her balance. Water tended to pool in the crevices between the road and driveway. When frozen over, those spots were especially slippery. It was easy for a person's foot to skid, sending them toppling back onto their tailbone.

Sarah opened the door and rushed out, leaving her jacket behind. She was happy to help out a neighbor in a pinch but she didn't intend to be outside long enough to bundle up for an extended conversation.

"You okay?" she called out.

The woman nodded, even as she rubbed her backside. Her long hair had fallen in her face.

"I slipped and landed kind of hard," she admitted. "I think I'm good but I could use a hand up."

The request made her a little uneasy. Approaching a stranger at night while alone was something she'd never do back in L.A. But this was a small town and word traveled fast. If she got a reputation as a bad neighbor, that would be hard to change. So despite some mild apprehension, she headed over, making sure to step in her own footprints so as to avoid the woman's fate and fall herself. When she got close enough not to have to yell, she asked, "Do you think you're all right to walk or should I call you a car?"

"I'll know more once I'm upright," the woman said sheepishly, extending her left hand.

Sarah offered hers. The woman squared her feet below her, grabbed Sarah's hand and tugged hard, lifting herself up. As she did, Sarah saw the woman's right arm appear from behind her back and rise above her head. Something metal gleamed in the moonlight. It took a second to process that it was a butcher knife.

She tried to let go of the woman's hand but the grip tightened. Before she could do anything else, she felt a deep, icy pain in her chest. She looked down and saw the knife had embedded in her chest all the way to the heel. Suddenly it was ripped out and the pain turned to agony. Blood began pouring out of her. She glimpsed steam leaking from the gaping hole in her chest.

Weird that I would notice a detail like that at a time like this.

She looked up and saw that the woman was raising the knife again. Staring at her face, she realized that she actually knew this person. But there was no time to process the knowledge before the knife slashed through her flesh again, this time at the neck.

3

The excruciating anguish mixed with weakness as she fell back into the heavy snow, and watched her own blood shoot into the air. She knew she should feel cold but she didn't. Instead she felt helplessness, softened slightly by the awareness that everything was getting soft and fuzzy.

And then not even that.

CHAPTER ONE

Jessie was already awake when she heard the floorboard creak.

Trying not to overreact, she fought the urge to reach for the handgun in the bedside table drawer.

Houses creak. This is normal.

She rolled over in bed and looked at Ryan, who was still fast asleep. He'd had a rough night, waking up with a jolt from a nightmare he described right afterward as him being suffocated with a pillow while underwater. He'd had many of those since last summer, when he was stabbed in the chest and spent weeks in a coma.

She didn't want to wake him over what was probably nothing, so she rolled out of bed, using the cracks of dim, pre-dawn light coming through the blinds as her guide to find her robe. She put it on while willing herself not to look at the drawer where the gun was calling out to her. She tiptoed to the bedroom door, unlocked it and poked her head out.

She could hear two voices speaking quietly from the end of the hall, where it opened up into the living room. After closing the door behind her, she shuffled quietly past the adjoining bedroom where her sister, Hannah, was sleeping. Her instinct was to hug the wall as she moved forward but she instructed herself not to do it, to just walk normally.

When she reached the living room threshold, she leaned forward, not quite furtively but not exactly naturally either. In the living room were two large men facing away from her, both armed. One of them seemed to sense a presence behind him and, with his hand resting on his holster, turned around.

"Good morning, Ms. Hunt," he said mildly, dropping his hand.

"Hi Sam. What's the word?"

"Nothing new to report," U.S. Marshal Samuel Mason replied casually. With his broad shoulders and meaty hands, he looked like a former college linebacker, which he was. "I wish there was."

"Me too," she sighed, before adding playfully, "aren't you supposed to be calling me Jennifer Barnes, by the way?"

"I thought we'd let you go with your real name inside the safe house. But out there, we'll stick to the fake identities."

"Out there? Is there still a world outside this house?" she asked wryly, trying to keep her voice from tipping into bitterness.

"Yes, Ms. Hunt, I assure you there is," Marshal Mason replied, not commenting on her tone. "Tommy made some coffee if you're interested."

"I am," Jessie said, nodding at Marshal Tom Anderson, who looked a lot like his partner, just in a slightly smaller package. "Let me just wash up and I'll be back out."

She headed back down the hall to the bedroom and delicately opened the door. Ryan was still sleeping. She silently moved to the bathroom and closed the door, where she finally allowed herself a deep sigh.

It had been a week since they'd been rushed to this safe house; a week since an elderly serial killer called the Night Hunter, who was playing a deadly game of cat and mouse with her, had insinuated his way into her home and almost poisoned her little sister and boyfriend while she was right outside.

Normally there would have been more red tape in getting protection. But Jessie had been through this whole protective custody routine once before when her own serial killer birth father was hunting her, so she had connections that expedited the process.

What kind of life do I lead where I have U.S. Marshal connections because I've had to go into hiding previously?

However messed up it was, one call to Patrick "Murph" Murphy, who had been the lead marshal on her protective detail the last time around, was all it took. Now a supervisor, he went straight into action, giving them a half hour to collect some clothes and personal items.

In fact, it was only twenty minutes after he hung up that a black SUV rolled up to their house that night. Three marshals escorted Jessie, Ryan, and Hannah into the vehicle and whisked them away, cutting through the Hollywood Hills to a nondescript ranch house in Sherman Oaks.

That was last Tuesday. The good news was that in the week since then, the Night Hunter hadn't killed anyone else, at least no one that could obviously be connected to his prior murders. In addition, they felt fairly safe where they were.

No one outside the Marshals Service knew where they were. All three of their phones had been replaced, at least temporarily and they had to get formal permission before giving their new numbers out to anyone. The list of approved people was small.

6

Captain Roy Decker, Ryan's boss at LAPD Central Station, took being in the dark in stride. He'd been through this before as well. But explaining the situation to the dean at UCLA, where Jessie taught a seminar in forensic profiling, was a little trickier. Hannah's high school was less of a hassle. They were so used to her leaving school for extended stretches that they didn't even ask why this time.

Beyond that, the marshals were a constant presence. There were always two inside the house and usually between two and four outside. The house was gated and set back from the street with unobstructed sight lines for fifty yards in every direction. The closest neighboring house was a football field away.

Despite the comprehensive protection regime, there were major downsides too. The Night Hunter may not have struck in a week, but he hadn't been caught either. Despite being elderly and scurrying out of her home only moments before a team of cops arrived, he'd somehow managed to escape their dragnet. Jessie knew that if they hadn't captured him in that first hour, the chances of finding him now, a week later, were remote.

This was a man who, after wreaking bloody havoc along the eastern seaboard for much of the 1980s and 1990s, had gone into hiding for the two decades since. In fact, many people assumed he'd died. But he hadn't. Instead, he'd learned how to hide in the shadows and bide his time. The question was, how long could Jessie, Ryan, and Hannah put their lives on hold, living cloistered, away from the world, while he was out there waiting?

They'd already missed the funeral of Delia Morris, the retired neighbor the Night Hunter had murdered and stolen the identity of to infiltrate their home. Nor could they attend the funeral of Detective Alan Trembley, who had been killed by the Night Hunter when he inadvertently came across him at the hostel where the killer had been staying.

Jamil Winslow, the unit's crack researcher had FaceTimed Trembley's funeral for them, but it wasn't the same as being there. The cemetery looked serene, with rolling hills, large overhanging trees, and not far from Trembley's gravesite, memorial benches surrounded by rose bushes. Still, there was something hollow about watching it on a screen, even with a massive contingent of LAPD there, all in their dress uniforms.

They listened to Captain Decker's words as he described how Trembley had started as a goofy rookie detective apt to potentially

7

contaminate a crime scene. But he went on to say that though the guy remained goofy, his acumen improved and his instincts sharpened to the point where he became an invaluable asset to the team. Beyond that, his good nature and unflagging enthusiasm for the job and the people he worked with often made the most difficult days more manageable.

Jessie had dabbed quietly at her eyes during the ceremony, trying to come to terms with the loss of yet another person in her life, used as a pawn by someone out to hurt her. Ryan had sat stone-faced beside her. He may have seemed unemotional but she knew he was taking Trembley's death even harder than she was.

She felt guilty because the Night Hunter was destroying others to get to her. But Ryan felt a different burden. He'd told her how he believed Trembley would still be alive if he had been physically able to go into that hostel with his young partner. He'd also confessed how he'd frozen when the Night Hunter emerged from the hostel, unable to grab his gun and fire at the man before he disappeared into the Santa Monica crowd. She knew the shame was eating at him but she didn't know how to help.

Less emotional than the culpability they both felt, but equally important, was the growing realization that working the investigation from a safe house wasn't practical. They couldn't go out in the field. They couldn't access evidence in person. They couldn't interview witnesses face to face to get a sense of what they might be hiding. It wasn't sustainable. And it was wearing on her.

Jessie turned on the bathroom light and stared at herself in the mirror. Part of it was just waking up, but she thought she looked drab. Her shoulder length brown hair was limp. Her green eyes looked dull. Her athletic five-foot-ten inch frame seemed somehow slouchy. Though she was just thirty, on this morning she thought she looked a half decade older.

Ryan seemed to be doing better than she was. Maybe it was that he'd spent much of the last few months home-bound, recovering from his injuries and rehabbing. He was used to casual confinement. In fact he seemed to be embracing it, using every free moment to do extra working out on top of his physical therapy exercises.

Jessie suspected it was primarily to get rid of his nervous energy, but it was working. Though he still held his cane as a security blanket, he mostly walked without it. Admittedly, it was more shuffling than normal walking, but it was a vast improvement from where he'd been just a few weeks earlier.

Hannah seemed to be doing okay too, but Jessie had lingering doubts. In the middle of the Night Hunter madness, she'd learned that her younger half-sister, Hannah Dorsey, had been secretly engaging in massively risky behavior. In the last year, she'd confronted a drug dealer, used herself as bait to bust up a sexual slavery ring, and broken into the home of a convicted pedophile to see if he had kidnapped a young girl.

On the surface it might have seemed like she was out for some kind of righteous justice on behalf of victims. But it eventually became clear that her actions were more about trying to get some kind of adrenaline high from putting herself in harm's way.

It was only after Jessie's best friend, Kat, admitted to her that she was aware of the behavior and had been hiding it from her that the full truth came out. Hannah had subsequently taken the initiative and resumed sessions with her therapist, Dr. Janice Lemmon. In fact, they'd had video sessions every weekday since going into hiding. But Jessie still sensed that her sister's grip on the situation was tenuous.

It was understandable. After all, this was a girl whose adoptive parents had been murdered before her eyes by her birth father, a serial killer who also happened to be Jessie's biological father. She'd also been kidnapped by another serial killer, an acolyte of their shared father, who hoped to seduce her into becoming a killer herself. It was a lot for anyone to handle, even if they didn't already have underlying emotional issues. Now she couldn't go to school, couldn't see friends, couldn't hang out in her favorite chair at the local coffeehouse.

Add that to the normal concerns facing a seventeen-year-old girl planning to graduate from high school in a few months—what she would want to do next year, if she'd ever meet a guy who wouldn't be scared to take her on a date—and it was no wonder she seemed a little shaky.

It also explained why she was on a cooking frenzy. Hannah was already the cuisine master in the family, usually making dinner, often elaborate ones. But now she'd taken it to the next level, giving the marshals a daily list of required ingredients for the full menus she'd planned out. Jessie knew she was considering going to culinary school instead of college but recently it seemed like she was taking an independent study course right here in the safe house.

9

A groan from the bedroom told her Ryan was awake. She finished brushing her teeth and opened the bathroom door to find him easing himself upright at the edge of the bed. Tufts of his short black hair stuck up randomly, a result of bed head. She couldn't see his kind, brown eyes but she pictured them blinking slowly as he took in the morning. He was shirtless and she noted that he'd regained some of the muscle tone he'd lost after the stabbing and coma.

She doubted that Detective Ryan Hernandez would ever get back to the chiseled six-foot, 200-pound specimen he'd once been, but it wasn't for a lack of effort. He looked so much healthier than last summer. For a few weeks back then he'd been comatose and unresponsive, at death's door. All of that was a result of her ex-husband Kyle Voss's elaborate plan to destroy Jessie's reputation before killing everyone dear to her. It had almost worked.

In the end, he'd murdered her friend and profiling mentor, Garland Moses, nearly killed Ryan, and tried to do the same to Jessie and Hannah. The man sitting on the bed in front of her now was unrecognizable from the weakened patient lying in a hospital with tubes sticking out of him only six months ago.

"Hey there, sleepyhead," she said, sidling up next to him.

"Morning," he replied, giving her a kiss on the cheek to spare her his morning breath, "how long have you been up?"

"Not that long. I checked in with the marshals. There's coffee brewing."

"Excellent," he said, stretching his arms above his head, "although I feel bad that those highly skilled professionals have been reduced to prepping our morning joe."

"I think they made it for themselves and just brewed some extra for us," she assured him. "Don't worry. They still consider their primary gig keeping bad guys away."

He kissed her again for no obvious reason. She loved that he didn't seem to need one.

"Is Hannah up?" he asked. "I've come to expect a massive morning spread."

"She wasn't out there earlier but who knows what's happened in the few minutes since. I wouldn't be surprised if she's whipped up a frittata in the interim."

As if on cue, there was knock on the door.

"Who is it?" Jessie asked.

"Hannah. Can I come in for a sec?"

Jessie looked over at Ryan, who nodded.

"Sure," she replied.

Her younger sister poked her head in. It was clear that she'd been up for a while. Her sandy blonde hair was brushed and styled. Her green eyes, the same as Jessie's, gleamed with energy. She was just an inch shorter than her big sister but right now she looked positively statuesque in comparison.

"Morning," she said sunnily. "I was checking to see if you guys were feeling more like crêpes or Belgian waffles this morning."

"Wow, "Ryan said. "Both sound great."

"Yeah," Jessie agreed. "I'm happy with either."

"Let's do crêpes then," Hannah said. "I've been meaning to experiment with a new, savory version. You can be my guinea pigs."

She was gone as quickly as she'd come in, leaving the two of them alone and suddenly hungry. Ryan pushed himself up from the bed, notably leaving his cane untouched. It was a good sign. Despite the self-doubt he'd felt of late, he was pushing to get stronger. Neither of them needed to say why out loud.

He moved slowly to the bathroom as Jessie tried to decide which pair of yoga pants she'd wear today. Ryan was about to close the bathroom door when her phone rang. He stopped in his tracks.

"It's Decker," she said, looking at the screen. "Should I answer it?"

Ryan nodded. Decker was on both their approved contact lists.

"I don't think he'd be calling at 7:14 a.m. just to say hi. Maybe it's good news."

"Good morning, Captain," she said, putting the call on speaker.

"Morning, Barnes," he said brusquely, pointedly using her alias as an extra precaution in case someone out of the loop was around. "Is Hosea there with you?"

"Right here, Captain," Ryan called out. He was currently going by the name Randy Hosea. "We're alone, by the way."

"Good. I need you both to come into the station as soon as possible."

"Did something break on the Night Hunter case?" Ryan asked excitedly.

There was a brief pause.

"No," he finally said. "But I have something else important to show you both. And it needs to be in person. Are you on some beach in Maui or can one of your marshal friends get you in here within the hour?"

"We're in driving distance but I think it will take longer than that," Jessie said. "They'll need to follow their standard security protocol. Plus there's the typical traffic. We'll be lucky to get there by nine."

"See you at nine then," Decker said, hanging up without another word.

"Still as charming as always," Jessie noted.

"You think we'll have time for crêpes?" Ryan asked.

"Maybe to go," she replied. "We shouldn't keep him waiting. Decker knows Marshals Service protocols as well as anyone. If he's asking us to come in on short notice, it must be big."

CHAPTER TWO

Even after everything she'd been through, Jessie still wasn't used to it.

As the large black SUV with bulletproof glass pulled into the underground LAPD Central Station parking lot, escorted by two additional vehicles, she felt mildly ashamed. She wasn't a head of state. This kind of security for a profiling consultant and an LAPD detective felt excessive. But it wasn't up to her. She'd asked for their help. That meant she had to follow their rules.

So she didn't complain when they waited in the vehicle while the marshals secured the garage, the stairs (no elevator for them), and the first floor corner storage room near the stairwell where Captain Decker would be meeting with them. The goal was for as few people as possible to know they were there. The chances that the Night Hunter might have a mole in the department were slim, but they weren't none. And he'd already proved adept at sneaking into places he shouldn't be, so the marshals weren't taking any chances.

As well as he was moving, it still took a little extra time for Ryan to navigate the stairs from the basement garage to the first floor and they had to wait in the stairwell until they got the all clear. When they did, Marshal Sam Mason held the door open for them. Marshal Tommy Anderson did the same with the storage room door.

Once they were inside, Tommy stepped in too, closed and locked the door, and stood with his back to it, his eyes on the people in the room. From past experience, Jessie knew that Sam would take up a casually clandestine position just down the hall, where he could watch the storage room and anyone approaching it. Both men wore earpieces, as did the marshal still in the SUV in the garage, the marshal watching the station lobby, and the two marshals circling the block in separate vehicles.

It gave Jessie a sense of security to know that the contingent back with Hannah at the ranch house (or the Ponderosa—the code name it had been assigned) was equally diligent. When they'd left, there were two marshals inside, two more just outside and one parked down the block.

For the first time since entering the small storage room, Jessie actually gave Captain Decker more than a passing glance. It was the first time she'd seen him in close to a week and a half and he looked worse than she felt.

His starched, dress shirt and jacket masked it well, but she could see that he was worn down. His few remaining strands of white hair were angling upward, fighting whatever gel he'd used to hold them down. Though he was a tall, skinny man, his whole body was bent over, as if pressed down by some invisible anvil. He seemed to have developed even more wrinkles since she saw him last. His forehead was one big crinkle. His long nose twitched nervously. The only things that looked younger than his sixty-one years were his piercing, hawk-like eyes.

She wasn't particularly surprised at how rough he appeared. In fact, she'd expected him to look even worse. The man was under fire from all sides, including the folks at police headquarters. Though he was responsible for everyone at Central Station, it was his favorite unit, Homicide Special Section, which was currently in danger being shut down.

HSS specialized in cases that had high profiles or intense media scrutiny, often involving multiple victims or serial killers. And while they'd recently had a big win when Jessie solved a series of connected murders, including one of a popular, high profile social media influencer, that didn't make up for the Night Hunter's escape.

His exploits weren't yet known to the media, but the police chief and his minions were well aware that HSS had yet to catch a notorious serial killer who was removing the flesh of victims before murdering them. It didn't help that the man was likely in his late seventies, or that he'd murdered Detective Trembley, one of their own. It seemed that unless this killer was stopped soon, HSS was in danger of being unceremoniously folded into another unit or worse, simply abolished. The weight of all of that was visible on Decker's face.

"How are you doing?" he asked the two of them in a lame attempt at perfunctory pleasantries.

Jessie knew he was just waiting to get to the reason they were here so she skipped any details about her feelings of impotence or Ryan's delicate emotional state and answered for both of them with a simple "fine."

"Good," he said, clearly happy not to have to continue the charade, "I have good news. I think I may have found a way to keep all of you

14

safe while we search for the Night Hunter and do some good at the same time."

Jessie was happy to hear the first part but couldn't help but be skeptical at the talk of "doing good." It sounded like he was opening the door to something she wouldn't like.

"Pray tell," Ryan said with the same caution she felt.

"I got a call from an old buddy of mine early this morning. His name is Richard McClane. We went to the police academy together. He was on the force for a half a dozen years before he decided to bail on city life. He moved to the San Bernardino Mountains and joined the Riverside County Sheriff's Department. He worked his way up and now he's the Undersheriff for the whole county."

"You're not really about to pitch us a case right now, are you Captain?" Jessie asked, cutting him off before he really got going.

"Just hear me out, Hunt," he replied, sounding mildly peeved. "This could actually be an elegant solution to multiple problems."

She tried to keep her own irritation at bay.

"Sorry," she said. "Go ahead."

"There *is* a case involved but it's more of a means to an end. A woman was killed last night in a mountain town called Wildpines. She was stabbed multiple times in her driveway."

"As ugly as that sounds, it seems like a pretty cut and dried murder," Ryan said, "certainly not HSS worthy."

"You'd be right if it was just one murder," Decker replied. "But it's the second one this week. Both were stabbings. Both victims were wealthy, successful women in their thirties. That's as many murders as this place usually sees in a whole year. Rich was calling me for some friendly professional advice since he knows we handle this kind of case all the time. But the potential connection between the cases and the brutality involved is unusual enough that I started to think it could justify bringing in some help from the fancy folks down in L.A. Rich wasn't opposed. In fact he'd be happy to have the help and he thinks he can spin the involvement of a specialized homicide team into a plus. But to be honest the investigation is just a smokescreen to get you up there."

"Why?" Jessie asked, though she was beginning to suspect the reason.

"Because it's isolated, away from where the Night Hunter is. Rich has a cabin just outside of town. He's offered to let you borrow it. I've visited him there many times for hiking and fishing trips. He rents it out

15

a lot as an Airbnb. It's nothing fancy but it's big enough for the two of you and Hannah to get by comfortably. It's away from the media spotlight. No one will know who you are. You can lie low up there while the rest of the team searches for the Night Hunter back here."

"You don't have confidence in ability of the Marshals Service to keep these folks safe?" Marshal Tommy Anderson asked, speaking for the first time.

"It's not that," Decker said quickly. "Your people do amazing work. I just thought that if your protectees were over a hundred miles away from the immediate threat to them and if the threat had no idea they'd gone, it would reduce the burden on everyone."

Anderson didn't respond but it was clear that he took at least some offense.

"That's a generous offer," Jessie said, trying to smooth things over. "But I can think of a few issues with it off the top of my head."

"Like what?"

Jessie debated how best to continue.

"I don't want this to come across as arrogant, but I think that even in an isolated mountain town, some folks might know who I am. The name Jessie Hunt has been all over the news the last couple of years. They have TV there, right? It's not like they're cut off from society."

"No, they're not," Decker said, smiling for the first time since they'd arrived. "That's why you wouldn't use your real names or mention any affiliation with HSS. You're just resources on loan from LAPD. You've all already been given fake identities as a precaution, ones that will hold up to most scrutiny, certainly from local law enforcement up there. Besides, people may have heard your name but your face isn't as well known. It's cold up there. Keep a parka on. Wear hoodies and caps. Unless you make a spectacle of yourself, no one will have any reason to be suspicious. Now you said there were a few issues. What are the others?"

Jessie looked over at Ryan, unsure how to explain herself without sounding like a jerk. She saw in his eyes that he understood. He nodded and spoke up.

"It's just that this is *our* case, Captain," he insisted. "I was with Alan Trembley when the Night Hunter murdered him. All the other murders are direct messages to Jessie. It feels wrong to just decamp to some idyllic mountain town while everyone else does the heavy lifting of finding the guy."

"I understand how you feel," Decker replied, "but it doesn't have to be that way. Yes, Detective Reid will be on point here. And Jamil will do the research. But that doesn't mean you won't be in contact, able to help as needed. Hernandez—you're not formally cleared to go back in the field yet anyway so this is just a change of venue for you, one where you will have more latitude to move about than you would here. And Hunt—with everything that's happened, I wouldn't let you out in the wild around here either right now. Hell, if you stay here in L.A., you're going to be stuck in a safe house until the Night Hunter is caught or killed. That could be days. It could be months. It could be…"

His voice trailed off and they all knew his next word was going to be "never." He continued quickly, trying to push past that thought.

"At least with my offer you get to be out and about, moving around as you see fit without bodyguards everywhere. Besides, wouldn't a different setting be a nice change of pace for Hannah? She's been cooped up here too, right? It's not like she can go back to school until this is resolved."

Jessie looked over at Ryan, who shrugged. He seemed to be acknowledging the same point that she couldn't deny: Decker made a compelling case. If they could go somewhere safe, where they—especially Hannah—could get outside and walk around and go to the store like normal people, *and* still participate in the search for the Night Hunter, all while solving a murder, that seemed like the best deal they would get anytime soon.

"Okay," she said. "We're in. But I have a few conditions, which I'll share with you later. So what happens next?"

Decker seemed more relieved than happy.

"Next, we call in the whole team. Catching this guy is going to require all hands on deck, whether from here or the mountains. We need everyone on the same page before you guys leave. By the way, I told Rich you'd be up there by around 2 p.m., which means that accounting for traffic, we have about two hours to organize everything before you leave. There's not a second to waste."

CHAPTER THREE

Walter Nightengale was annoyed.

He'd spent a lifetime trying to control his emotions so that when he finally let them have free rein, it would be doubly satisfying. There was nothing more exhilarating than keeping everything bottled up inside only to release it all as he cut into the soft flesh of a target while watching the terror in their eyes.

But Jessie Hunt was testing his self-control. Only one week ago, he'd been so close to making his vision a reality. He'd actually walked right into her home, invited in by her when she'd fallen for his disguise as an old neighbor woman. He'd had multiple syringes full of the paralyzing agent ready for use on Hunt, her detective boyfriend, and her sister.

Only bad luck had foiled him. The boyfriend stepped away from him at just the wrong moment. The old neighbor woman's dog barked at him, arousing suspicion. The detective and Hunt's sister had managed to get to a panic room just before he could administer the shots.

Even then he'd managed to flood that room with poisonous gas before Hunt found a way into the house to rescue them. He'd had to leave before finishing the job. The cops were closing in and Hunt was armed. He'd barely made it out of the neighborhood before they closed down all the nearby streets.

Despite that, he wasn't certain that he'd completely failed. Had Hunt had arrived in time to rescue Detective Hernandez and Hannah Dorsey? There was nothing on the news about their deaths and certainly the passing of the decorated detective Ryan Hernandez would have been newsworthy. Had they somehow kept it quiet to deny him the satisfaction? Were the two of them on life support in a hospital room? He'd carefully pursued that angle and found no evidence that either had been admitted anywhere.

He had to assume that Hunt had saved them, that she was as good as he'd imagined—a worthy protégé of her mentor, Garland Moses, Walter's one true nemesis. He had to assume that his near-perfect opportunity to kill all of them in one long, happy night of torment was forever gone.

That night seemed like a lifetime ago now. Despite his best efforts Hunt and her family had dropped off the map. He'd staked out their home and the police station where Hernandez worked. He'd surveilled the university where Hunt taught and the high school that her sister attended. There was no sign of them anywhere. They had gone into hiding, and very effectively.

He had considered kidnapping Hunt's best friend, a woman named Katherine Gentry, to use as bait to draw Hunt in. But that came with complications. His research indicated that Gentry, a former Army Ranger, would be difficult to surprise or subdue. Furthermore, he feared that Hunt would have her friend watched, aware that this might be his next move. It was too risky.

Still, she was his best remaining lead, so for the last hour he'd been reduced to watching and waiting as she went about her private detective business. Right now he was well disguised and sitting on a park bench not far from where she was hunched over in her car, taking photos of a guy who wore a neck brace but seemed able to twist around without trouble.

After so many years, he was used to the boredom of waiting. Patience was one of his greatest attributes. But usually he applied it on his own terms, not out of necessity because he'd been outmaneuvered by some upstart criminal profiler.

The man in the brace disappeared inside a building. Gentry put away her camera and drove off, apparently satisfied with what she had for now. Walter was tempted to get in his car and follow her but decided to let her go. It wouldn't be hard to catch up with her later.

Besides, he needed a moment to gather himself. Now that the monster within him had been unleashed, now that he'd fully re-embraced his role as Night Hunter after so many years in the shadows, it was hard to shut down the murderous urges on command.

Even now, he felt the itch growing inside him. At some point soon, if he couldn't get to Hunt, he would have to take out his frustration on another target. Maybe this one would have Hunt's initials, J.H., as two previous casualties had. Or maybe the initials would be H.D., which the previous casualty shared with Hannah Dorsey. Perhaps he'd try someone new—R.H? K.G.? None of that was preferable. It put him at risk of being caught. Besides, he was tired of the facsimiles. He wanted the originals.

19

As maddening as these delays were, he knew the disappointment was temporary. Eventually Hunt, or someone around her, would make a mistake. And he would be there to capitalize on it. He had waited a long time and he could wait longer.

If his seventy-eight years on this earth had taught him anything— other than that there were few pleasures greater than causing others pain—it was how to endure. He would bide his time. And when Jessie Hunt revealed herself to him, he would hunt her down and pounce. After all, he was the Night Hunter. That's what he did.

CHAPTER FOUR

Jessie was impressed.

Decker had set up a special room for the meeting. It was on the second floor of LAPD's Central Station, at the very end of the hall in what had once been a break area but was now an overflow records room. This was where the oldest case files were kept, cold cases from 1900-1950. They were in the process of being digitized, but it was slow going and far from a top priority, so the room was rarely visited.

That meant that, other than the officer assigned to patrol the second floor, there was no staff to contend with. Decker had sent that officer downstairs until further notice, which meant that the locked records room was guarded by Marshal Tommy Anderson, who sat in a folding chair, out of sight in a nook across the hallway.

Marshal Sam Mason remained in the room as an extra precaution, just in case one of the people Jessie worked closely with was actually in thrall with the Night Hunter and intended to take her out with a half dozen cops in the room. As crazy as the notion was, Jessie didn't bother to object. It was challenging enough to convince Mason that she, Ryan, and Hannah should be permitted to go to Wildpines without a Marshal escort. There was no way she was going to keep him out of this room if he insisted on being there, which he did.

She and Ryan waited as the others filed in. All of them looked surprised and delighted when they entered the room. Detective Callum Reid, with his burgeoning belly pudge, receding, brown hair, and black-framed glasses, gave her a big hug upon entry. He'd been her partner in solving the social media influencer murder. While working the case, he'd privately shared that he had a heart condition and planned to retire imminently. She'd told no one in the department about his plans.

Next in was Jamil Winslow, the researcher extraordinaire who had been so instrumental in closing many of her cases. Short and skinny, the frail-looking twenty-four-year-old was actually a relentless investigator who seemed to absorb energy from uncovering minutiae that escaped others. Unfailingly polite, he smiled and shook Jessie's hand. She was having none of it and pulled him in for a hug too.

21

Next was Detective Jim Nettles, who had spent fifteen years as a patrol officer before finally getting his detective's shield last fall at age thirty-seven. Burly, grizzled, and taciturn, he had flecks of gray in his black hair. Jessie silently noted the long, horizontal scar across the front of his neck, the remnant of a knife wound he'd gotten back in uniform while trying to protect her from Xander Thurman, her serial killer father. He didn't hold a grudge but she knew his wife still did.

As Nettles was shaking hands all around, Jessie got her first real surprise of the morning. Walking in next was Detective Karen Bray. Karen was a detective with Hollywood Station who had helped guide Jessie through several cases in her neck of the woods, including the recent murder of a "past her prime" actress.

Her petite figure and self-effacing manner were deceptive. Karen had repeatedly proven to be a savvy, efficient investigator who didn't take any crap but managed to be diplomatic about it. Jessie also considered her a friend. In her late-thirties, Karen's dirty blonde hair was currently tied back in a utilitarian ponytail. There were no bags under her alert gray eyes, a sign that her young child had let her sleep through the night.

"Oh, yes," Decker said, clearly amused to see the surprise on Jessie's face, "I've been meaning to share this news and was waiting for the appropriate time. Detective Bray requested a transfer to Central Station to join the HSS unit. Based on her exemplary work with Ms. Hunt on multiple cases, I was happy to bring her on board. She's on a week's vacation and was officially supposed to start next Monday but insisted on coming in today to help out."

"Well, this is a pleasant surprise. Tired of kowtowing to the rich and famous?" Jessie teased.

"Are you telling me that you guys don't have to do that over here?" Karen asked skeptically.

"Not *every* day," Jessie assured her.

"And in her fancy consultant capacity, almost never," Ryan added.

Jessie suddenly realized that the two of them had never met.

"Karen, this is Ryan Hernandez. He's the lead detective for Homicide Special Section. Ryan, meet Karen Bray. She was my rock in several cases last year, as I believe I may have told you."

"Nice to meet you, Karen," Ryan said, extending his hand. "Jessie speaks very highly of you, even when you're not around."

"That very nice," she replied, "though I doubt she blushes when she talks about me the way she does when she mentions you."

"You might be surprised," Ryan countered.

Jessie could feel her face starting to flush at that very moment. The process was abruptly cut short when the next person walked through the door: it was Kat.

As usual, she was dressed in blue jeans, a casually professional shirt, and a brown leather jacket. The unremarkable outfit masked the powerfully built woman underneath. At five foot seven and 140 pounds, she didn't look like what she was: an elite military veteran capable of easily killing someone with her bare hands. Like Karen, her dark blonde hair was pulled back into a no-fuss ponytail. Her focused eyes missed nothing.

Suddenly embarrassment was replaced by awkwardness. Maybe it was a result of Jessie's closest friend, who had so recently betrayed her trust, seeing her so chummy with another female friend. Maybe it was the fact that they hadn't seen each other since the evening the Night Hunter had invaded Jessie's home, just after she and Kat had established a delicate détente while solving a murder together. Whatever the reason, the discomfort lingered in the air. Ryan tried to make it dissipate.

"Glad you could make it, Kat," he said warmly.

He was the one who had called her, albeit at Jessie's request. That was one of the conditions she had insisted Decker meet if she was to go to Wildpines today. Whatever personal issues still remained unresolved between them, she wanted Kat on the Night Hunter case.

Part of the reason she wanted Kat on board was so her friend would be working with and under the protection of the LAPD. Jessie knew that with herself, Ryan, and Hannah under protection, the Night Hunter might decide to go after someone else close to her, either as punishment or as bait. Katherine "Kat" Gentry was her best friend and the logical next choice. It would be harder to get to her if she was working with cops.

The other reason she wanted Kat around was more selfish. Unlike employees of the Los Angeles Police Department, Kat was a private detective and therefore, not subject to all their rules and regulations. She could immediately go places they needed a warrant to access. She wasn't constrained by the same rules when questioning witnesses and suspects. If they needed something done fast and dirty, Kat was more likely to have success.

Additionally, Kat's Army Ranger experience while in a war zone in Afghanistan meant she was unlikely to lose her nerve in a sticky situation. Her shrapnel-pocked face and the long vertical scar under her left eye, permanent gifts from a run-in with an IED, were evidence that she wasn't afraid of sacrifice. Finally, it didn't hurt that she clearly still felt guilty about her deception regarding Hannah and would do almost anything to make up for it.

"How's it going?" she asked when Kat walked over.

"I'm fine," her friend replied. "More importantly, how are *you* guys doing? The last time I saw you, we were celebrating catching a killer. The next thing I hear, you all are in hiding because the Night Hunter snuck into your house."

"Waltzed right in is more like it," Ryan corrected. "We were idiots. If not for Jessie's obsession with panic rooms and a few spare gas masks, Hannah and I wouldn't be here right now."

"Well, I'm glad you are," Kat said, and then looked directly at Jessie, "all of you."

"Thanks," Jessie replied. "I know we were going to have lunch and…catch up. But obviously some stuff came up. Maybe we can reschedule *after* the old-timey serial killer is captured?"

"It's a date," Kat replied.

"I think we have everyone," Decker announced loudly to let them know the time for chit-chat was over. "Our guests of honor are on a tight timetable before they have to leave us, so we should get started. Let's discuss how we're going to catch this bastard."

He was about to continue when there was knock on the door. Jessie watched Marshal Sam Mason listen to a message in his earpiece.

"Copy that," he whispered, "Opening up now."

He unlocked and opened the door. As the latest entrant walked in there was a collective gasp of surprise from almost everyone. But not from Jessie.

Standing in the doorway was Hannah.

CHAPTER FIVE

"Hi everyone," her sister said, in a faux chipper tone. "Didn't you all know that this was 'take your sister to work' day?"

No one laughed. Decker glared at Jessie and she knew what he was thinking: this was a bad idea.

This had been her second condition before she agreed to go to Wildpines today. Hannah had to be brought into the loop. Despite Jessie's desire to protect her sister from the ugliness they were facing, the days of hiding the truth from her had to end. Technically she'd be an adult in just a few months. And in reality, her childhood had ended the day she saw her adoptive parents slaughtered in front of her by her own father.

She deserved to know what was going on. Just as importantly, Jessie had come to believe that having access to this information was crucial to her recovery. If Hannah felt like she was part of the decision-making process, maybe it would curb her reckless need to make sneaky choices which put her safety and stability at risk. Jessie wasn't sure it would work. But keeping secrets from Hannah had only led her to respond in kind. Maybe uncut honesty would serve them all better.

"Go ahead, Captain," she said to Decker, motioning for Hannah to come sit next to her. "You were about to explain how we plan to catch the Night Hunter."

Decker paused for a second and Jessie thought he might be about to bail on their agreement. But he seemed to sense they were past the point of no return and shrugged.

"Okay," he began, "here's what we're thinking. The problem up until now is that we've been handling this case piecemeal. We only recently learned that this guy was back in circulation. It took a while after that to realize that he was killing his victims as a way to send a message to Hunt."

"Why would he do that?" Detective Nettles asked.

Jessie took the question.

"It's complicated," she said. "We believe that he viewed Garland Moses as his nemesis, the one person who ever came close to catching him. Twenty years ago, Garland caught up to him. Their physical confrontation almost killed him. Most people thought it killed the Night Hunter too. But Garland never bought that. He had extensive files in his house that show as much. Our theory is that once the Night Hunter learned of Garland's murder at the hands of his protégé's ex-husband, he was intrigued."

"What does that mean exactly?" Karen asked.

Ryan picked up from there.

"We think he wanted to see if Jessie was as good as her mentor, if she was a worthy adversary. That's why started killing people with her initials, and later with Hannah's. He also changed his method of murder. Back in the old days when he was on the East Coast, he hacked people up with a machete. But here in L.A., he injects them with a paralyzing drug, then removes their skin with an X-Acto knife. We found a reference in Garland's files to him doing that once before he went into hiding. He likely wanted to see if Jessie could make the connection, which she did."

"Unfortunately," Decker jumped in. "Things have escalated. Last Tuesday night, he managed to get into their house. He intended to do his X-Acto routine on all of them and when that didn't work, he tried to poison them with gas. His days of sending messages seem to be over. Now he just wants blood. That's why you haven't had your friends around lately. It's why our colleagues from the Marshals Service are joining us here today. And it's also why Hunt, Hernandez, and Hannah won't be with us after this meeting. Once we're done, they'll be taken to an undisclosed location until the Night Hunter is caught or killed."

"But how are we supposed to catch one of the most notorious serial killers of the last half-century without the help of the people who know the most about him?" Detective Reid asked.

"They won't be around," Decker acknowledged. "But that doesn't mean they won't be available to help."

"That's right," Jessie said. "We won't be here in the office or in the field with you. But we still plan to coordinate with the teams doing the active investigation. If you have questions, call. If you need information, let us know. Just because we're not out there with you doesn't mean we're not engaged."

"The plan is for Winslow to provide leads," Decker added. "He's been diligently going through surveillance footage for the last week. We caught one murder on video, clearly by the Night Hunter's design. He was performing for us. We also know he prefers to drive older cars, mostly from the 20th century. He likes clunkers without GPS systems in them. Winslow's been tracking down any vehicle from near the crime scenes that fit the description. Based on video clips and descriptions from folks in this room, there's a decent shot we may find him via facial recognition. The guy is good at hiding—very careful—but all it takes is one slip-up and we're on him."

"I've already got a list of seven potential haunts that he might have used recently," Jamil volunteered. "I may also have a lead on a couple of used car dealerships where he got his vehicles. We know he's used at least three different cars in the last few months. We found all of them abandoned. Two were burned out. None had fingerprints or DNA. I wouldn't be surprised if he has at least that many still available to him. He prepared for this adventure well ahead of time."

"Which is why we've got a lot of catching up to do," Decker said. "We're going to split into two teams. Detectives Reid and Bray will work together. Detective Nettles will partner with Ms. Gentry. I know it's rare to allow a non-LAPD investigator to join a unit investigation, but we're short-handed and Hunt assures me that Gentry will be an asset. She certainly was in resolving the recent wedding murders."

Jessie wondered if Decker suspected the real reason she'd suggested Kat be paired with Nettles: he was the least experienced detective and might defer to her reputation as a war-hardened badass. She had a feeling that he knew and didn't mind. Sometimes even a police captain liked having someone at his disposal that wasn't bound by department regulations.

Jessie looked around the room and sensed a confidence in the group that she found disconcerting. Though they all knew that Alan Trembley had died at the Night Hunter's hands and a few of them had watched the video of him torturing Hallie Douglas, she got the feeling that some of them still thought a serial killer in his late seventies wasn't a mortal threat to them. She decided to disabuse them of that impression.

"Listen up," she said, her voice quiet but forceful, "don't think this is going to be a walk in the park. The man you're after isn't just an elderly gentleman with a few tricks and a small blade. He's brilliant, he's experienced, and he's crafty. He walked into our home right under our noses when we were on high alert. He took Alan Trembley by surprise and left him bleeding out on a hostel floor. He's killed at least three people in the last few months just because of their initials. Prior to dropping off the radar two decades ago, he killed over eighty people that we know of—hacked them to death with a machete. He's probably murdered at least that many that we'll never know about."

Everyone in the room was silent. Hannah had gone white. Jessie felt a brief rush of guilt at subjecting her teenage sister to so much horror. But that was the downside of deserving to know the truth—it was sometimes hard to hear. So she kept going.

"Remember, this guy gets off on killing. It's what brings him joy. And right now, he's probably frustrated that he hasn't gotten to us," she said nodding at Ryan and Hannah. "He's not going to give up on that. But his frustration is likely to make him lash out, maybe at other innocents who just happen to have the wrong initials, and probably soon. He may have already done so. Don't underestimate this guy."

She looked over at Decker who didn't have much to add. She could tell he thought that was a good note to end on.

"Let's wrap this up," he said. "Say your goodbyes to these three and get to work. If we don't solve this, they can't resume their normal lives and Homicide Special Section will likely be disbanded. No pressure though."

He left the room without another word. The others lined up to offer their well wishes. No one asked where they were going. Everyone knew better than that. After everyone else but the marshal had filed out, Jessie approached Kat.

"Ryan told you why we want you on this thing, right?" she asked under her breath.

"Yep," Kat assured her. "You need someone who can go places and do things legitimate cops can't."

"Is that going to be a problem for you?"

Kat looked at her as if she'd just been insulted.

"What do you think?" she asked, before adding, "I'm your girl."

"Good," Jessie replied, "Because I think we're going to need your skill set before this is all said and done."

"Sorry to interrupt," Marshal Mason said from behind them, "but if you're going to get to your destination by your target time, you need to leave now."

"You should go," Kat said. "Just stay safe. You never know what this guy is capable of."

"Same to you. Don't let your guard down for a second."

"Don't worry," Kat said, "I don't know how."

She gave Jessie's hand a squeeze and walked out. Now it was just the three of them and their U.S. Marshal protector. He closed the door again. When he spoke, his voice was quiet but firm.

"You'll have a driver for the first leg of the trip, just until you get out of the city. Three identical vehicles will leave the garage at the same time as you. Your driver will use evasive maneuvers to look for tails in conjunction with the rest of the team. Once you're out of town and we're confident you're not being followed, you'll change cars. One that's a little less conspicuous than a large black SUV has been assigned to you. You'll take that the rest of the way to Wildpines. It's tagged with GPS, but only the Marshals Service will have access to your location, and even then, just a select group of agents. In addition, we have a small field office in Palm Springs. Here's the number. Ask for Marshal John Troy if you have any trouble. They can be at your door in forty-five minutes. Understood?"

"Got it," Jessie said.

"I just want to reiterate that I think this is a terrible idea," Mason said. "You'll be unprotected, vulnerable, and away from immediate assistance."

"We understand, Sam," Jessie said quietly, pulling him to the corner of the room so Hannah couldn't hear. "But my sister needs to be able to get out and walk around a little. She's in a sensitive emotional place and keeping her locked up for weeks on end is going to take a toll. If we do this right, no one will know where we are. Just the thought of that is like a breath of fresh air."

"I'm all for fresh air and nice walks," he said. "But I'm also a fan of darting, alert eyes and heads on swivels. Promise me that you'll take those with you."

"I promise," Jessie said with a confidence she wasn't sure she felt.

She really did believe that Hannah needed a chance to get away from the constant stress. Stir craziness was a real thing. But what Sam said was true. They were taking a risk leaving the city and the protection it afforded. She hoped it was worth it.

CHAPTER SIX

It took over two hours for traffic to finally subside.

By the time they were actually able to drive the speed limit, they were in Redlands, only twenty-two miles from the exit to Wildpines. Ryan was driving. Initially Jessie balked at the idea, worried that he might have mobility issues, as he hadn't been behind the wheel since last July. But he was insistent and within minutes, seemed completely comfortable. In the backseat, Hannah was immersed in her phone. Jessie spent the entirety of the time focused on the cars around them, watching to see if they were being followed.

She had Ryan change lanes unexpectedly, speed up and slow down repeatedly, at least as much as they could when going twenty-five miles an hour on a packed freeway. Twice she had him get off at exits without warning, only to get right back on the freeway. In those two hours, she never saw one suspicious vehicle. If the Night Hunter was following them, he wasn't just an effective serial killer, he should also apply to be a driver for the FBI.

When they got off the freeway for good in Banning, they headed south on Highway 243 toward the mountains, passing the local high school and a penitentiary that seemed disturbingly close to it. After crossing a small bridge, they immediately began a sharp, winding incline up the barren mountainside.

It was a two lane road and there was no way for any trailing vehicle to follow them without being noticed. Still, Jessie had Ryan pull into two turnouts to let vehicles behind them pass, then watched to see if they lingered. None did.

Despite the constant hairpin turns, after only five minutes they were several thousand feet up. In the dusty distance of the desert, Jessie could see a huge tower reaching skyward. She knew it was part of a massive casino complex that had been built in the middle of nowhere. Somewhere well beyond that, at least another twenty miles east, was the desert oasis of Palm Springs, where U.S. Marshals were apparently ready to take her call.

Before she could think about that too much, they began to cut across the mountains.

"Thank God," Hannah muttered from the backseat.

"What?" Jessie asked.

"All those twists and turns were making me nauseous," she said, rolling down her window despite the forty-something degree temperature.

"It might have something to do with trying to read on your phone," Jessie suggested. "Maybe try keeping your eyes on the horizon."

"Don't get too comfortable," Ryan added. "I have a feeling this straightaway won't last for long. Once we get on the other side of the mountain we'll be back to the hairpins. We're 3000 feet up right now. The town is at around 5400 feet, so we've got a ways to go."

Jessie had been so busy marveling at the terrain that it hadn't even occurred to her to be bothered by the sharp turns or the sheer drop-offs. She did notice that as they cut across this relatively flat section of road, the landscape changed. On the north side of the mountains, which they were leaving, the earth was scorched brown, with brush and skinny gnarled trees. There were long stretches with no foliage at all. That was likely due to one of the many wildfires that tore through this region every few years. As if to confirm her suspicions, they passed a collection of charred, black trunks, a tree cemetery.

Soon they were on the other side of the mountain. The trees were suddenly taller and greener. Snow began to appear out of nowhere, first in small patches and then everywhere, covering the hills in a white blanket that came right up to the edge of the recently plowed, two-lane road. It was amazing to think that less than three hours earlier, they'd been in sight of the ocean and now they were in what could be easily misidentified as the Rocky Mountains.

After another fifteen minutes of endless, twisty ascent, they saw a cabin, then a Christian-themed lodge, then more cabins. And after one last long, slow curve they passed a sign that noted the population of Wildpines as 2,477, and all at once they were in the town. They pulled off Highway 243 onto Central Circle Drive and were suddenly in what appeared to be the main square.

"This place is cute," Hannah said, expressing how they all felt.

The entire area was a collection of homey, log cabin-style storefronts. They'd barely gone a block before passing two cafes, a coffeehouse, an artisanal soap store, a glass-blown art gallery and a one-screen movie theater that was apparently only open Friday through Sunday. A banner tied to two telephone poles above the main road announced that the Pines JazzFest was only twelve weeks away.

"I want to drive around more but I guess we should go to the substation," Jessie said. "Undersheriff McClane said he'd meet us any time after 2 p.m. and it's almost three now."

"I think that's the best call," Ryan agreed. "He can give us the case details along with the keys to the cabin. Then we can drop off our stuff and start doing interviews."

"Maybe you could let me off here in the main square," Hannah suggested. "There's no reason for me to be in that meeting, right? And while you're talking to the sheriff, I could walk around a little bit, get a feel for the place. Maybe I could even find a good spot for dinner."

Jessie couldn't think of a reason to object. Once again she remembered that one of the reasons they'd come here was so that they could actually move about without the constant fear that they might encounter the Night Hunter at any moment. Getting out and about would actually be good for her sister.

"That's fine," she said. "Enjoy yourself but please stay aware. All those maneuvers we made coming out here give me confidence that we weren't followed. But if you see anyone suspicious, let us know. Otherwise, we'll call when the meeting's over. Sound good?"

Hannah nodded as she got out and gave the broadest, most genuine smile Jessie had seen from her in days. She closed the door and headed straight for the coffeehouse, as Jessie had silently predicted she would.

Jessie gulped hard, trying to swallow the rising desire to call Hannah back. This was the first time her sister would be truly alone in well over a week and the realization was more stressful than she'd expected. Next to her, Ryan gently put his hand on her forearm.

"She'll be okay," he whispered, reading her mind. She nodded, though she wasn't entirely convinced.

Once they saw her safely enter the place, Ryan pulled back out onto the road and drove the additional two hundred yards to the Wildpines substation, which, unlike most of the other structures on the street, was made primarily of concrete. The building was square and squat, designed for utility more than aesthetics.

Jessie's phone buzzed and she looked down. Reading the message, she couldn't help but chuckle.

"What is it?" Ryan asked.

"It's a text from Marshal Sam Mason. He says now that we're securely in town, he's pulling the tail that followed us here."

"Wow," Ryan marveled, shaking his head. "Those guys are impressive. I never saw anything suspicious the whole drive out here."

"Me either," Jessie said. "Either we're getting sloppy or they're just that good."

"I choose to believe it's the latter."

Jessie did too, because if the marshals could track them without their knowledge, someone else might be able to as well. And that person's intentions might not be so pure. She tried not to linger on that possibility. Worrying wouldn't do any good. Besides, the people inside the tiny police station she was staring at needed her help. She had two murders to solve.

CHAPTER SEVEN

The wind was biting.

As soon as they got out of the car, Jessie zipped up her coat. She glanced at her phone and saw that the temperature was thirty-six degrees. They hurried up the steps and into the station. When Ryan opened the door for her, Jessie was hit with a blast of warm air. Just as quickly as she'd put on her jacket, she peeled it off.

Looking around, she saw that there wasn't much to the place. A tiny waiting area with two chairs was separated from the rest of the place by a Formica countertop. A woman in her sixties with coke bottle glasses sat behind it on a high swivel chair. She was on the phone and barely glanced up as they entered.

Behind her at one of the two desks in the station, a heavyset, straw-haired deputy in his late twenties was also on the phone, desperately scribbling down notes as he listened intently to the person on the other end of the line. At the rear of the station was a second deputy with his back to them. He was talking to a man seated on metal bench in the substation's solitary cell. The man on the bench looked like he was still hung over from whatever adventure he'd had the previous night.

Jessie recognized the fourth person in the station from the photo Captain Decker had shown them. Sitting in a chair along the side wall, reading the paper with his feet propped up on a coffee table, was Undersheriff Richard McClane. Though she gathered he was about was the same age as Decker, he didn't look nearly as worn down as his friend.

His thick hair was still as much pepper as salt and his weathered skin looked more sun than work-wrinkled. His cheeks were ruddy and his forearms, visible because of his rolled up sleeves, seemed like they were used to chopping wood. He was a healthy looking guy. Maybe that's what bailing on city life for the mountains could do. He looked up at them and smiled.

"Detective Hosea and Ms. Barnes, I presume?" he asked, using the fake identities they'd been assigned as he stood up to greet them. He was taller than Jessie had realized, with just the beginnings of a belly, which he didn't try to hide.

"That's right," Ryan said. "Nice to meet you, sir."

"You can call me Rich," he said, waving away the formalities.

"Should we join you back there, Rich?" Jessie asked.

"Actually, why don't we head out back behind the station?" McClane suggested. "This place gets toasty when it gets more than a half dozen people inside."

He raised the lift-up countertop, stepped through, and led them out the front door, then back down the steps and around the side of the building to his vehicle in the back.

"Trip go okay?" he asked.

"Not too bad," Ryan replied. "The traffic opened up after about Redlands."

"It could have been worse," McClane said. "Sometimes it's bumper to bumper out past Palm Springs. Is the girl okay—Heidi, right?"

"Sure," Jessie said, sticking to the façade, despite how weird it felt. "We dropped her off in the main square to look around. She wasn't all that interested in this."

"Understood. I have a fifteen-year-old granddaughter. If it's not on Tik Tok, it doesn't exist for her. You want to talk in the car or outside?"

"Maybe we start outside until I can't handle the cold anymore?" Jessie offered.

"Sounds good," McClane said, looking impervious to the weather, "So Roy filled me in on the basics of your situation. He said the fewer details I know, the better off I am and I tend to agree. As far as I'm concerned, you're regular LAPD detective types who are helping out because of the unusual nature of this case."

"We're happy to stick with that story too," Ryan said.

"Good. For now, I've managed to conceal your involvement from my boss, the County Sheriff. He wouldn't like having LAPD here. Besides, his interest will only complicate matters. But I have to admit that two murders in such a small community, especially within days of each other, both using the same method, well that's pretty rare. At some point, he's going to find out. Once he does, he'll get antsy and want to defend his turf. I'd say you've got about forty-eight hours before he pulls rank. When that happens, you may need to step back if you want to keep that low profile. You'll still have access to my cabin of course, but you may have to take a backseat to detectives from the County. I assume you don't want too many people asking personal questions about you, and these County guys are liable to."

"Seems reasonable," Jessie said. "I say the fewer questions, the better."

"That's been our policy as well," Rich told them. "In fact, while it might seem a little unconventional to city cops like yourselves, we've done our best to keep the particulars of these cases under wraps for now. We don't want a panic."

"How have you managed that with two murders?" Ryan asked, incredulous.

Rich smiled ruefully.

"It's not as difficult as you might think. Hardly anyone knows about the second case yet since her body was just discovered this morning. And while people know about the first victim's death, we agreed with her husband that getting into the gory details doesn't serve anyone at this time. Most folks still assume she died of natural causes and we haven't seen the need to correct the record just yet."

While she understood Ryan's shock, Jessie didn't have a problem with the decision. The fewer people who knew the truth, the bigger advantage she had as an investigator. In a town this small, once word got out, it would be hard to conduct interviews. Beyond that, more attention on the victims meant more attention on her and Ryan, which put their identities at risk of discovery.

"So how do you want to start?" she asked, choosing to move on.

"I figured we'd dive right into the cases to maximize time, if that's okay," McClane suggested, pointing for them to hop in the car. "I'll give you keys to the cabin and you can check it out later."

"Sounds good," Ryan said as he opened the front seat for Jessie.

"Okay then," Rich replied, before adding, "and if you find that the cabin doesn't work for you, just let me know. I won't be offended. There are other options. I'm friends with a couple that rents out cottages, Leanne and Paul Tobias. They might have a few left. And there's always Riggs Mountain Resort off 243. It's not as fancy as the name sounds, more of a motel really. But because they're off the beaten track, they don't get a ton of traffic. You might even have the place to yourself. I'm sure Stanley and Charlotte would cut you a deal just to get the business."

"I'm confident your place will work fine," Jessie assured him, not adding that she didn't want to involve any more people in their personal circumstance than necessary. She changed subjects. "So Decker only gave us the basics. Can you fill us in on the situation?"

They all got in the car and closed the doors before McClane answered.

"Sure. Our two victims are Clarice Kimble and Sarah Ripley. Clarice is a long-time local; grew up here, moved away briefly before returning for the last decade; married, no kids. She ran an aromatherapy shop and was vice-president of the local chamber of commerce. She was killed on Sunday night outside her house. She was stabbed three times in the upper torso and neck. Her husband found her soon afterward."

"And the other victim?" Ryan asked.

"Sarah Ripley. We'll be going to her place first. She's not a local but a frequent visitor. She and her husband live in Los Angeles but they own a place up on Rockview Drive. My understanding is that the husband doesn't come up often but that Sarah was here pretty regularly. She was supposedly on the verge of opening a second location of a store she has back in L.A. She was killed last night. I can fill you in on what else I know when we get up there. It's only a five minute drive from here."

"Before we head up there, I was wondering what resources we're working with here?" Ryan wanted to know.

"In terms of forensics, mostly what you're used to. Both bodies were taken to the coroner down in Perris. It's about an hour west of here but it's the closest option. As far as human resources, the substation has one residential deputy. That's Garrett Hicks. You saw him talking down the drunk in the cell. He's young but he's smart; grew up in this community, knows most folks and has an unassuming manner. He'll be an asset. I'm going to call him out now," he said before speaking into the radio. "Garrett, can you join us out back? We're going up to the Ripley place."

"Yes, sir," came the immediate reply.

"Normally, we assign a daily second deputy to the town on a rotating basis," McClane continued. "Because of the murders, the second deputy is on semi-permanent status of late. Today it's Pete Traven. He lives just down the mountain in Hemet but knows the area well. He'll handle the non-murder calls for the day. Otherwise, I can be here in an hour if you get in a real jam, but I'm hoping to avoid that. The more I come up here, the more attention it attracts."

"We'll try to keep you out of it as much as possible," Ryan said.

Deputy Garrett Hicks walked out the back door. Jessie hadn't gotten a good look at him earlier when he was talking to the drunk in the cell. But now she saw that he was a human oak tree. He was easily six foot five and 220 pounds, with broad shoulders and thighs as thick as Jessie's waist. His black hair was crew cut short, and his face was warm and open. She doubted he was more than a couple of years out of high school.

"By the way," McClane added, "Garrett doesn't know anything about who you really are or your personal circumstance. He just knows you're here to help solve these murders and that he's not to get too curious about you. Except for case details, you can count on him to keep his eyes open and his mouth shut."

Deputy Hicks got in the backseat next to Ryan and the conversation stopped.

"Sorry for the delay," he said. "Rusty was threatening to puke on the floor instead of in the toilet until I told him he'd have to clean it up."

"Not a problem," Rich said, "Garrett, this is Randy Hosea and Jennifer Barnes. They do detective work for LAPD. You'll be assisting them with anything they need."

"Nice to meet you, Deputy," Ryan said, shaking his hand.

"You all as well," he replied. "But please call me Garrett. Not even Rich here calls me deputy."

"Okay then, Garrett, I'm Jennifer," Jessie said, the name sounding weird coming out of her mouth. "Rich tells us you know the folks around here pretty well."

"Yes, ma'am," Garrett replied. "Born and raised here. Whatever you need to know about folks, I'm your guy."

Despite how old it made her feel, Jessie didn't insist he not call her "ma'am." She was more likely to respond to that than her fake name.

"Well, where do you recommend we go first, Garrett?" she asked.

He thought for a second before responding.

"Well, if Rich agrees, I think our first stop should be the Ripley place. It's the most recent crime scene and, since the weather hasn't changed much since the murder last night, there could still be some physical evidence you might find that we missed."

"I think that's a wise choice," Rich agreed.

"Sounds good," Jessie added, impressed with Garrett's humility.

"Just one thing to keep in mind," he added as they pulled out. "The scene out there is pretty brutal. Even without the body, there's blood everywhere. You should prepare yourselves."

38

Jessie nodded. Ryan did the same. Neither of them mentioned that they'd seen and experienced horrors he couldn't possibly imagine. Jessie touched her collarbone, where she still bore the neck-to-shoulder scar from the torture her own father had inflicted on her when she was six, just before he gutted her mother right in front of her.

Garrett didn't need to know about that. He still had a belief that the world was more good than bad. It wasn't her place to tell him otherwise. He'd find out soon enough.

CHAPTER EIGHT

It took a while before Hannah finally allowed herself to relax.

She'd spent the entire last week essentially locked up. Admittedly, it was in a large ranch house in the San Fernando Valley. But that didn't change the fact that she was never even allowed use of the large pool in the back yard. She had to be indoors at all times, away from windows, and with the exception of the bathroom and her bedroom, always with at least one agent in close proximity. Adjusting to actually being alone and free to move about was taking some time.

After ordering a macchiato and settling into a worn, leather easy chair in the corner of the coffeehouse called Elevated Grounds, she watched the comings and goings of the customers, at first with a cautious eye, but then more out of curiosity. It took a few minutes for the small bell that rang every time the door opened not to make her inhale quickly in apprehension. But after a while, she settled in. In fact, the people-watching was so good that she barely looked at her phone.

It was one of the more eclectic groups of people she'd encountered in some time, and she lived on the outskirts of Hollywood, where eclectic was the norm. On the patio just outside where she sat, an older, hippie-ish woman with long, braided hair of at least three colors was talking to two bikers in leather jackets with chains on their belts.

In the corner of the coffeehouse, a skinny, nervous-looking guy in his late teens with unkempt hair unpacked his cello for an imminent set. As he did, he talked to a female barista who looked like a model who had just left a photo shoot advertising some coffee product. She was breathtakingly gorgeous, and though the cellist was well aware of it, she seemed breezily oblivious to the impact she was having on him.

Hannah's attention was diverted by a loud ruckus near the door. Her shoulders involuntarily tensed up until she realized it was just a bunch of teenagers, all around her age, coming in for an after-school snack and caffeine hit. But they definitely didn't look like the kids from her high school.

Several carried instruments. One had a large portfolio case and an easel under his arm. Another had a camera bag slung over her back. There were tattoos and piercings everywhere and the attire varied from punk to goth to one girl who removed her jacket to reveal what looked like a debutante gown. None of them seemed to think they looked out of the ordinary. Neither did any of the coffeehouse regulars.

Jessie tried not to stare, but glanced up from her phone as often as she could without drawing attention to herself. After they ordered, a couple of them sat down on a large love seat adjacent to her chair. The debutante gown girl, who had long, flowing blonde hair with intermittent green and pink streaks, looked over at her and smiled.

"You starting new this semester?" she asked.

"Excuse me?" Hannah replied, not sure what she meant.

"I didn't recognize you so I just assumed you had come up for the spring semester at the conservatory."

"The conservatory?" Hannah repeated, knowing she sounded foolish.

"The Wildpines Arts Conservatory," the guy beside her with the easel and portfolio said. "It's just off 243 on Brookgate Road. We're all students there."

"Oh, no—I'm just here visiting the town," Hannah admitted. "I didn't even know there was a school here."

"Sorry for assuming," the debutante girl said. "You just had the look. I'm Patrice by the way."

"Hi, I'm Ha...Heidi," she quickly corrected. "What look do I have?"

Patrice looked over at the easel boy and smiled before turning back to her.

"It's hard to put my finger on it," she explained. "Everyone at the conservatory has an artistic bent. That's why we're there. You just gave off the vibe. Are you sure I pegged you wrong?"

"I love to cook," Hannah offered. "Does that count? I was actually thinking about going to culinary school after graduation."

"That must be it," Patrice said.

"And sure it counts," the easel boy added. "I'll bet you like your meals to look like works of art, am I right?"

Hannah pretended not to be gob smacked by his sky blue eyes or the thick blond hair that was almost as long as hers.

"Now that you mention it, I do spend a lot of time on presentation."

"See, we knew it," the boy said. "Also, I'm Chris."

"Hi," Hannah said, sensing she was on the verge of doing something she never did: blush.

"You know," Patrice said, "They have a summer program in Indigenous Culture and Cuisine. It might not be the same as training under a James Beard Award winner, but I guarantee it'd be a kick. You should look into it; have your folks schedule a campus tour."

"Thanks, I'll mention it," Hannah said, her guard suddenly going up at the reference to "folks." Hers—both birth and adoptive—were all in the ground.

"I hope so," Chris said, grinning broadly, his white teeth gleaming in the late afternoon sun. "Unfortunately, we have to get out of here. Salvatore over there always starts his solo cello gig at 3:30 and he considers it rude if people leave once he begins."

"Besides, even though it's an arts school, we still have homework," Patrice added. "Speaking of, it's sweet that you can visit up here on a Wednesday. Are you still on winter break or something?"

"No," Hannah said, unable to think of a convincing answer, "it's a little complicated, kind of a family thing."

"Don't interrogate the girl, Patrice," Chris chided. "Anyway, we're all going to be hanging out later tonight at Wildyology around nine. They have an outdoor patio overlooking Blueberry Creek. We like to play board games by the fire and listen to bad cover bands. It's cheesy fun. You should come, Heidi."

Hannah's insides bubbled nervously. It had been a while since she'd been invited to any kind of social event she felt safe attending, especially by someone as cute as Chris.

"I'll think about it, thanks," she replied, hoping she sounded appropriately casual.

The rest of their group had gotten their food and drinks and were waiting politely by the door, so Patrice and Chris got up to join them.

"Remember my warning about Sal," Chris whispered in her ear before walking off. The heat of his breath on her skin sent a shiver down her neck.

Once they left, she decided to do the same. She wasn't sure how much longer she'd have before Jessie and Ryan came to collect her and she wanted to get more of a sense of the town while she could. She watched all the students pile into a van with the conservatory logo on the side and waited until it was out of sight to step out of Elevated Grounds.

She looked around for a minute, trying to determine which way to go. After a moment, she decided to walk up the hill on Central Circle Drive in the direction of a funky-looking strip center that included a clothing shop, a stationery store, and a place that apparently sold both ice cream and beef jerky.

Even though it was less than fifty yards away, by the time she got there she was wheezing slightly. Her recent lack of exercise, combined with the elevation, was doing a number on her. She stopped into the ice cream joint and got a small mint chocolate chip cone to tide herself over until dinner. Then she went to the stationery store next door.

An older woman stood behind the register. She was pleasantly plump, with curly, gray hair and glasses attached to a cord, so that she could take them off without losing them. The glasses frames were adorned with what looked like hand-drawn flower petals. She wore a green apron, also decorated in a floral design. In cursive letters near the top of the apron was the name "Maude."

For some reason, she reminded Hannah of the elderly man she'd found lying in the street just over a week ago. He was having a heart attack and she had rushed him to the hospital, where he'd died holding her hand. Later she'd learned that he was a Holocaust survivor named Edward Wexler who eventually established a legal foundation that repatriated family heirlooms stolen by the Nazis and brought the perpetrators to justice.

Whenever she felt sorry for herself, she remembered what that man had suffered through and how he'd overcome it. Looking at the woman now, she realized the connection between them. They shared the same eyes: weary but kind.

"Is it okay if I bring this in?" Hannah asked the woman, holding up her cone.

"Yes, dear," the woman said, her voice all grandma warmth, "just be careful please."

"Thanks," Hannah said.

There was no one else inside so she didn't feel bad about taking her time perusing the greeting cards section. After that she came to a wall of souvenir-style trinkets. One of them was a charm bracelet with a lone pine tree. She was just trying it on when three middle-aged couples entered the store, loud and boisterous.

Somehow, she knew immediately that they were from L.A. Maybe it was their clothing or the way they talked, but she had no doubt. Grandma Maude, as Hannah had mentally taken to calling her, looked briefly bewildered. One of the couples immediately headed for the register as the wife asked something about personalized printing. Grandma Maude seemed not to understand the question.

43

Without even thinking about it, Hannah found herself ambling casually toward the door. No one was paying any attention to her. She felt a familiar surge of adrenaline as she realized she was on the verge of walking out of the store with the unpurchased charm bracelet on her wrist. Just one more step.

CHAPTER NINE

As she pushed the door open, the thrill of the moment was muddied slightly by another, far less familiar emotion: shame.

What the hell are you doing? After all the work you've done with Dr. Lemmon, are you really going to throw it all away for the excitement of shoplifting a $13 charm bracelet from the store of a local grandma?

She stopped on the porch front just outside the door and stood there silently, debating how to proceed. After several seconds of unpleasant churning in her stomach, she turned and walked back in the store. The couple who had been accosting the employee had moved back over to their friends. They were all chirping at each other loudly.

Hannah walked over to the register and to Grandma Maude, who looked relieved to be talking to anyone other than the couple who'd just left her.

"I'm sorry," Hannah said quietly, leaning over the counter. "I was in such a rush to leave when those noisy folks came in that I walked right out with this charm bracelet on my wrist without thinking. Unless you'd rather have me arrested, I'd like to buy it."

"What a darling you are," Grandma Maude said. "Thank you for coming back. You know some people wouldn't have."

"Really?" Hannah asked, doing a solid job of feigning shock.

"You'd be surprised," Grandma Maude conspiratorially. "So let's see, I believe that charm is $13. How about I give you a mid-week honesty discount? Let's call it $8."

"On no, I couldn't," Hannah replied. "You shouldn't reward me for being belatedly honorable."

"I insist," Grandma Maude said. "$8. Will that be cash or charge?"

"Let's make it cash. I don't want you stuck with the service fee after you're already giving me a deal."

"See, you are a darling," Grandma Maude said, taking the $10 dollar bill from her.

Hannah wondered if this might be a worthwhile racket—leaving stores with items, then immediately returning, all apologetic, in the hopes of getting a solid discount. She shook her head in frustration at her seeming inability to just function like a normal person in society.

As she watched Grandma Maude count her change, the ding of the door opening sounded and an unsettling feeling came over her. She turned around to see that a burly man wearing all black had just entered the store. He looked to be in his forties, with a thick, well-trimmed beard and dark sunglasses. Despite the shades, she could tell he was staring at her.

"Here's your change, dear," Grandma Maude said, handing over the bills.

Hannah thanked her and quickly pushed past the man, who only made a token effort to stand aside so she could get out. Glancing back as she walked along the porch front, she saw that the man was still watching her. On instinct, she stopped into the clothing store next door and moved immediately to the back corner, behind a rack filled with mittens, gloves, and earmuffs.

A few seconds later the man walked in and took off his sunglasses. His dark eyes surveyed the store. Hannah did the same and noticed that there were no other customers inside. In fact, she didn't see any employees either.

The man began to move in her general direction and she felt her heart start to thump louder. Just then, a young guy in his twenties stepped out from the back of the store. He saw Hannah in the corner and smiled.

"May I help you?"

"Yes," Hannah said quickly, aware that the burly man would now be alerted to her location. She stepped toward the young guy and leaned close. "Do you have a bathroom I could borrow? I'm not feeling great all of a sudden."

"Of course," he said, clearly not wanting to press the issue. "It's just back there to the left."

"Thank you so much," she said and then added in a whisper. "By the way, I saw that man looking at your Merino wool scarves. You may have a big spender on your hands."

"Thanks for the tip," the young guy said and immediately moved in the man's direction.

Hannah walked back, noticing the store's back exit was right next to the restroom. She opened the bathroom door and looked back. The burly, bearded guy was watching her but his attention was diverted when the salesman began speaking to him. Hannah used the opportunity to dart out the back door.

Once outside, she found herself in a narrow alley behind the strip mall, which abutted the edge of the forest. She hurried back down the hill along the back alley in the direction of the town square, passing behind a second strip mall. Then she cut between two strip centers so that she was near the main road again.

She looked back up the hill in the direction of the clothing store. The burly man was nowhere in sight. Hoping that he'd fallen for her ruse and was waiting for her to exit the restroom, she joined a family of four crossing the street, walking on the right side of the father to hide herself.

Once across the street, she hurried back to the coffeehouse and went inside. It was less crowded than earlier. Apparently not everyone loved Salvatore the cellist, who was in the zone, his eyes closed and sweat on his brow. Hannah moved to the small alcove where the restrooms were and tried to open the ladies' room door. It was locked.

She poked her head around the alcove corner and looked up the street. She had a clear view of the strip center she'd just left. She also had a clear view of the burly man, who was now on her side of the street, walking back downhill in the direction of the coffeehouse.

This was weird at best and bordered on truly scary. She didn't know if the guy was a marshal secretly assigned to watch her. If so, he was doing a terrible job of making her feel safe. She knew he wasn't the Night Hunter. She'd seen him up close and he was about half this man's size. Was he just a standard variety creep? Could he be the person Ryan and Jessie were here to catch?

Despite her pride and hating herself as she did it, she pulled out her phone. With her fingers trembling and her eyes fixed on the front door, she texted Jessie.

CHAPTER TEN

There was no one guarding Sarah Ripley's cabin. Jessie was about to raise a stink when Rich beat her to it.

"I know what you're thinking," he said as he parked on the side of the road, "no one here to ward off looky-loos or troublemakers. That's true but we didn't have much choice with our limited manpower. We closed off the area for most of the morning, took lots of photos and video. And even though the house isn't even a mile out of town, this road isn't highly trafficked. There are only three other homes further up the hill and two of them are currently unoccupied. Like I said earlier, word hasn't gotten out about Sarah Ripley's death yet. No one has any legitimate reason to come up here. That's why I'm not too worried about contaminating the scene."

Jessie wasn't entirely satisfied but held her tongue. From his sharp exhale in the backseat she could tell that Ryan felt much the same way that she did. Rich must have sensed that they were holding back and continued even before they were out of the car.

"Having said that, we can't just assume the best of folks. Someone out here is a killer, seemingly two times over. That's why I left this little fella here."

He walked over to the stone mailbox at the edge of the driveway and pulled out a camera embedded in the snow next to it. It had been well hidden among a pile of dead leaves.

"I set it up when we left this morning," he said. "It's motion-activated and records to the camera, our phones, and to a server back at the station. We get an alert when there's any activity. I haven't gotten any. Like I said, we've got limited resources up here so we have to get creative."

Jessie nodded and walked over to the area that had piqued her interest even before he had finished speaking. There was a thin, dark line of frozen liquid that extended midway from the mailbox to a large, dark section in the snow. The latter was almost like a tracing on a piece of paper. The long line was where blood must have sprayed out after Sarah Ripley was stabbed. The dark section was clearly where her blood had pooled and eventually frozen along the edges of her body. It formed a loose outline of a person from the head down to about the stomach. Inside the outline was an indentation where Sarah Ripley had lain, and slowly sank, until she was discovered.

"Who found her?" she asked.

"Eddie Tillman," Garrett said. "He's one of our snowplow drivers. There wasn't much snow last night but our drivers always check these isolated roads in the morning. Because of the lack of traffic they tend to ice over more easily than the streets in town. He drove by around 5:15 a.m. The sun wasn't even out yet, but he saw a weird mound in his headlights and pulled over. He said at first he thought that someone might have hit a deer. But then he noticed that the front door was wide open. He pulled over and checked it out. Then he called me. Once I confirmed it was a body, I called Rich. She wasn't even wearing a coat."

"That's when I reached out to our mutual friend in the department," Rich said, obliquely referring to Captain Decker. "This combined with the incident on Sunday made me feel like we could use some specialized assistance."

Jessie stared at the sunken snow where Sarah Ripley must have lied unattended for hours. Had she died quickly or suffered for a while?

"How many times was she stabbed?" she asked.

"It was pretty bloody, hard to tell definitively," Rich said, "But I saw at least five distinct wounds. The coroner will have more information later today."

They were all quiet for a few seconds, taking in the scene.

"You said she was married?" Ryan eventually asked.

"Yes," Rich confirmed. "His name is Dwayne. I spoke to him briefly, earlier on the phone. He was in L.A. but he's down in Perris right now identifying the body. He promised to be in town in the next hour or so. I told him to go straight to the station rather than here when he arrives. You can meet him there to conduct a formal interview. In the meantime, was there anything else you wanted to check out before we stop by the Clarice Kimble crime scene?"

Jessie took a moment to look around.

"I see there are no street lights," she noted.

"That's true," Garrett conceded. "But the place has motion-activated floodlights. And there was a full, cloudless moon last night."

He seemed to be anticipating the conclusion she had come to.

"This area is wide open," she said. "It's hard to imagine that anyone could have snuck up on Sarah."

"Yes, ma'am," Garrett said. Rich nodded as well.

"You said the front door was open?" she reconfirmed.

"That's right," Garrett answered. "Eddie said it was open and the foyer light was on. There was also smoke coming out of the chimney, which meant the fireplace was cooking. I shut that down when I got here. It's a fire risk with no one inside."

"No sign of forced entry or anything stolen?" she asked.

"Not on the former," Rich answered. "We won't know for sure about missing items until the husband gets a chance to look around, but nothing seemed disturbed."

"Do we know where she was last night?" she pressed. "Home all night? Doing something in town?"

"We don't have that yet," Garret replied. "We're waiting for her GPS phone data and we didn't want to start asking around town yet. We convinced Eddie to keep quiet for the sake of the case, but the second we start asking questions, word will spread like wildfire. I hope that wasn't a mistake."

Jessie had started to tune him out. Her focus was elsewhere. She barely heard Ryan say "no, you did the right thing."

"How cold was it last night?" she wondered.

"It got down to about twenty-six at one point," Garrett answered.

Jessie nodded absently and walked up the path to the front door. Even under the circumstances, she couldn't help but notice how impressive the cabin was. Comprised of massive logs that must have required enormous effort to get in place, it looked like a Swiss chalet that could simultaneously withstand a snowstorm, avalanche and earthquake all at once. When she reached the door, she turned and looked back to where the three men stood.

"What are you thinking?" Ryan called out.

Jessie didn't answer at first. After a few moments she returned to them so she wouldn't have to yell.

"Sarah wasn't wearing a coat when something got her attention outside. She didn't think whatever it was would take that long or she'd have put it on and she wasn't that scared or she never would have come out in the first place."

"You think she knew the killer?' Garrett asked.

"Possibly; or maybe whoever it was just didn't appear like a threat. There's no sign that she was dragged to where she died. She walked there. That means she felt comfortable enough to go from her front door to the end of the driveway in the dark in just a sweater. She didn't realize she was in danger. She had no idea she was about to die."

Everyone stood silently for several seconds. Ryan finally broke the spell.

"Why don't you show us where Clarice Kimble was killed," he suggested.

Rich nodded and they all quietly returned to the car. No one spoke until they were back down the hill and on the main road again.

They turned off Circle Center Drive onto Cedarwood Street. It was residential, with several large cabins tucked into secluded spots among the pines. They stopped in front of one that looked like a gingerbread house on steroids. It was built of brown, wafer-like squares separated by white lines that looked like frosting, and had bright red shingles on the roof.

"We can walk around if you like," Rich offered, "but there's not much to see. There was a big snow on Monday that blanketed everything; wiped out any residual evidence. Luckily we got all our photos and crime scene work down before then. Everything's at headquarters in Riverside, but we have digitized files at the station. We can make copies for you."

Jessie glanced back at Ryan and saw that he felt the same way she did.

"We don't want to disturb the husband until we have some constructive questions to ask him," she said. "If you don't think we'd get much out of walking around right now, it can wait."

"I think you might be better off holding off until you've had a chance to look at the file," Rich advised. "Her husband, Martin, is pretty broken up right now. In fact, the whole town is. Clarice was a known quantity around here. Learning that she died has been unsettling for everyone in the area. Once word starts to really circulate that she was murdered, it'll only get worse. I can't imagine what it'll be like once folks learn about Sarah Ripley too."

"That's fine," Ryan agreed. "If you can just point us to where it happened so we have a sense of it, that would be helpful."

"Garrett took the call," Rich said, looking back at the deputy.

Garrett gulped hard before responding.

"Right, so Martin called it in," he said, his voice getting stronger as he went on. "I came right over. As you can see, it's literally a forty-five second drive here from the station. When I got here, she was lying in the snow by her car. She was on her stomach. There was blood on the hood of her car. I think she had just gotten out, was taken by surprise, stumbled back onto the car and then collapsed forward."

"What makes you think she'd just gotten home?" Jessie asked.

"For one thing, her hood was still warm. They tend to cool off pretty quick around here in winter so it couldn't have been more than a few minutes. Plus, Martin said she called earlier in the evening from her aromatherapy store to tell him she'd be coming home after nine. He was in the house when it happened and tried calling her when she didn't arrive by 9:15. She didn't answer her phone so he was actually heading out to the store to check on her when he found her lying in the yard."

Jessie looked over at Ryan and saw that he was doing the same mental calculations she was, trying to determine how much time the killer would have had to commit the crime. Before they could come to any conclusions, her phone buzzed. It was Hannah. The message was short: *at coffeehouse. ready to get picked up now.*

Though there was nothing overtly urgent about it, she got an odd sensation. It wasn't like Hannah to give up her private, independent time, especially after having been confined in a safe house for so long. Something felt off.

"I think we've seen everything we need to here," she told them all while looking directly at Ryan, willing him to get the urgency of the moment. "Why don't we head back to the station? You can make copies of the file for Ry...Randy while I pick up my sister, Heidi. I think she's all coffee-housed out for now."

Ryan's expression told her that he understood, even if he didn't know the details.

"That sounds good," he said. "Besides, I've needed to use the restroom for a half hour now. The sooner we get back the better."

Rich didn't need any further incentive, putting the car in drive and making a u-turn. Even thought the station was less than a minute away, Jessie had to fight the urge to tell him to go faster.

CHAPTER ELEVEN

Hannah darted out of the coffeehouse and jumped in the car.

"Is something wrong?" Jessie asked, trying to discern why her sister would ever give up even a moment of freedom.

"Let's go," Hannah said brusquely in response.

Jessie let it lie for a few minutes. Only when they had started winding their way up the road to the cabin did she try again.

"How did you like the town?" she inquired, hoping another tack might be more successful.

"Fine," was the only answer she got.

They pulled up at the cabin and got out. It was nothing fancy, just a standard log cabin like many others in town. But it did have a large front yard with a charming wagon wheel bench, which was currently covered in snow.

They grabbed their bags and headed for the front door. It was unlocked.

"Ryan?" Jessie called out, making sure that everything was okay.

"In the bathroom," he yelled back.

Hannah went to the room with the smaller bed and sat down. Jessie decided to try one more time.

"Are you sure there's nothing bothering you?"

"I'm sure," Hannah replied definitively.

"Okay," Jessie said, giving up for now. "Then I'm going to unpack."

Maybe she was reading too much into the text. Maybe Hannah had just gotten tired of the coffeehouse. She wasn't convinced but with her sister completely unresponsive, there wasn't much she could do. She retreated to her room and took the stuff out of her bag. All of it fit into one drawer. Ryan came out the bathroom. He had already put away his clothes and sat on the bed as she finished up.

"What do you think of the place?" he asked.

"Nothing fancy but it's charming," she said, "especially for the price. I think it will do for a few weeks. Anything longer than that and we might get a little stir crazy."

The cabin was on Beaver Drive, only a three minute drive from the center of town. But because it was near the top of a long hill and around a long bend from any other homes, it felt isolated.

"I noticed that there are deadbolts on the all the doors and that the windows are reinforced," he said. "I guess that's one advantage of crashing at an undersherriff's place."

"Yeah," Jessie said, before reluctantly adding. "I guess I'm just paranoid, but I wish it had cleaner sight lines. There are lots of trees near the cabin, lots of places to hide."

"What are you worried about?" Ryan asked, unable to mask the surprise in his voice.

Jessie didn't love his tone, which suggested he thought her concerns might be overkill. When she responded it was with an edge.

"Once it gets out around here that we're investigating these murders, someone in possession of a large knife is going to get pretty nervous. If they decide to come calling on us, I'd like to be prepared."

"Fair enough," Ryan said, holding his arms up in surrender, realizing he'd hit a sore spot. "Speaking of the case we're here to solve, do you want to go over the file Garrett copied for me before Sarah Ripley's husband arrives in town? We've got a lot to review and not a ton of time before he gets here."

"That sounds like a productive use of our time," Jessie said, still slightly miffed at his hint that she might be overreacting but trying not to give in to her irritation.

"Okay then," he said, pulling out a laptop and plugging in the thumb drive Garrett had given him, "While I was waiting for you and Hannah to arrive, I did a cursory review of both victims' backgrounds. On the surface there are some similarities."

"Like what?" Jessie asked, looking at the screen.

"Both women were in their mid-thirties and married with no children," he explained. "Both were attractive. Both were successful entrepreneurs who ran retail businesses. But after that, their differences become more noticeable."

"For example?"

"Like Rich said, Clarice Kimble is a local. She lived here until she went away to college in Arizona; met her boyfriend there. After a couple of years in Tucson, they came back here and got married. They've been here ever since. A few years back, she opened her aromatherapy store, Sense of Scents. She's the vice-president of the chamber of commerce and from what I can tell, is incredibly active in the community. She's on the board of her church and of an arts high school in town called the Wildpines Arts Conservatory."

"Sounds like a pillar of the community," Jessie said drily. She'd learned to be suspicious of such spotless resumes.

Ryan was about to continue when Hannah poked her head in the door.

"Everything all right?" Jessie asked.

"Yeah, sorry to interrupt but this cabin's small and I couldn't help but overhear you."

"That's okay," Jessie said. "What's up?"

"I heard you mention the Conservatory and it reminded me—I met some students who go there at the coffeehouse earlier. They invited me to hang out tonight at a café bar. I looked it up and it's only a half mile walk from here, just down the hill. I'd like to go if it's cool. After all, the whole point of coming up here was to let us get outside a little, right?"

Jessie looked over at Ryan, who shrugged. She could tell he didn't want to get in the middle of this and though she understood the urge, she didn't exactly love being left out on an island to deal with it. She turned back to Hannah.

"I think you can definitely go. I'm less sure about the 'walking there' part. It's partly true that we're here so we can get outside. But the other reason we're up here helping out is because, over the last few nights, someone has been stabbing women who were alone late at night. I know that the pattern so far suggests that victims are older than you, but I don't really want to test the theory. So if you don't mind being driven there and back, I'm okay with you going."

She could see Hannah's mind racing and recalled her own teen years, when prior to having a car, she'd insisted that her adoptive mother drop her off a block from the mall so none of her friends would observe the horror of her getting a ride from a parent.

"I'll park next door so no one sees you get out of the car," she offered preemptively.

Hannah smirked.

"You think I'm so shallow that I'd be bothered by you dropping me off right in front of the place?" she asked, trying to gin up a sense of moral outrage.

"Maybe," Jessie said. "At your age, I was. I'd actually consider us to be in a pretty healthy familial place if our conflicts are about you being embarrassed by people seeing you with me."

Hannah looked torn between wanting to be snarky and not wanting to upset her chances of going.

"They're meeting at nine," she finally said before disappearing from the doorway.

"Lovely, dear," Jessie called out to the empty space, "I'll be sure to remove my apron and curlers before we head out."

She looked over at Ryan who shook his head disapproving.

"I don't think she's as amused as you are," he chastised.

"Mind your business, coward," she instructed. "You were about to tell me why Sarah Ripley is nothing like Clarice Kimble."

"Yes, ma'am," he said saluting elaborately. "As I was saying, Clarice is a local through and through. Sarah lives in Los Angeles—Silverlake specifically. She has a shop there called SEE, or Sarah's Everyday Essentials. It's kind of a gift store. They have everything from leatherbound journals to body scrubs to tote bags with quips about 'wine o'clock.'"

"Sounds like the kind of place I'd like to visit," Jessie admitted.

"Apparently you're not the only one because she was planning to open up a second location here. She leased a space at the start of the year and, according to Garrett, hoped to open for business by April."

"But she doesn't live here?"

"Not yet," Ryan said. "Garrett said she was a familiar face around town, usually here on weekends. She was well-liked, from what he says, friendly and enthusiastic about being here. They own the place where she was killed, though her husband came up far less often, and he wasn't well-known. But Sarah had joined the chamber and was ingratiating herself with the local powers-that-be."

"Any suggestion that her attempts at ingratiation had alienated anyone?"

"Garrett said he hadn't heard anything like that but I guess we can see if her husband tells a different story."

Jessie nodded, her eyes scanning the files on the laptop.

"Do we know if the women knew each other?" Jessie wondered. "Maybe they were in the same social circle?"

"I asked Garrett that and he said he wasn't aware of them knowing each other socially. But he also admitted that he wasn't totally plugged in to the over thirty female social scene."

"I see one connection at least," Jessie noted, pointing at the screen. "They were both part of some online group for local business owners called 'Wildpines Business Association.' It looks like it's not formally associated with the chamber of commerce, although I see a lot of cross-over in membership."

"Good catch," Ryan said, typing in the web address for the WBA.

When it loaded, they saw that the site was pretty bare bones. There was a list of local businesses in the association, with addresses and phone numbers, one-line business descriptions, and website links. There was an events tab, which included monthly coffee klatches and occasional workshops. And there was members-only chat forum, which required a log-in and password. That was pretty much it.

"Why do they need this, if there's also a chamber of commerce?" Jessie asked. "Don't they do the same thing?"

"From what I can tell, the WBA is more informal, intended as a resource rather than an official group representing the town. What I'm wondering is whether it's just a coincidence that both women were in the group."

Jessie was inclined to think so.

"This town is so small that it looks like half the businesses here are listed," she noted. "I'd be more surprised they *weren't* both members. I have a different question. I know we only have two victims. But they have comparable profiles and were killed only two nights apart with the same weapon. Does this killer have a type?"

She knew Ryan couldn't answer that question yet any more than she could. But it seemed hard to buy that in a town as small as Wildpines that two women with such similar traits were killed within forty-eight hours of each other.

Jessie stood up and began pacing, officially to stretch but more to clear her head. Even though she'd never known either of these women, she felt for them. Both Clarice and Sarah looked to be in great places in their lives, at least professionally. Clarice was a community leader. Sarah was starting an exciting new endeavor. They seemed set.

On good days, Jessie imagined herself potentially being as settled as these two appeared to be. She already had a good job, a loving boyfriend, and a challenging but interesting sister that she hadn't even known existed just over a year ago. When she wasn't being stalked by elderly serial killers, her life wasn't half bad. What was possible five years from now? Maybe great things; or maybe she'd end up stabbed to death, lying alone in a pile of snow, waiting for a snowplow driver to come by and realize she wasn't a deer hit by a car.

Before she could go too far down that rabbit hole, her phone, resting on the end table, buzzed. Ryan's did the same a half-second later. He looked down.

"It's from Garrett. Dwayne Ripley just arrived in town. He's waiting for us at the station."

"Good," Jessie said, pushing thoughts of her own future out of her head for now. "It's time we get some answers."

CHAPTER TWELVE

Ryan thought he was pretty smooth.

They were just leaving the cabin when he pretended like he'd forgotten something, gave Jessie the car keys, and told her he'd be right out.

Technically he was being honest, though he couldn't reveal what he'd forgotten: an engagement ring. He'd bought the ring the previous week, on the same day that he and Hannah had almost been poisoned by the Night Hunter. In fact, he'd concealed it in the very panic room where they'd gone to hide from the killer's paralyzing syringes.

He'd subsequently taken the ring to the safe house in Sherman Oaks and now brought it here. But since the cabin was small and he didn't trust Hannah not to snoop, he'd decided to keep it on him. So he rushed back to their bedroom, removed the black engagement ring box from the rolled up pair of socks in the cabinet drawer where he'd put it earlier, and then headed back out.

He kept it in his front pocket, where it burned an imaginary hole in his pants during the entire three-minute drive to the station. The only distractions from its weight against his leg were the questions that consumed him.

Was he really going to propose to Jessie soon? Of course, he was. Otherwise why bring the ring? Why *buy* it? So if it was inevitable, when was the right time? Logic suggested maybe waiting until after they were free of the Night Hunter threat.

On the other hand, asking her to marry him might be a way for them to take back control of their lives, a way to prove that they could find happiness in the middle of chaos and violence. Of course, that led to the question he couldn't answer: when he asked her, what would she say?

Even beyond that, there was one final question, which loomed larger than all the others. Did he even deserve her? With his still-withered body, his post-trauma mood swings, and most of all, his shameful failure to save Alan Trembley from the Night Hunter, had he lost the right to be with her? He felt himself slipping into a dark place and shook his head violently to break the spell. *That's all the worrying you have time for right now.*

He pulled into one of the two parking spaces in front of the station. Glancing over at Jessie, he was briefly worried that she'd read his thoughts. But then he saw that she was lost in her own.

"You ready for this?" he asked.

"As ready as I can be."

They were just getting out of the car when his phone buzzed. He read the message, then shared it with her.

"I reached out to Jamil earlier back at the cabin while you were talking to Hannah," he said. "I wanted to get confirmation that Dwayne Ripley was in L.A. last night."

"What did he find?" Jessie asked as they walked up the stairs to the station entrance. Even though he felt much more confident walking these days, he took it easy on the icy steps.

"According to Ripley's phone and vehicle GPS systems, he was in Silverlake from 7:15 last night until 7:30 this morning. Then he went to the Perris coroner's office and here after that—nothing overtly suspicious."

"Okay, then I guess we can rule him out as a suspect, at least directly," she replied. "It doesn't mean he didn't pay someone, although then we're really getting out there. Would this guy hire someone to kill his wife *and* have another woman killed to throw off suspicion? It's a stretch."

"We've seen crazier," Ryan countered.

"That's true," Jessie conceded. "Still, let's give him the benefit of the doubt and start easy. We can always go harder if need be."

Ryan nodded in agreement and started to hold the door open for her before quickly closing it again.

"You should keep your beanie on," he reminded her as she was about to pull it off, "Maybe your coat too. Don't forget—this guy is from L.A. It's possible he's seen you on TV. Anything you can do to prevent him from recognizing you is worth it."

He could tell that she wasn't excited by the prospect of keeping everything on in the warm station but she didn't fight him on it. Once inside, they found that the station was marginally quieter than earlier in the afternoon. Rusty the drunk had been released and Undersheriff Richard McClane was gone too. So was the other deputy who'd been here before, Pete Traven.

That left only the receptionist, Deputy Garrett Hicks, and the man he was quietly talking to at a table near the back. Ryan assumed it was Dwayne Ripley.

"May I help you?" the sixty-something woman with coke bottle glasses asked.

Ryan was a little surprised but made no mention that he and Jessie had been here earlier that afternoon, accompanied by the county undersheriff. She was either unimpressed or very forgetful. Before he could answer, Garrett called out.

"They're with me, Bitsy," he said. "Remember, they're the city detectives helping out on the recent cases."

Bitsy gave no indication that she remembered but motioned for them to pass behind the Formica barrier. Garrett stood up to greet them. The man he assumed was Ripley stood as well and turned around.

He had on slacks, a dress shirt, and a blazer. Ryan noticed that he was wearing dress shoes that were completely inappropriate for the snowy surroundings. Footwear choices likely hadn't been a priority for him today. In his late thirties, with thick brown hair, tan skin and a trim physique, he would have been considered good-looking under normal circumstances. But in his current state—unshaven, with red, puffy eyes—he looked rough, more like a guy coming down from a bender.

"Mr. Ripley," Garrett said by way of introduction, "this is Jennifer Barnes and Randy Hosea. They're detectives with LAPD who agreed to help us out. Detectives, this is Dwayne Ripley. He's just come in from Perris to answer your questions."

"We appreciate that, sir," Ryan said, walking over. "And we both want to offer you our deepest condolences. We can only imagine how difficult it is to get this horrible news and then have to spend your day driving all over Southern California to confirm it."

"Thank you," Ripley said. His voice was hoarse, probably from a combination of yelling and crying.

"Why don't you sit back down," Jessie suggested. "We'll pull up some chairs."

Once they were all situated, Ryan decided to ease in as he and Jessie had discussed.

"Why don't you tell us a little about Sarah," he said gently. "What made her decide to open up a second location of her store here?"

It was a question intended to get Ripley talking without putting too much pressure on him right away. Ryan liked to think of it as a crime-adjacent question. Nonetheless, the man sighed heavily, as if even that straightforward inquiry might be too much for him. Finally he gathered himself.

"Mostly I think it was just an excuse to spend more time in Wildpines. She just loved it up here. She'd take every opportunity to visit and the idea that she could come up with a legitimate professional reason to do so really appealed to her."

"You didn't feel as strongly about the town though, right?" Jessie asked, keeping any accusation out of her voice.

"I like it," Ripley said, looking at Garrett as he answered, as if he felt an obligation to make his feelings clear to a designated local. "We bought the cabin here, so I'm obviously fond of the place. But my business doesn't allow for me to get away as much. I work for a brokerage firm and am bound by the timing of the markets. Sarah didn't have that problem. Her shop is a finely tuned machine. Usually she'd be there for most of the day on Monday through Thursday. But on a lot of Fridays she might only stop by for a few hours, sometimes not even that, all so she could get a head start on coming up here."

"That sounds nice," Ryan said. "I have to admit I'm jealous just hearing about it. Did you ever feel that way?"

"Jealous?" Ripley asked. "Not really. Like I said, I like it here but part of that was because it made her so joyful. Her passion was contagious. Even when she came up here alone, the good vibes could last for days after she got back. She always seemed so happy after a visit, giddy even."

He stopped for a moment to blow his nose, giving Ryan a chance to make eye contact with Jessie. She glanced back knowingly. He knew immediately that they had the same thought. What could be going on up here that had Sarah Ripley giddy with enthusiasm for days afterward without her husband around? It could be a passion for long walks in the woods. But more likely it was an affair, or at least the potential of one. Neither of them lingered on the idea.

"Did she ever talk about moving to Wildpines?" Ryan asked.

"Not for good, but she did suggest that she split her time up here for a few months when the store opened. She'd be starting with fresh staff and want to be around more to supervise. She talked about being in L.A. Monday through Wednesday and here Thursday through Sunday until the place got going. She was going to just open from Friday until Sunday at first."

"You were cool with that plan?" Ryan asked.

"Like I said, this place made her happy. I didn't want to get in the way of that."

"Did Sarah ever mention having a falling out with anyone up here?" Jessie asked, making a sharp turn. "Or even just someone who made her uncomfortable?"

Ripley was quiet for moment, searching his memory.

"Not that I recall," he finally said. "Sarah got along with just about everybody. That's one of the reasons her store did so well. It's not like it sold anything all that different from other gift places. Customers just liked being around her. I can't remember her having a heated argument with anyone."

"Not even you?" Ryan pressed slightly, having to at least test out the hitman angle. "I saw that you were married five years last fall. There had to be a few hiccups."

Ripley shrugged.

"Sure, we disagreed like any couple. But heated stuff? No. We're both level-headed people. Yelling isn't our thing. In fact, I think I've raised my voice more today when trying to get answers than I have at any time in the last half-decade."

"No one resented her starting a new business up here?" Jessie asked, wisely moving away from the couple issues. They didn't want the guy to shut down or get defensive. "Nobody viewed her as competition, as a threat?"

"I'm sure some folks did," Ripley answered. "But she never mentioned it. In fact, she was invited to all kinds of stuff. I know she'd been encouraged to attend a 'women in business' seminar next month. She told me she'd joined some local business group too, with an online forum to exchange ideas."

"The WBA?" Jessie asked.

"That's it," he said.

"We'll need her login info for their chat room," Jessie told him. "It's possible someone made a threat against her on there and she didn't want to worry you with it."

"Sure," he said, seeming to consider the idea for the first time. "She kept all her sign-on information in her phone, which they're holding as evidence in Riverside. I can give you the password."

"That'd be great," Jessie said. "And we'd appreciate it if you could send us a couple of good, close-up photos of Sarah as well."

"Okay. When do I go up to the cabin?" he asked, writing down her code on a slip of paper. "Deputy Hicks said he wanted me to take a look around to see if anything was missing, that it might help with the investigation."

Ryan looked over at Jessie to see if she had any opposition. She indicated that she didn't.

"You can go do that now," he said. "Deputy Garrett can accompany you and let us know if there's anything amiss."

They all stood up and shook hands. Ryan and Jessie offered a second round of condolences and watched the men leave. Ryan wanted to get her thoughts on the idea of a potential affair but he could tell that she didn't want to broach the subject in front of Bitsy the receptionist.

"Want to get some air?' he asked casually.

"Yeah, it's warm in here," Jessie said dramatically.

Once outside, they stood on the porch, watching Garrett's vehicle drive up the hill toward the Ripley cabin. Once it was out of sight, she ripped off the beanie in relief. The hair on her forehead was sticky with sweat.

"Sounds like Sarah was really enjoying her alone time up here," he said leadingly.

"Assuming she was alone," Jessie added. "I think that's an avenue we need to explore a little more. Dwayne may have liked how 'level-headed' their lives were. But maybe Sarah had started to find it a little boring. I'd be curious to know if she was home all last night or if she spent time anywhere else."

"It's funny that you say that," Ryan replied. "I just got an alert from Rich McClane saying they have the location data from Sarah's phone."

"Why didn't I get that alert?' she demanded, a second before her phone buzzed too. "Oh, never mind."

Ryan studied the information.

"It looks like she spent a few hours at a bar called Wild Things, stayed until 9:30. It's just down the road if we want to stop by."

"Around here, everything's just down the road," Jessie pointed out. "We also need to talk to Martin Kimble. I want to find out if he's aware of any connections between his wife and Sarah that we might be missing."

"Okay," Ryan replied. "Where do you want to go first?"

He watched his girlfriend ponder the question. He loved to watch her ponder. Her forehead got a tiny wrinkle just above her nose when she concentrated extra hard.

"Let's start at the bar," she suggested. "It's late afternoon and I'd rather talk to the folks there before it gets too rowdy. Let's meet the drunks first. We can grill the grieving widower after that."

"You are such a delicate flower," he teased.

"That's why you love me," she replied, sticking out her tongue.

He pretended to act casual, but hearing the word "love" out loud suddenly reminded him of the ring in his pocket, and on cue, the invisible burning sensation returned.

CHAPTER THIRTEEN

It was hard to make believe everything was normal.

Walking through the aisles of Brightside Market, it was a challenge not to imagine that everyone knew. How could they not realize that they were standing next to someone who had snuffed out two lives this week? How could they not know that the hand beside them reaching for milk had only hours earlier plunged a knife deep into the chest of a vital young woman? It seemed absurd. And yet no one batted an eye or gave a sideways glance.

The same thing happened at the bank, and later at the furniture repair shop. People just talked casually, like you hadn't had to shower late last night to wash dried blood off your hands. No one suspected a person so normal-seeming could be capable of such brutality. Having the secret was almost as delicious as doing the deed.

Soon, there would be another deed to do. The excitement was already building somewhere deep in the chest. The heart was beating faster. The breath was quicker and shallower. The memory of the knife puncturing and then shredding flesh returned in an orgasmic rush. It was almost too much to bear.

Luckily there were only a few hours left to wait. The next perpetrator had been selected. Actually, that wasn't quite accurate. This one, like the others, hadn't been selected—rather, she had presented herself for reprisal. Just like the others, she deserved what was coming to her. Just like the others, she had brought it on herself.

CHAPTER FOURTEEN

Jessie felt like kicking herself. They had waited too long.

By the time Ryan pulled into the Wild Things parking lot at 4:34, the sky was darkening fast and the lot was already filling up.

"Ugh," Jessie said as they got out.

"What's wrong?" Ryan asked as they got out of the car.

"A crowded bar is going to make things infinitely more difficult," she replied. "Not only will we have to navigate rowdier folks, it's going to make it that much harder to keep a lid on Sarah's murder."

"That's true," he acknowledged, "But to be honest, I'm surprised it's stayed quiet this long. In a town this small, information like that spreads fast. We're lucky Garrett got that snowplow driver to keep quiet."

As they approached the bar entrance, she noticed that he didn't take his cane and knew it wasn't only because he felt he didn't really need it anymore. He also didn't want to look vulnerable in what could be a rough place. She didn't comment on it.

It took a second to adjust to the darkness. When she could see clearly, she found that the place was a real dive. There was sawdust on the floor, much of it dried after mixing with any number of liquids. The lamps above the pool tables in the backroom were dim and one of them flickered, adding an extra level of difficulty for the players. Most of the cocktail tables looked rickety and the bar itself appeared to be comprised of rotting wood.

They walked straight for it. As Jessie got the attention of the bartender, Ryan held back a little and stood slightly apart when he eventually came over. The bartender was in his thirties and looked like he probably drank more than most of his customers. He had greasy black hair, three days of stubble, and a crooked grin that Jessie suspected he busted out often on well-lubricated ladies.

"Hey there," she said, going into coquettish mode.

"Hey there yourself," he quipped, his voice gravelly.

"You look familiar. Were you working last night?" Jessie asked coyly.

"I was," he answered, assuming she was flirting with him, just as she hoped he would. "But I know you weren't here. I'd have remembered you."

"Are you sure about that?" she asked, batting her eyes. "Were you here around 9:30?"

"Sure was," he said proudly. "I worked 'til closing. Don't tell me I somehow missed you. If I did, let me make it up to you with a free drink."

"I might take you up on that later," she said, stretching out languorously as she leaned over the bar and beckoned for him to get closer. He bent forward to meet her.

"What's your name?" she whispered in his ear.

"Tim," he told her. "You?"

"I'm Jen," she cooed. "I need to ask you a personal question, Tim. But I don't want to do it with all these people around. Can someone take over for you for a minute?"

"Sweetheart, I promise you it'll take longer than a minute."

"Tim," she replied, feigning bashfulness at his comment as she fought off the urge to vomit, "Why don't we start with the question and see where it goes from there?"

"You got it," he said, waving at a server across the room. "Take over for a spell. I need to assist this lady briefly."

"Is there somewhere a little more secluded?" Jessie asked.

He nodded, came out from behind the bar, and led her down the hall past the restrooms to a swinging door marked "employees only." He held it open for her and she glanced back at him as she entered. She saw that his eyes were focused on her backside so he didn't notice that Ryan was only a few paces behind him.

He had led her into the small employee break room just off to the side of the kitchen. Cooks and servers darted back and forth just out of sight. Being so close to the kitchen and still wearing her jacket and beanie to disguise her identity, Jessie felt like she was in a self-contained steam room. Ryan lingered just outside the swinging door, though Jessie could see him through the small, round, porthole window.

"So what's up, darlin'?" he asked, leaning against the entryway.

"I wanted to show you a photo on my phone and see what you make of it."

"Oh wow, Jen," he said, clearly intrigued. "You really don't waste time, do you? Let's see it."

Jessie clicked on one of the photos of Sarah Ripley that her husband had given them and held it up for Tim.

"Do you recognize this woman?" she asked.

Tim looked at it and then back at her. He was clearly surprised. This wasn't the kind of photo he'd been expecting.

"Why?" he asked, still titillated but slightly more on guard. "Is she a friend of yours? Did she have nice things to say about me?"

"Is there any reason she'd have a strong opinion about you?" Jessie asked, trying to keep her voice playful but finding it increasingly difficult. "Did you spend some quality time together last night?"

Tim's half-smile disappeared.

"What is this?" he said warily. "You made me think you wanted to have a little fun but now you're asking all these questions. If your friend said I did something wrong, she's lying. I sold her some drinks and I flirted with her and her friends. She left. The rest of them stayed and none of them seemed to think I was out of line. So what's the problem, *Jen?*"

The way he said her fake name had an air of hostility to it. Any chance that she could tease answers out of him was gone now, not that she minded.

"What time did she leave, Tim?" she asked, dropping all pretense of playfulness.

"I've had enough of this," he said. "Worst break ever. Why don't you head on back out there? Or better yet, try another bar. The service here is about to get real slow for you."

He turned around to find Ryan, who had quietly slipped through the swinging door during their conversation, standing in his way.

"I think you should answer the lady's question," he said, holding up the badge and ID that said his name was Detective Randy Hosea.

He stood with his shoulders squared and his jaw set. His open jacket revealed his holster and the gun inside. Anyone who didn't know about his injury would find him an intimidating presence.

Jessie was overcome with pride. Just last summer, Ryan was comatose in a hospital. As recently as a few weeks ago, he was still using a cane for everyday support. But in this moment, he looked almost like his old self.

Tim turned back to Jessie, who held up her own fake ID saying she was Jennifer Barnes.

"Still waiting," she said quietly.

He looked like he wanted to object, but seemed to sense that combativeness wouldn't serve him well and sighed.

"Okay, let me think. I remember her saying she had to bail because she was meeting someone around ten. One of the other girls told her she had time because it was only 9:30. But she said it would take a while to get home because she wanted to walk. She paid her tab and left a little after that."

"Do you have a receipt that can confirm the time?" Ryan asked.

"I can check but I think she paid cash," he said, then added. "Is she okay?"

"That's what we're looking into," Jessie said, not lying but not wanting to reveal any more than necessary.

"Why don't you check those receipts just to be sure," Ryan suggested.

As he spoke, Jessie noticed one of the female servers in the kitchen whispering to a cook as they both looked in her direction. Though she couldn't be sure, she thought the server's expression was more than just generally curious. She seemed to be trying to remember something, almost like she was attempting to place a face, like she thought she recognized someone.

"We should go, Randy," Jessie said suddenly as she touched her head to make sure the beanie hadn't fallen off. "We have somewhere to be. Just give Tim your number and he can text you once he's checked the receipts."

Ryan followed her gaze and immediately picked up on what had her worried.

"Sure thing, Jen," he said. "I'll meet you out at the car."

Jessie nodded and quickly brushed past Tim.

"Thanks for your help," she said quietly. "And keep this to yourself. We don't want to worry folks unnecessarily. If we start hearing rumors about this woman, we'll know where they got started, understand?"

Tim grunted that he did. Jessie didn't stick around, pushing through the swinging door and hurrying out of the bar and into the cold, near-dark night as fast as she could. She had to hope that the server hadn't recognized her. If she did, she might tell others and eventually—inevitably—that would get back to L.A. and potentially the Night Hunter. The thought gave her more of a chill than the weather.

70

It was only exacerbated when she remembered where they were going next: to talk to the widower of a woman who was murdered right outside his front door less than seventy-two hours ago.

CHAPTER FIFTEEN

Jessie steeled herself for what she knew was coming.

Unlike tricking a bartender into answering a few questions, the interview they were about to conduct had to be more straightforward. It would also likely be much more painful.

Just after 5 p.m., as the last embers of the sun dipped behind the westernmost mountain, Ryan pulled up outside the gingerbread-style house where Clarice Kimble had died.

Neither he nor Jessie had commented on their shared concern that the server at Wild Things might have identified her. There was no point in worrying about something they couldn't control. Any attempt to remedy the situation would only make it worse. Instead they focused on the task at hand: questioning Martin Kimble.

"How do you want to play it?" Jessie asked.

"Sympathetic, at least at first," Ryan said. "His wife just died and he may be beating himself up, wondering if he had come out of the house earlier, would she be alive?"

Jessie couldn't help but wonder if he wasn't projecting a little. She knew that's how he felt about Alan Trembley's death—that the detective might still be here if Ryan had been able to walk up those Santa Monica hostel stairs with him. She didn't dare comment on that specifically but she felt it wise to give him a reminder.

"I think that's a good starting point," she said. "But let's not forget that this guy is a potential suspect too. He could have been waiting for his wife to get home, then killed her and gone back inside. The GPS won't help us much since it can't distinguish whether his phone was inside or out at the time she died. That's awfully convenient for him."

"If he did it, it is," Ryan acknowledged. "But if he didn't, it's pretty inconvenient. He won't have a convincing alibi to fall back on when he might have just been watching TV on his couch."

Jessie shrugged. "I guess it's time to find out."

They got out of the car. Jessie noted that just like at the bar, Ryan didn't take the cane with him. But unlike then, there was no need to project an air of toughness for this interview. She hoped he'd left it in the car this time simply because he was feeling more confident moving without it. Even so, she stayed close in case he lost his balance or slipped on the ice.

Ryan knocked on the door. They heard someone moving inside and after about half a minute, a lock clicked and the door opened. They were met by a chunky, balding man in his late thirties. He was blandly pleasant-looking but it was clear he hadn't slept much recently. He was bleary-eyed and his face was blotchy. He was also wearing a red and green Christmas-themed sweater with Rudolph on the front. It struck Jessie as wildly inappropriate considering his situation. Then again, maybe he was too out of it to notice.

"Mr. Kimble," Ryan began, "I'm Randy Hosea and this is Jennifer Barnes. We're with the Los Angeles Police Department. Undersheriff McClane asked us for assistance in your wife's death. Do you mind if we come in?"

"Rich told me you might be coming by sometime soon," he said, opening the door wide so they could enter. His voice sounded as tired as he looked. "Please forgive the state of the place. I haven't had the energy to do much cleaning up since…it happened."

"Not a problem," Jessie said, stepping inside. The house didn't look all that messy, though it was packed with knick-knacks. Every shelf and counter in sight was covered with baubles and trinkets, most of which looked like they'd been collected from garage sales. There were a *lot* of gnomes.

Kimble guided them to the couch in the living room and he sat across from them in an easy chair. He seemed oblivious to the fact that the TV was on and the volume was loud. An infomercial about a wrinkle-defying cream blasted at them.

"Do you mind muting that?" she asked politely.

"Oh, sorry, I barely noticed it," he said, reaching for the remote and accidentally knocking it to the ground.

While he fumbled with it, Jessie glanced at the photo of him and Clarice on the table beside him. They were sitting on a log in front of a creek, likely somewhere not far from here. The picture looked to be a couple of years old. Martin was slightly less pudgy. Clarice looked much the same as in the photos Deputy Garret Hicks had provided them.

Like Sarah Ripley, she was attractive. She had blonde hair and porcelain skin. But she didn't look anywhere near as friendly as Sarah. With her tight smile and no-nonsense hazel eyes, the photo looked more like a DMV photo than a couples' portrait.

Once Kimble managed to mute the television, Ryan launched in.

"We know you've already had to answer a lot of questions and we read the reports so we won't go over every detail, but we did want to address a few things."

"Of course," Kimble said. "I'm ready to do anything I can to help find out who did this."

"So just to be clear," Ryan began, "you were home and decided to leave when Clarice didn't return on time?"

"It wasn't that she wasn't on time," Kimble said. "She's often late and she told me she was running behind on Sunday night too. What concerned me was that she wasn't returning my texts or calls. So I figured that I'd just go check on her. Everything around here is so close that it's not a big deal, you know?"

Sure," Ryan said, "and that's when you found her—around 9:15?"

Kimble nodded, seemingly unable to speak.

"You never heard anything unusual prior to that?" Jessie asked, trying not to sound accusatory.

He shook his head. "We hear things all the time. Raccoons and squirrels get into trash. Deer walk through yards. A bear once broke into my storage shed. But nothing that night made me perk up more than usual."

Jessie glanced over at Ryan, who seemed content to let her take the lead, so she continued.

"Why was Clarice late that night?" she asked. She watched him closely to see if the question upset him but he didn't react.

"She was working," he said non-responsively.

"On something for the store?" she pressed.

"No. She said it was for her business group."

"The WBA?" she prompted.

"Right, so you've heard of it?"

"We were looking at the website this afternoon," Jessie told him.

"Okay, then you're familiar. Well, Clarice runs it—ran it. She hadn't updated some new members to the group so she wanted to get them in fresh for the new week."

"Yes, we saw the list of members," Jessie said. "But we couldn't access the chat area."

"That's a forum for members only," Kimble said. "You need a login to get in."

"We'd appreciate getting Clarice's administrator login, Mr. Kimble," she said. "Having full access to the membership data and chats might be very helpful to us."

Kimble looked aghast.

"Oh, I couldn't do that," he said as if she'd asked for her medical records. "That information is private. Clarice always assured her members that they could speak honestly and confidentially in that forum. I couldn't betray their trust."

Jessie wasn't amused. The confidentiality of a small town business chat forum didn't take precedence over a murder investigation. Ryan must have sensed her annoyance because he spoke up.

"We can respect that, Mr. Kimble, but it's just that, in a situation like this, it could be quite helpful—."

"Is there something untoward in the chats, Mr. Kimble?" Jessie demanded, interrupting. She was tired of Ryan's diffidence. "Something illegal perhaps?"

"Of course not! Why would you even suggest such a thing?"

"If there's nothing to hide, then why hide it?" she answered his question with one of her own. "Don't you want to help us solve your wife's murder? This list could be a great resource. It could reveal financial misdeeds or infidelities, perhaps even—and forgive me for saying this—on the part of your wife."

"I doubt the latter," Kimble said, coming as close to cracking a smile as she'd seen since they arrived.

"Why do you say that?"

"Because there isn't much cause for cheating around here, Ms. Barnes," he said. "We don't talk about it publicly, but Clarice and I were part of a swingers' group."

"I'm sorry?" Ryan said, unable to help himself.

"I know it must shock you fancy Los Angeles types to learn that we provincial mountain folk like to have a good time, but it's true. We were swingers."

"Is that why you don't want to share the login info?" Jessie asked, refusing to be baited by the city "types" jab. "Is it a list of swingers or something?"

"Heavens no," he said as if the idea was absurd. "It's just a chat forum for business owners. But I don't know if someone made a passing mention of a liaison in the chat. Since I'm a naturalist and don't own a business, I wasn't a member. But I'm not going to allow you to go rooting around in the website on some fishing expedition."

"Even if accessing it might reveal a threat against Clarice?" Jessie pressed.

"I can answer that for you now. My wife told me everything and she never mentioned any threats. Sure, she'd get nasty comments from people. Sometimes, she'd even read them out loud to me. Clarice was a strong-willed woman and that rubbed some people the wrong way. But it was never anything serious. You have to remember, most people around here have known each other for decades. Yes, there's a lot of baggage, but there's a lot of love too. No one would hurt her."

Jessie was dumbfounded by the statement.

"Bu the thing is, Mr. Kimble," she pointed out, "someone *did* hurt her."

The comment didn't have the desired effect. His back stiffened and he sat upright in his chair.

"Nonetheless, I won't act in opposition to her wishes. You may *not* access the WBA website chat forum without a warrant." The way he said it suggested that the conversation was over.

Even before looking over at Ryan, whose eyes were pleading with her to pull back, she had decided not to push any farther. She wasn't sure what he was hiding, if anything at all. But there was no point in arguing. There was also no point in alienating a pillar of the local community any more than she already had. That would only make things more challenging for them when they reached out to other residents.

"Thank you for your time, Mr. Kimble," she said, standing up.

He walked them to the door and they exchanged goodbyes. As she and Ryan returned to the car, he leaned over and whispered to her.

"What now?"

"Now," she said, making sure that she didn't reply loud enough for Kimble to hear her, "we go back to Rich McClane's cabin to check in on Hannah and see how our friends back at HSS are doing in the search for the Night Hunter."

"I think I hear an 'and' in there," Ryan said with trepidation.

"Oh yeah, *and* we get a frickin' warrant to check that website."

CHAPTER SIXTEEN

It wasn't as simple as that.

When they got back to the cabin and called Rich, they learned that crossing the Kimbles, especially one in mourning, was frowned upon.

"We can get the warrant," Rich told them, "but it's delicate. We have to go to the right judge at the right time. And that means we have to wait until around midday tomorrow, when the ones who might cause trouble are out to lunch. Can you wait until then?"

"It doesn't sound like we have much of a choice," Jessie said. "We'll wait."

More out of frustration than enthusiasm, they began reviewing everything they'd compiled. But eventually the long day and the altitude started to hit them. Jessie changed tactics. They moved into the living room to call Jamil for an update.

It was the first time any of them had spent time in the room, which could politely be called rustic cozy. There was a weathered couch and an easy chair with loose stuffing, separated by a small end table. Resting on a slightly larger, well-dented coffee table was the remote control and a three-year-old issue of a backpacking magazine. The TV, which actually had rabbit ears, was pressed up against the wall, not far from the fireplace, which was full of patiently waiting logs. Everything felt crammed together.

As they settled in on the couch, Jessie put Jamil on speaker so Ryan could hear. Hannah wandered into the room too. Jessie's initial inclination was to make her leave but then thought better of it. Maybe hearing the updates would help set her at ease. Regardless, she deserved to know. Unfortunately there wasn't much at all in the way of new information.

"The teams have been driving all around town," Jamil told them, "following up on every recent camera sighting of an old dude driving an old car but they've come up empty. Detectives Reid and Bray have been interviewing employees at all the hostels where we know the man stayed for the last few months, hoping to discern a pattern. So far we've got nothing. Detective Nettles and Kat have been visiting multiple used car dealerships where the man bought cars. But they've come up empty too. None of the dealers recall the guy. He did an amazing job of being unmemorable. They've called it quits for the night, although I think Kat was going to check out one last dealership on her way home. I wouldn't hold your breath that she finds anything."

"You're really filling us with optimism here, Jamil," Ryan said acidly.

"I'm sorry Detective. I wish I had better news. But don't lose hope. Tomorrow's another day. I'll have brand new camera data to work with. We'll start fresh then. How's it going there?"

"A lot of dead ends," Jessie sighed. "But don't worry about us. And don't forget to stop working for the night. You're no good to us if you're half asleep, Jamil."

"You know I don't operate like the rest of you humans, Ms. Hunt," he replied, coming as close to a joke as Jamil was capable of.

"Goodnight," she chuckled and hung up. She was just about to call Kat when Hannah waved to get her attention.

"Remember the thing I wanted to go to tonight at Wildyology?" she said.

"I do."

"Are you still cool with me going?" Hannah asked.

"Are you still cool with me dropping you off and picking you up?"

"Yes," Hannah said flatly.

"And you understand that there's a killer on the loose and that you're not to go anywhere other than Wildyology?"

"I understand," Hannah said coolly.

As much as Jessie still wanted to say no, she knew she couldn't. Hannah had agreed to all her restrictions. She hadn't rolled her eyes once. And something in the oven was making her mouth water.

"I'll have you there at nine," she said.

"Thank you," Hannah replied, breaking into a wide grin. "By the way, your friend Rich the undersheriff had duck breasts in the freezer. I've taken possession of them, as well as some mushrooms and couscous. Dinner will be ready in an hour."

She left without another word. Jessie looked over at Ryan, who nodded approvingly. Apparently she'd handled the situation well. Feeling surprisingly good about herself, she grabbed the phone and called Kat.

It went straight to voicemail. She decided not to leave a message for now. She could always check in later.

Wildyology wasn't exactly what Hannah would call "wild."

It was more like an amped up version of the Elevated Grounds coffeehouse, with alcohol and live bands instead of a lone cellist.

After Jessie dropped her off and—to her credit— left without issuing any additional warnings about avoiding knife wielding killers, she walked into what looked like a converted hunting lodge.

She was immediately met by multiple large, stuffed, animal heads on the walls near the entryway. Directly in front of her was a large sitting area with a roaring fireplace that took up a whole wall. Several worn couches had animal hide blankets draped over them for anyone who felt chilly despite the flames. Off to the left was a traditional dining room. To the right was a long bar packed with people, all yelling orders at the lone, frazzled-looking bartender.

Hannah didn't see anyone she recognized so she walked to the sliding door beside the fireplace wall and stepped outside onto the top floor of a massive, two-level deck. The lower deck down below overlooked what she assumed was Blueberry Creek, though it was hard to see it in the dark. A band was playing Bad Company's "Feel Like Makin' Love." Surrounding the performers in a semi-circle were a dozen rickety cocktail tables, all full.

On the top level where she stood were multiple picnic tables. People were eating at all of them but a few also had board games spread out between the plates. Hannah was just about to check out the lower deck when she heard someone call out "Heidi!"

It took a second to process that the person was probably shouting to her. Luckily she knew she could play it off as not hearing the name because of the music. She waited until she heard the name a second time before looking around. Patrice, at a table at the corner of the deck, was waving wildly to her. She had switched out of her debutante dress into a tie-dyed sweater, army fatigue pants, and an honest-to-goodness hair bonnet. Hannah waved back and walked over.

As she approached, she saw that Chris was there, smiling shyly at her. In his black turtleneck and corduroy pants, he looked like he'd just left a Jack Kerouac fan club meeting. She loved it. She identified two people that she'd seen at the coffeehouse. The remaining two folks at the table were new to her. When she arrived, Patrice gave her a hug. Chris stood up and did the same.

"Everybody, this is Heidi," Patrice said by way of introduction. "She's visiting from out of town with her family. Heidi, you remember Chris. And this is the rest of the crew for the night: Carlos, Annie, Melina, and Doug. Guys, make room for Heidi."

"Hi," Hannah said to the group, not even pretending to try to remember all their names as they scooched over, opening up a space for her next to Chris. She felt her cheeks flush slightly as she settled in next to him. In an attempt to divert attention from herself, she nodded at the game on the table.

"You're playing Scattergories?" she asked.

"Are you a fan?" the guy she thought was named Doug asked.

"I've played before," she said.

"So where are you from, Heidi?" asked a pretty girl she believed was Melina. The girl had long, curly black hair and her tone was a little more edgy than the others. It only took Hannah a second to ascertain why. Prior to her arrival, Melina had been seated next to Chris and it seemed she wasn't happy about the reconfiguration.

"I'm sorry, what was your name again?" she asked, less out of real interest but rather to give herself a moment to stall. She wasn't sure how honest she was supposed to be with people. After all, she was using a fake name but did she have to give a fake hometown too?

"Melina," the girl said before resuming the interrogation. "I'm guessing you're from the L.A. area?"

"Good guess. Yeah, I live in the San Fernando Valley," Hannah said, deciding to just be vague rather than outright lie. After all, before her adoptive parents were murdered, she had in fact lived there.

"Oh, a valley girl," Melina said jokingly, though her eyes were daggers. She really felt threatened.

"Sure," Hannah said, losing interest in appeasing her, "so how's the game going?"

"We're on a little break," Patrice said, holding up what looked like a mojito. "Do you want something? I should warn you not to get too excited. It's a mocktail."

"Actually, a hot chocolate sounds really nice."

Patrice waved to the server. After she gave her order, they started a new round of the game. She and Chris were on the same team, which seemed to irk Melina even more. They eventually changed up the teams and switched to Taboo. Melina got to partner with Chris for that but they didn't seem to be on the same wavelength and finished in last

80

place. Hannah and Annie won. After that got old, she decided to run to the restroom.

"You want company?" Patrice asked.

"No, I'm good," Hannah replied. She actually wouldn't have minded but wanted avoid making a conversational mistake while waiting in line. It was hard enough remembering she was Heidi from the Valley. The more questions she was asked, the more likely she was to screw up.

She walked back inside, closed the sliding door, and dodged the feet of the people sitting near the fireplace on her way to the bathroom. The line wasn't too long. To pass the time, she turned back to the main room and enjoyed some people watching.

A couple was making out on the loveseat closest to her. They were covered in an animal fur blanket and it appeared that they were keeping as busy under it as they were up top. A little farther away, a guy was clumsily hitting on a girl near the bar. Hannah could tell he was too drunk. Every time he gesticulated, it looked like liquid was going to overtop his glass. Finally, as she knew he would, he moved too quickly and some of his beverage splashed on the girl. She squealed in exasperation and headed over to get in line for the bathroom.

Hannah was about to offer a sympathetic comment when she suddenly felt eyes boring into her. She looked around the packed room. Then she saw him. Standing behind the clumsy drunk amid the crowd at the bar was the burly, bearded forty-something guy from this afternoon. He was still wearing all black, though he'd disposed of the sunglasses. And he was staring at her unblinkingly.

Before she could decide what to do, the girl behind her line tapped her shoulder and pointed at the restroom door. It was her turn. She stepped inside and moved to the open stall. Locking the door, she sat down and debated what to do.

She could call Jessie. After all, there was a killer at large and though the two victims were roughly twice her age, it was possible that this was the culprit and he was scouting out a new target. But she doubted it. He was so overt that it was hard to imagine he'd act this brazen in public if he intended to come after her later.

But that didn't mean he wasn't dangerous. He might just be a standard issue pervert. But he could also be a guy waiting to assault her the second she moved somewhere secluded. She'd seen enough of both types to know that you couldn't be sure what you were dealing with just by looking.

But calling Jessie would end her night out and probably prevent any future ones in the foreseeable future. Besides, why should her evening have to be cut short because of some asshole? She determined that if he was still around when she got out of the restroom, she'd take matters into her own hands.

Sure enough, when she returned to the main room, he was there. He'd changed spots, now loitering closer to the fireplace, but his eyes fixed on her the second she walked out. Pretending not to notice, she returned to the sliding door, making sure to go the long way around so she didn't have to get near him. She returned to the table and leaned over to Patrice without sitting down.

"Is there a big guy with a beard dressed in black over by the sliding door?" she whispered in her ear.

Patrice glanced over and nodded.

"Yep, that's Gunnar. He works at the hardware store."

"Is he staring at me?" Hannah asked.

"He is," Patrice confirmed. "I guess that means you're official now."

"What?"

"Gunnar's the local mouth-breathing creep. He's a big fan of ogling girls half his age and especially loves artsy types. He's gross but he's harmless. He just doesn't seem to understand social mores like not engaging in open-mouthed staring."

"So you all just put up with it?" Hannah asked, appalled.

Melina, who had been listening in, spoke up. "I complained to security at the Conservatory once and they said that the cops technically couldn't do anything because it wasn't a crime to have a pedo vibe if he doesn't act on it. I mean, what are we supposed to do other than ignore him?"

Hannah looked at Melina and her irritation with the girl's prior pettiness faded away. Now she simply felt sorry for her, for all of them. One good thing about having endured so many traumas in her life was that when she faced a menace she could actually do something about, she wasn't inclined to shrink from the opportunity. In fact, the idea of taking action caused the old, familiar thrill to return to her belly. She felt her fingers tingle.

"I'll tell you what *I'm* going to do," she said, standing up straight, "put an end to it."

CHAPTER SEVENTEEN

Hannah turned and headed back toward Gunnar.

Chris grabbed her wrist and stood up.

"I'll go with you," he whispered.

"Thanks, that's sweet," she said, pleased at the gallant gesture even though she doubted he'd be much help. "Just don't get in the way."

She walked directly over to Gunnar, who made no attempt to move or even avert his gaze as she got closer. His arrogance only emboldened her. She felt that familiar euphoric surge that she only got when she was taking a chance that put her at risk. She stopped less than two feet from him. His breath was heavy with booze and garlic but she didn't flinch.

"Is there something you wanted to say to me?" she asked in a loud, clear voice.

"No," he said mildly, "I'm happy looking."

Hannah heard a slight gasp beside her from Chris, who clearly hadn't been expecting that response. But it didn't surprise her.

"Well, I'm *not* happy with you looking," she said. "So I'm going to ask you politely to stop."

"And what are you gonna do if I don't?" he snarled more than said. "It's not like I'm breaking any laws. We still live in a free country, don't we?"

Hannah had a good idea what she was going to do about it. For the last week, she'd been working hard not to let her impulses determine her choices. That was a major focus of her video therapy sessions with Dr. Lemmon. But this situation was different than the ones where she'd sought out trouble. Today it had come looking for her in the form of Gunnar and she wasn't having it.

"Please, just leave me alone," she pleaded, before turning to Chris and burrowing her head into his chest, pretending to choke back tears. She heard Gunnar grunt in malicious amusement as Chris held her. The cover band was wrapping up their latest song and she knew the moment she needed was fast approaching.

"When I let go of you, shove me into him," she muttered in Chris's ear as she wrapped her arms around his neck. "But not too hard, understand?"

She looked up at him, her eyes brimming wet. He nodded, his own eyes wide. She removed her arms from around his neck and winked. He took that as his cue and gave her a little push, just enough so that she bumped into Gunnar.

"Don't touch me!" she screamed, shrinking back from the man.

"I didn't," he protested and for the first time his voice was tinged with something other than arrogance. He sounded slightly apprehensive. Just then, the song the band was playing ended. That was *her* cue.

"Yes, you did!" she yelled in the relative quiet that followed the final wallop of the drums. "You won't leave me alone and now you rub up on me. Get away!"

Gunnar was formulating a response when a man in his thirties emerged from behind the sliding door and came over.

"Is there a problem?" he asked, trying to speak quietly. It was pointless. No one else was talking and the other customers could hear everything he said.

"There's no problem," Gunnar said quickly.

"Are you the manager?" Hannah demanded.

"My name's Todd. I'm the assistant manager," he said.

"In that case, yes there is a problem," she said, making sure her voice could be heard by everyone on the deck. "This guy was following me all around town today. Everywhere I went, he showed up. He wouldn't stop staring. I had to run out the back of a clothing store because I wanted to get away from this stalker. Then I show up here tonight and he comes in and starts doing it again."

"That's not true," Gunnar tried to interject.

"Oh, were you *not* following me at the ice cream jerky store this afternoon. Did you *not* come into the place next door right after me? I wonder if they have security cameras. You think they'd back you up on that?"

"Miss," Todd said, "can you please lower your voice? I'm sure we can work this out."

"Work it out, Todd?" she repeated angrily. "How does one work out dealing with a stalker? And no, I won't lower my voice. I already tried the polite method. I asked this guy to please stop staring at me like

I was a piece of meat. You know what he said—'what are you gonna do about it?' Is that working it out, Todd?"

"No, but I'm not sure what you want us to do?"

Though she had been putting on a show up to this point, she now stared at him in genuine disbelief.

"What do *you* think you should do, Todd?" she asked. "This guy is harassing me. And just now, he rubbed up on me. I'm seventeen years old. I'm still in high school. Are you saying that this is the kind of establishment that's cool letting some guy more than twice my age perv out on me? Is that the reputation you want for your place?"

"Of course not," Todd said miserably.

"Should I call Deputy Hicks?" she wondered, using the name she'd heard Jessie mention earlier.

"That won't be necessary," Todd assured her before turning to the burly guy. "Gunnar, I'm going to have to ask you to leave."

Gunnar looked astounded.

"Are you kidding me? You're gonna let this lying bitch run me out of here?"

"Please just go," Todd pleaded. "Let's not make this any worse."

"I can't believe this," he said, looking around at all the suddenly unfriendly faces. Realizing he couldn't win, he started to leave, then turned back and growled so low that only Hannah and Chris could hear him. "Next time, I won't be so obliging."

Hannah wasn't going to let him get away with that. Her fury rose right along with her voice.

"Next time?" she repeated loudly. "What does 'next time' mean, Gunnar? What are you going to do the next time you see me that's not so obliging? Are you going to try to force me to like you? That sounds like a threat. And everyone out here heard it. So I guess if something happens to me, they'll all know who was responsible."

"It wasn't a threat," Gunnar muttered.

"We'll see if the authorities agree. I think the young women of this town have had just about enough of you leering at them. How about the next time you get the urge to salivate over a teenage girl, you walk the other way? Because I have a feeling it's not going to be too well received from here on out. I think you're going to get called on your crap from now on."

"Damn straight!" Melina yelled from the table.

"Get the hell out of here," one of the guys in the band shouted from the lower deck.

85

Gunnar seemed surprised by the suddenly vociferous crowd.

"You should go," Todd said firmly, if still under his breath. "You're only making things worse for yourself."

Gunnar didn't respond, simply turning and reaching for the sliding door handle.

"And I swear if I catch you eyeballing me again," Hannah added, even though she knew it wasn't necessary. "I'm going straight to Deputy Hicks, maybe even to Sheriff McClane. We'll see who they find more credible. Bye, Gunnar."

He slammed the door without another word. Through the glass, she watched him stomp back through the main room and out the front door. When she turned around, there were about three dozen sets of eyes on her. For several seconds, there was silence. Then Patrice broke it.

"Whoo, girl!" she screamed gleefully. "I wish you'd come to visit two years ago."

A few people applauded and the band broke into an impromptu rendition of Hall & Oates' "Maneater." Hannah looked over at Chris, who seemed both impressed and slightly intimidated.

"If that's your bark, I'm afraid to see your bite," he marveled.

The rush she'd felt during the confrontation only escalated as she looked around at the admiring faces and then back at Chris, whose expression suggested he was feeling more than just admiration. She allowed herself to ride the wave of good feeling, happy that, for the most part, it was well deserved.

Patrice and the others had gotten up from the table and were walking over. Melina came close and Hannah briefly worried that she was going to make a dig.

"I'm pretty sure you just made my last semester of high school appreciably less creepy. Please transfer here," she said. Apparently all the Chris-centric water was now under the bridge.

"Hold on ladies. Before we make plans for Heidi to come to school here, which we really need to discuss," Patrice said, "I think we should nail down our plans for the rest of the night. We've probably worn out our welcome here. Heidi, some of our friends are doing a set just down the road at Café Bouquet."

"Where is that exactly?" Hannah asked.

"It's literally a hundred yards to the left after we walk out the door," Chris told her. "Come on, it'll be fun."

The offer was tempting. She was still feeling the rush from her confrontation with Gunnar and the crowd's enthusiastic reaction to how she'd handled him. Chris was clearly interested in getting to know her better and the feeling was mutual. Besides, it was just nice to be out with friendly people, moving about freely, behaving like a normal high school senior.

She told herself that nothing awful could happen walking a hundred yards down the road from one busy place to another, surrounded by half a dozen people. Thirty minutes at this Café Bouquet wasn't a big deal in the grand scheme of things. And as she'd learned well in her seventeen years on earth, the old cliché was true: it was easier to ask for forgiveness than permission.

"Okay," she said quietly.

They all gathered their things and headed back inside the bar, past the fire and mounted animal heads, to the exit. It was only as Chris opened the door for her and the cold blast of air hit her face that she had second thoughts.

It might be easier to ask for forgiveness, but if she violated Jessie's faith once more, she wasn't sure she'd get it. She had made a promise to her sister not to leave this place. If she broke that promise, how could she ever reasonably expect to be trusted again?

"I just remembered I can't go," she abruptly said to Chris. "I told my folks that I'd come back in decent time tonight. If I screw up my first night here, there might not be a second, and I'd like there to be a second."

Chris nodded, though he looked disappointed.

"I would too," he said, "so I don't want to mess that up for you. Are you staying nearby? I can walk you back."

"No, it's up the hill a ways. Besides, I don't want you to miss your friends' performance."

"Okay," he said. "Would it be cool to exchange numbers? I can let you know where we'll be hanging out tomorrow."

Hannah was about to pull out her phone when she realized that sending him her info would reveal that her name wasn't Heidi.

"Actually, my phone died earlier. But we could trade them the old fashioned way. If you have a pen I can write my number on your hand."

Chris desperately searched his pockets.

"I have a pen," Patrice said, handing one over with a wry smile.

Hannah wrote her number down and made sure to write "Heidi" underneath the digits. She returned the pen to Patrice, who gave her a hug. Chris did the same. The rest of the crew waved to her as they started down the road to the Café.

"Talk tomorrow?" Chris asked as he jogged to catch up.

Hannah nodded and waved. She stood there watching them go for a few seconds, then turned and trudged slowly in the direction of the hill that led to Rich McClane's cabin. When the others rounded the corner out of sight, she turned and hurried back to Wildyology.

She was still on a high but she wasn't an idiot. Gunnar might be lurking out here somewhere looking for payback. The killer with the knife might be around too. Though she was loath to admit it, she actually felt comforted by the idea of Jessie picking her up. But before she called her sister, she needed to reach out to someone else.

She had to acknowledge that she'd almost given into her impulse to court danger. It was one thing to confront a stalker-ish creep in a crowded bar. She gave herself a pass on that one, even if she'd pushed it farther than she had to. But she'd almost broken her promise to Jessie, almost backslid into the dangerous territory of justifying risky behavior just because it made her feel something. That it had come so easily, after all her hard work scared her more than Gunnar ever had.

She returned to Wildyology and asked for a quiet table in the back room of the place. Just about everyone else was in the main dining room, at the bar, or outside on the deck, so she had the space to herself. After ordering a slice of apple pie and another hot chocolate, she pulled out her phone and made a FaceTime call. After three rings, Dr. Janice Lemmon picked up. It was clear that she'd been asleep.

"Hi Hannah," she said groggily. "Are you okay?"

"I'm sorry for calling so late," she replied. "I wasn't thinking about the time. I can call back tomorrow."

"Don't be silly," Dr. Lemmon said, putting on her familiar, thick glasses. "I told you to call me if you ever felt you had to. And you clearly felt the need. So, let's talk."

That was all the permission Hannah needed. She launched in. A half hour later she was still going strong.

CHAPTER EIGHTEEN

If it was anyone else, Kat would have been long gone by now.

But it wasn't anyone else. It was Jessie Hunt, her one-time (and hopefully future) best friend, assuming she could win back her trust.

That's why Kat Gentry was sitting in the bookkeeping office of a used car dealership on Pico Boulevard, poring over sales records at 10:30 at night. She'd spent the day teaming up with Detective Nettles, but parted ways with him hours ago, as she couldn't in good conscience ask him to join her on what looked to be a wild goose chase. So even though no one on the team was supposed to investigate alone, she was working solo.

And as unpromising as it seemed, this was a potential lead in the search for the Night Hunter, the elderly killer who had put the lives of Jessie, Hannah, and Ryan in danger. If there was even a glimmer of hope that she might learn something of value here, it was worth the time and effort.

The accounting manager assigned to stay might be feeling differently. She glanced over at the guy, sprawled out and snoring on the couch in the office. He'd drawn the short straw, ordered to stick around by his boss, who'd gotten a scorching phone call from Captain Roy Decker when he'd initially refused to allow Kat access to the files.

She would have left by now except for one thing. This was the one dealership where the Night Hunter appeared to have bought a car but never collected it. Jamil had discovered five-week-old street camera surveillance of him near the lot, though there was no useful footage from the dealership itself. Unfortunately, they used old-school videotape, which they recorded over every two weeks.

Despite that, Jamil had found a record of an older man purchasing a black 1988 Ford Tempo on the same day he was seen in the nearby street footage. The strange thing was that, according to the salesman who sold it to him, he never even got in the car much less took it for a test drive. She planned to have a crime scene team from the station confirm that tomorrow, just to be sure. There was always the possibility that he'd inadvertently leaned on the thing and left a fingerprint.

But if the salesman was right, he simply walked around the vehicle a few times, paid for it in cash, and said he'd be back to pick it up in a few hours. But he never returned to collect it. It was still sitting on the lot, where Kat had gone to look it over a few hours ago.

That should have been the end of it. The Night Hunter bought a car and for whatever reason, never took possession of it. Maybe he got spooked. Maybe he found something better and decided he didn't need it. It didn't really matter if he never bought the thing.

But something about the situation just didn't sit right with Kat. Everything she had learned about the guy suggested that nothing he did was by accident. If he purchased this car, there was a reason. And if she could figure out what that reason was, maybe it would lead her somewhere useful.

She punched up the camera shot of the lot with the Tempo and zoomed in to study it again. There was nothing remarkable about it. In fact, other than the white 1991 Honda Civic nestled beside it, the Tempo was the most forlorn looking vehicle on the lot. At the least the other old cars nearby—like the maroon Oldsmobile and the lime green Fiat—had some kind of cheesy, retro panache. But not those two; they were just a sad pair of sedan siblings, waiting for drivers that would likely never come.

She was about to give up for the night and head home to get a few hours sleep when her phone rang. She looked down and was surprised. The call was coming from the downtown Twin Towers Correctional Facility. Though she was familiar with the place, having been there many times, she had no idea why she was getting a late night call from the most notorious prison in Los Angeles. Worried that it might be related to one of her unresolved P.I. cases, she answered. An automated voice began talking.

"Collect call from Twin Towers Correctional Facility- Women's Forensic In-Patient Unit. Will you accept a collect call from: *Andrea Robinson?*"

The last words were spoken by a live person that Kat assumed was Robinson. She recognized the name, but in her exhausted state of mind, she couldn't immediately place where from.

"Yes," she said hesitantly. There was a clicking sound, followed by a fuzzy connection. She could hear loud voices and clanging in the background.

"Hello?" she said.

"Is this Katherine Gentry?" a female voice asked.

"Yes," she said. "Who is this again?"

"Andy Robinson," the woman said, sounding mildly offended that she had to repeat herself. "I have some important information for you."

Hearing the name "Andy" made everything click in Kat's memory. Jessie had mentioned Andrea "Andy" Robinson to her in the past and not with warmth. Robinson was part of Jessie's first case working for the LAPD as a criminal profiler.

Kat remembered Robinson being described as a bored, rich society girl with a biting wit and a sharp tongue. But after a wealthy wife at their shared country club was murdered, she also had an apparent willingness to help Jessie navigate the cutthroat world of the club.

Kat also recalled Jessie telling her how she was immediately drawn to Andy's sardonic charm and, after the case was seemingly solved, decided to hang out with her new friend. Unfortunately, Andy Robinson turned out to be a sociopath who had poisoned her married lover's wife and framed an innocent maid for the crime.

When Robinson sensed that her new criminal profiler friend might be on to her, she poisoned her too. Only Jessie's quick thinking saved her from meeting the same fate as the murdered wife.

Since her capture, Robinson had been held at the Twin Towers Facility, which was not unlike the facility for criminally insane male prisoners that Kat used to head security for; that is until it all went wrong. Kat recalled how even now that Jessie still occasionally beat herself up for allowing Andy's charisma to blind her to the woman's true nature.

"How are you able to call at this hour?" she asked. "Shouldn't you be in your cell right now?"

"I should," Robinson said, sounding mildly amused. "But I made a big fuss and the folks here have learned that it's easier to let me have my way than deal with my fusses. Now do you want to keep asking stupid questions or do you want to know why I called?"

Kat could already sense the woman trying to manipulate her by boasting of her relative freedom at the jail and trying to belittle her. Standing up, she walked out of the small office into the dealership showroom to get the blood pumping and clear her brain. Whatever this was about, she needed to be on her game.

"Go ahead," she said. "What's so important?"

"First of all, I wanted to make sure Jessie was okay."

"What would make you think she wasn't?" Kat asked, not wanting to give anything away.

"Please don't insult my intelligence, Katherine," Robinson said with disdain. "I'm incarcerated, not lobotomized. You don't think I have access to information outside this place? I know that Jessie is facing danger at the hands of an old-timey serial killer. I know that she's been in hiding—probably under U.S. Marshal Protection—for at least a week. And I know that her friends in the LAPD are no closer to finding this guy now than they were then."

Kat was stunned at just how plugged-in someone in the in-patient lockdown unit of a prison was, but did her best to hide it. This woman was calling for a reason more complicated than simple concern and if she wanted to tease that out, she needed to match Robinson's focus.

"Then why are you calling me?" she asked as she pulled up a photo of the woman on the other end of the line. "If you know so much, then you must know that I'm just a lowly private investigator. I'm not in the loop on protection procedure."

"We both know that's not true," Robinson replied. "After all, you replaced me as Jessie's bestie, though you seem like a poor substitute based on what I've gleaned so far. I'm sure she's been in touch. I'm sure she's poured her fragile heart out to you. I'm sure you are very much in the loop. And since there's a court order legally prohibiting me from calling Jessie directly, I thought I'd check in with the new but not improved me."

Kat was increasingly skeptical that Robinson actually had anything useful to offer. She seemed to be fishing. Under normal circumstances she might have just hung up. But she remembered that Jessie had described the woman as brilliant and if she really knew something valuable, ending the call might be a mistake.

But continuing like this was useless. She decided to up the ante. Robinson might be a devious mastermind, but she was also arrogant, and more importantly, imprisoned. That made her the desperate one. Plus, Kat had one extra advantage. When she ran security at the non-rehabilitative division of the state hospital in Norwalk, she dealt with unstable, violent offenders on a regular basis. They didn't scare her.

"Well, this has been great, Andy," she said, letting the sarcasm drip off her words. "But it seems like you called me more out of loneliness than helpfulness and I'm pretty busy. So unless you have something useful to share in the next ten seconds, I'm going to say goodnight and let you get back to your padded cell."

She waited for a response. For several seconds, there was no sound other than the distant howls of what she assumed was another disturbed prisoner. Suddenly, the automated voice returned saying "there are 60 seconds remaining in this call." Still she didn't speak. The ball was in Andy's court.

"It's not wise to alienate me, Katherine," Robinson finally said. "I'm already inclined to dislike a usurper like you. It took enormous humility for me to even call you. But I did it anyway, out of concern for Jessie."

"The clock is ticking," Kat said coldly.

She heard the woman inhale sharply, obviously trying to control her resentment. When she responded, it was in slow, clipped language.

"I know how this man—this Night Hunter—thinks. He is ten steps ahead of you and your LAPD friends. Despite that, he's growing frustrated that he hasn't gotten to Jessie. But he will have made contingency plans. And those plans involve you, Katherine. You are the weak link. I promise you that he knows about you. After all, I do and I'm locked up. He will manipulate you, without you ever knowing it, to get to her. He may have already laid the trap. And if you're not careful, you'll fall into that trap and put your dear friend's life in jeopardy. And since I can't protect her from in here, you have to do it out there. I know this is counterintuitive, Katherine, but don't trust your instincts. Just like your eyes, they can deceive you."

The line went dead. Kat didn't know if Robinson had hung up or been abruptly cut off. Leaning against the showroom wall, she realized that she'd been holding her breath ever since the woman mentioned the Night Hunter. She exhaled and sucked in a new breath, and then another.

When her breathing returned to something close to normal, she tried to decide what to make of the call. She looked down at the picture of Robinson that she'd pulled up on her phone. It was from before she was convicted, at some kind of gala back when she seemed to be a philanthropic pillar of the community.

She was attractive in a nondescript sort of way. Her blonde hair was shoulder-length and far less fussy than the other women around her in the photo. About five foot five and 125 pounds, she seemed unremarkable in almost every way. That is, except for her eyes. They were a deep blue and twinkled with a mischievous sharpness. In retrospect, "malicious" might be a better description than mischievous.

She knew that Andrea Robinson was incredibly intelligent. She also knew that despite trying to kill Jessie, the woman harbored a genuine affection, if not obsession, for her. It didn't make sense that she would call merely to bait the person she thought had replaced her in Jessie's circle. It was possible that she was legally insane, but she still needed to be taken seriously.

Kat briefly considered reaching out to Jessie to tell her about the call, but then thought better of it. Until she had something substantial to work with, these were technically just the musings of an unbalanced, jailed murderer. Besides, Jessie had enough on her plate without having to worry about another person fixating on her who had once tried to kill her. It could wait.

She returned to the accounting office and looked at the screen with the video of the purchased but never collected Ford Tempo sitting forlornly beside its Honda Civic friend. For some reason, Andy Robinson's words popped into her head: *Don't trust your instincts. Just like your eyes, they can deceive you.*

A thought popped into her head, one she was embarrassed hadn't occurred to her until now. All this time, her eyes had been preoccupied with the Tempo, mainly because she assumed the Night Hunter was too. But that wasn't a certainty.

How could she be sure that when he first walked onto the lot, he hadn't come across the two old cars side by side and been drawn to the Civic first? What if he had already looked at that vehicle—maybe even sat in it—by the time the salesman arrived and saw him expressing interest in the Tempo? There was no video of the visit and therefore, no reason to think he'd looked at anything other than the one car...until now. Suddenly invigorated, she walked over to the sleeping accountant and shook him awake.

He looked up at her blearily and muttered, "What?"

"I need you to get the keys to the Civic in the used lot."

Looking confused and irritated, he wiped a line of drool from his mouth.

"Why?' he whined.

She didn't have time to waste or patience to spare.

"Just get up and get the goddamn keys!"

CHAPTER NINETEEN

She knew she was going to catch hell.

It was almost 11 p.m. and for the second time this week, Ellen Wade was essentially closing the gym down. She waved goodbye to Teddy, the night manager of Mile High Muscle, then hurried through the nearly empty parking lot to her car, bundling up tight against the cold. Hypothermia was always a risk during a Wildpines winter, but especially so when one was sweaty after a workout. She zipped the puffy jacket all the way up to her chin.

As she walked, she looked at the text from her husband, Gerard. As usual, he was complaining about her being out so late. It was another in his nonstop series of grievances. She worked endless hours. She was never around, even at night.

It didn't seem to occur to him that she was never around because she was constantly running ragged. In addition to operating the only quality website services firm in town, she was also the primary caregiver to their two children. That meant dropping off both Geoff and Estie at school and picking them up later. It meant going to rock-climbing practice and ballet. It meant making breakfast and dinner every day and getting guilt trips if it wasn't ready on time.

Gerard liked to gripe that because he worked down the hill in Banning, he had the rougher go of it. But that commute gave him a perfect excuse to never be on call. It was getting old, which was why she insisted on her private gym time. After all, at the hour she went the kids were in bed asleep. Besides, most nights he was just going to watch re-runs of *Law & Order* while pounding beers anyway. Her absence wasn't noted specifically because he missed her, but because it meant he had to find the detergent or put a kid back to bed after a nightmare. So she allowed herself this lone personal perk. Well, this and one other, but that was her little secret.

After getting another text asking when she was getting back, she shoved the phone in her coat pocket. She'd answered the question less than five minutes ago. He'd simply have to wait until she pulled into the driveway at home to get his answer. She reached her car and unlocked the door. She was about to open it when she caught a glimpse of herself in the one, dull overhead parking lot light.

She had to admit that she looked pretty good. She'd had two kids before thirty and worked a job that had her at a desk in front of a screen for about ten hours a day. But she'd managed to keep something close to her college-age figure. She pulled off her beanie and her dirty blonde, ponytailed hair flopped out. It wasn't too arrogant to think she could pass for twenty-seven instead of the thirty-three she was.

She opened the door and tossed her beanie and workout bag across to the passenger seat. She was just about to get in when she heard a frustrated "damn." She jumped, slightly startled. She'd thought she was alone in the parking lot. Looking around to find the source of the curse, she saw something she'd missed earlier. A woman with her back to her was about fifty feet away, leaning over her car engine with her hood up. The woman seemed to be using her phone flashlight to discern her problem.

"Are you okay?" Ellen called out.

The woman didn't respond. Ellen was debating whether to just leave when she saw that the woman had ear buds in. No wonder she hadn't replied. Between that and her hushed, repeated muttering "damn, damn, damn," it was clear that her focus was elsewhere.

Ellen sighed. She couldn't just leave her alone in a near-empty parking late at night. She'd never be able to live with herself. So she shut her door and headed over.

"Excuse me," she called out as she approached not wanting to scare the woman, who was small, with long black hair. Ellen couldn't see her face and had no idea if she knew her from around town. Again she called out.

"Excuse me, ma'am. You know the gym over there is open if you need to call for a tow. Better to wait inside where it's warm than—."

She hadn't finished the sentence when the woman spun around. Ellen's eyes opened wide in confusion, then surprise. She knew who this was. But something wasn't right. That's when she saw the knife coming toward her. There was no time to block it. She barely had time to move at all. Only her hyper-alertness after the recent workout allowed her to shuffle to her right. Out of the corner of her eye, she caught a glimpse of the blade as it sliced the air just to her left.

She started to turn and run but lost her footing on the slick parking lot pavement and narrowly avoided falling down. Once she regained her balance, she looked up to see that her assailant had recovered as well. The knife was coming toward her again. For a brief moment she thought that maybe her thick jacket would protect her. But as the knife plunged into her throat, she realized she was wrong.

CHAPTER TWENTY

For a second when the call first came in, Jessie panicked.

She opened her eyes and didn't recognize where she was. This wasn't the bedroom in her Mid-Wilshire home. It wasn't the one in the Sherman Oaks safe house either. It was only when she felt the bitter cold sneak in under the covers that she remembered she was in Undersheriff Rich McClane's cabin in Wildpines.

She fumbled for the phone and knocked it off the end table beside the bed. As she scrambled to retrieve it, she heard Ryan moan in frustration. From the other room, Hannah yelled out "answer it!"

Finally, she got hold of the thing and picked up without even looking to see who it was.

"Yeah?"

"Ms. Barnes?" asked a hesitant young male voice that sounded vaguely familiar.

"What?" she demanded, about to ream out someone for misdialing her at what appeared to be 4:57 a.m. Then she remembered who she was and added, "Yes, this is she."

"This is Garrett, er, Deputy Hicks. I'm sorry to call you so early but we found another victim. It's a local woman named Ellen Wade. I thought you and Detective Hosea would want to know right away."

Jessie sat up in the bed. She allowed herself a moment for the wave of frustration and growing anger to pass through her. When she was sure she could respond professionally, she put the phone on speaker.

"Of course, Garrett. Where and when was she found?"

"In the Brightside Market parking lot about ten minutes ago. I'm here now. There are several other businesses that share the lot. One of them is a local gym that opens at 5 a.m. and Don—he's one of the trainers there—was opening up the place. He noticed Ellen's car in the parking lot, which he said was unusual because she usually works out late at night. Then he saw some blood in the snow a little ways off. He followed it to the side of the lot, where there's a steep drop off. He looked down and saw her in the ravine. I just checked myself and it's her. I didn't get too close but it looks like she was stabbed—a lot."

"Okay," Jessie said, rolling out of the bed and putting her feet on the chilly wooden floor. "Block off the area. Call whoever you normally call to handle crime scenes. We'll be there in ten minutes."

*

They got there in eight.

To Jessie's surprise, when they arrived the lot was still mostly empty. It was still pitch black out. Sunrise wasn't for almost another two hours. They parked and got out. The bitter mountain wind whipped through the car, slicing into her. She looked at her phone. The wind chill was nineteen degrees. They walked over to where Garrett was standing, an anxious look on his face.

"How are you doing?" Ryan asked him.

"I've been better. I knew Ellen pretty well. She helped me set up the website for my band in high school. Even though she gets paid a lot from most of her clients, she didn't charge me a thing. She even taught me a few basics about coding. I know everyone in this town and I felt bad for Clarice Kimble and Sarah Ripley, but this one is different somehow. I really liked her. Plus she has two kids in elementary school. I don't know what's going to happen to them. Her husband's kind of a jerk. I don't think he's going to be a great single parent."

Jessie allowed herself a few seconds to take in the enormity of the loss. Not only did a woman die, but a whole family may have been destroyed. After the pause, she blinked a few times to refocus and decided to help Garrett do the same.

"Garrett, I'm sorry. It sounds like she was a nice person. I want you to take a moment to process this. I know it's lot."

He nodded and stepped away, looking at the not-yet-visible mountains to the east. She and Ryan stayed quiet for close to a minute before she spoke again.

"What I'm going to tell you now may sound harsh and I apologize for that, but hopefully you'll understand. Whatever remaining feelings of grief and pity are still weighing you down; you need to set them aside. There will be opportunities to work through all that later. But right now, time is of the essence. You're a Riverside County Sheriff's deputy. The best way for you to honor Ellen is to help us catch her killer. And that means concentrating on doing your job well. Would you agree with that?"

Garrett nodded.

"Okay, then we have a lot to do and not much time to do it in. So let's get started. Why don't you show us the body?"

Garrett led them to the spot where the parking lot ended, meeting the dirt at the edge of the hill. They looked down. About twenty feet below them, just above where the ground flattened out, a woman was lying on her back. She was wearing black tights and a heavy coat stained in blood. Her eyes were open. Her face was white.

Jessie looked at the spot at the top of the hill where the blood ended. That was where she was dumped from. The blood trail retreated to a snow-dusted parking spot about thirty feet away.

"Whoever did this had to be strong to drag her that far," she noted.

"They must have surprised her too," Garrett added.

"Why do you say that?" Ryan asked.

"Ellen was pretty tough. She was in good shape. I know she took a Muay Thai class at the gym. She wouldn't have just accepted her fate if she saw it coming. She was a fighter."

Ryan nodded. Looking around he asked, "Is that her car?"

"Yeah," Garrett confirmed. "Like I said, that's what got Don's attention. Occasionally people are already waiting when he opens the gym doors at five. But he said Ellen was a late-nighter. She usually showed up around 9:30 or 9:45 and stuck around until they closed at 11."

"Where's Don now?" Ryan asked.

"He's inside," Garrett said, pointing at the gym, which was only about fifty paces from Wade's car. "Don't worry. I told him to keep his mouth shut until I gave him the okay."

"Is that why there are no curious onlookers?" Jessie asked.

"Partly; none of the other businesses are open yet. The market opens at seven, most others around nine. There'd be no reason for anyone to stop by unless they were working out. That's why I didn't use any police tape to block off the scene yet. I figured that would draw more attention than just a few folks standing here. I hope that's okay."

"It's good thinking," Jessie told him. "We'll hold off on that as long as we can. When are the crime scene people arriving?"

"I actually called Rich McClane so he could coordinate that. He's got more pull than me and he said I should go directly through him on this case, on account of you two not being local. He doesn't want politics to get in the way of the investigation. Anyway, he told me a team will be here within the hour, and that was ten minutes ago. He

100

also wanted me to let you know he'd be calling you directly once he has a spare minute."

"That should be fun," Ryan said, pulling out his phone and using the camera to zoom in on Ellen Wade's body. "What about the on-call deputy, Traven? We'll need a little more manpower once things get busy around here."

"Yes sir," Garrett said. "I told him that I needed some backup this morning. He's coming up from Mountain Center. The road hasn't been cleared yet but even so, it shouldn't take more than fifteen minutes. I didn't want to tell him to hurry because he'd ask what the rush was. Pete Traven's a good cop but he's not the most discreet guy I ever met. I worry that telling him too much too early could lead to those crowds we're trying to avoid."

"Okay," Ryan said approvingly, "in the meantime, I think Jennifer and I are going to go down to get a closer look. It's pretty windy this morning and I want to get some photos in case anything gets blown away. Can you keep an eye on things up here?"

Garrett nodded.

"Be careful," he warned. "The hill is steep and with the snow and ice, it's easy to slip."

*

He was right. Jessie almost lost her balance twice. As they made their way down, she noticed that, though Ryan took his time, he was navigating the terrain better than she would have expected. Still, even though Ellen Wade was only twenty feet down, it took about three minutes to get to her. When they arrived they gave the body a wide berth.

"It looks like she was stabbed at least a half dozen times," Ryan said.

"That's more than either Clarice or Sarah," Jessie noted. "It's like the killer is getting more frenzied every time."

Ryan nodded in agreement though his attention seemed to be elsewhere. He was staring intently at the body.

"What is it?" Jessie asked.

"I can't tell for sure," he said slowly, "and I don't want to get any closer and contaminate the scene, but do you see that long dark fiber in the dried blood on the front of her jacket?"

Jessie peered closer.

101

"Yes," she said. "It looks like a strand of hair."

"Right," Ryan said. "And it's black. Ellen Wade is blonde. I think we might have found a piece of the killer's hair."

CHAPTER TWENTY ONE

Jessie knew there was a problem when Rich McClane didn't call them for another hour.

By then the crime scene unit had bagged the black strand of hair and was preparing to do the same to Ellen Wade's body. With the big CSU van in the parking lot, as well as both Garret's and Traven's squad cars, a small crowd had assembled. Reluctantly, the police tape was brought out.

They got a text saying McClane would call in two minutes so they left Garrett in charge and went to the car so they could talk without being heard. Ryan had just turned on the engine so the heat could circulate when the call came in.

"Sorry your quiet mountain retreat is turning into a cluster," Rich said without offering a greeting.

"We're used to it by now," Jessie assured him, as she wiped at the windows, which were already starting to fog up.

"I'll bet. You got any good news for me? Any hot leads?"

"Maybe," Ryan said. "We found a strand of hair on the victim's coat that we're pretty sure isn't hers. It was mixed with the blood. We're hoping it's the killer's."

"Great," McClane said. "I'll make sure that gets top priority when CSU gets back here."

"How's it going on your end?" Jessie asked. "I'm assuming you couldn't call until now because you've been pretty busy."

"Let's just say I've been putting out some fires down here," he replied.

"What does that mean?" Ryan asked.

"It means it's been hard to keep a lid on this thing. We've now got three murders in four days; all in a town that usually gets that many in a typical year, total. Plus they were stabbed to death by what appears to be one person. There's just no way to keep that quiet for much longer."

"How long do we have?" Jessie pressed. She felt her heart starting to beat faster. It was one thing if people in Wildpines gossiped about what was happening. But once word got out at Sheriff's Department headquarters, things would spin out of control fast.

"Well, Sheriff Nick Kazansky likes to ease into the office in the morning," McClane said with something less than admiration. "He usually shows up around nine. I've got things pretty buttoned up so he won't he hear about the case until he arrives. But once he does, there will be an overnight report on his desk. The Wade murder will be in it, along with the possible connection to the other deaths. It's buried in there but he'll find it."

"What happens then?" Ryan asked. Jessie heard the dread in his voice.

"First he'll get pissed that I didn't make him aware of it right away. I'll play a little dumb, say info was slow to come in so the connections weren't obvious at first and that I've been too busy following up on everything to loop him in. That won't help much but it will buy you a little extra time. He'll yell for a while, throw his weight around. But eventually he'll get down to business. He'll want to assign his own detectives. That'll be a turf battle. It might add a little time to the process. But he'll ultimately pick the guys he can control the most, not necessarily the best investigators, and a few hours after that, some of his guys will arrive in town, ready to bulldoze everything. I'd say you have until early afternoon before they show up and take over."

"Great," Jessie said, looking at the clock in the car, "that gives us between six and eight hours to solve three murders."

"I wish I could say that was your only problem," McClane told them.

"What else?" Ryan asked.

"The media," Jessie muttered under her breath.

"That's right," McClane said. "You know word is probably spreading around town about the murders. Even if it hasn't, I can guarantee you that Kazansky will change that. He won't just put out a release; he'll do a press conference. I'm hoping that even though he loves media attention, he'll give his guys a chance to get up here and look around before starts spouting off. But by mid-afternoon, you should expect a horde of TV trucks from all over Southern California."

"Oh God," Ryan groaned. McClane continued, undeterred.

"Once that happens it going to be difficult for you guys to keep that low profile you value. Even if you're close to solving this thing, you may be better off stepping back from the case for your own privacy and security. If you don't, the press will definitely recognize you. I wouldn't be surprised if the assigned detectives do too."

"He's right," Jessie said. "It's one thing for us to walk around a quiet mountain town in beanies and puffy jackets. No one pays us any mind. We're just like all the other out-of-towners. But after it gets out that these particular out-of-towners have been asking questions about local murders, folks will start looking at us more closely, just like that server at the bar last night. Once anyone recognizes me, it'll be on social media and the word will spread everywhere in minutes, including back home. We can't have that."

The silence after that comment lingered in the air. Looking at Ryan, she could tell he was thinking the same thing she was: the idea stopping in the middle of an investigation was anathema to them both. It almost made her feel ill.

"Another reason to move as fast as you can," McClane finally said. His business-like tone suggested he wanted to wrap up. "While you do that, I'll try to keep things under control here as long as I can. I'll also try to warn you when Kazansky sends his people your way."

"Thanks," Ryan started to say before realizing the Undersheriff had already hung up. "I guess that's that."

"Shall we get back out there?" Jessie wondered.

"Yep," Ryan said. "It would seem that every second counts."

He was just about to turn off the car when Jessie's phone rang. It was Kat. Jessie's stomach did a small flip. It was barely after 6 a.m., too early to call just to say hi.

It was either very good or very bad news.

CHAPTER TWENTY TWO

"Hey," Jessie said, "I'm here with Ryan. You're on speaker."

"Okay," Kat said. "Sorry to call so early. I hope I didn't wake you guys up."

"We've actually been up for over an hour," Ryan said. "We're working a case."

"I thought you were supposed to be lying low," Kat said.

"It's a bit complicated," Ryan said. "Unfortunately, I doubt we'll be under the radar much longer. Twelve hours from now this place will be overrun with media and there will be nowhere to hide in our little hideaway. We can't tell you where we are but it won't be hard to guess."

"I'm sorry," Jessie cut in, her antsiness got the better of her. "Is everything okay? Why are you calling so early?"

Suddenly there was a rap on the driver's window, making both her and Ryan jump. With the fogged-up windows it was impossible to see who it was. Ryan rolled his down. It was Garrett.

"Sorry to bother you but I need to show you something," he said.

"I'll check it out," Ryan said, then turned to Jessie. "You can catch up when you finish your conversation."

Jessie waited until he closed the door before continuing.

"You still there?' she asked.

"Yup," Kat said.

"So what's going on? I know something happened."

"It did but you can take a breath," Kat reassured her. "No one else has died and we haven't caught him. But I did come up with something and I wanted to run it by you if that's cool."

"Of course," Jessie said, unable to contain the tingle of anticipation in her gut.

"I'll give you the short version. I was following up on lead at a used car dealership last night. The Night Hunter bought a car there but never picked it up. We don't know why. But I noticed another car for sale parked right next to it and checked it out. It had a piece of paper crumpled on the floor in the back. I called in a team to check it out, pull for prints, all of that."

"Find any?" Jessie asked, not getting her hopes up.

"No. But the scrap of paper was interesting. There was an address written on it. I looked it up and it's for a hostel in Pasadena. Decker has the place under surveillance now. In a few hours, he's going to have a few officers go in undercover as Canadian students on vacation. They'll scope the place out."

"Are you going to be there?" Jessie asked.

She had mixed feelings about the idea. This lead held some promise and having Kat there as her eyes and ears would be reassuring. But she didn't want her friend to put herself in danger. Of course, the very fact that she thought Kat's safety was at risk was a sign that she was involuntarily letting optimism slip into her head.

"No," Kat said. "Decker doesn't want anyone the Night Hunter might recognize in the area just in case. He figures that if the man was stalking you for weeks, he's probably seen me."

"Makes sense," Jessie acknowledged. "So why are you calling? This doesn't sound like the sort of thing that would normally make you reach out before breakfast."

Though she didn't mean for that to sound harsh, a little terseness slipped out and she knew why. She and Kat still hadn't had time to really discuss her friend's betrayal of trust. Of course, that conversation couldn't happen in person until it was safe to meet. If Kat picked up on her tone, she made no mention of it when she replied.

"It's just that it seems too easy," she said. "The Night Hunter doesn't seem to leave much of anything to chance. He's incredibly meticulous. And yet he buys a used car and never picks it up? That's inevitably going to raise red flags. And then he accidentally leaves an address for a place like the others he's stayed at in the only other car on the lot similar to the one he bought? It seems awfully convenient."

"Do you think he planted it?" Jessie asked.

"It seems like something he might do, right?" Kat said. "On the other hand, maybe I'm giving him too much credit. The dealership never called in anything about the car. I only went there because Jamil found camera footage of him nearby. Would he really set all this up counting on someone to find the footage, connect it to the dealership, learn about the car that wasn't picked up, notice the *other* car next to it, see the scrap of paper in the back, look at it, check the address and tie it to him? That's putting a lot of faith in the collective investigative powers of the LAPD, and all for what purpose? It seems a little outlandish to me."

"Listen, Kat," Jessie said. "I don't know if this is all by design, but I do know one thing: you're better off giving this guy too much credit than not enough. Better to keep your guard up, you know?"

"I do," Kat answered, sounding glad that she didn't seem crazy to be so suspicious. "Speaking of keeping your guard up, how are you guys doing?"

Jessie decided to keep it light. Kat had enough going on. She didn't need to be worrying about them too.

"Busier than I expected but we're getting by."

"And Hannah?" Kat wondered.

"Surprisingly well, actually. She met some kids her age yesterday and I let her go out to meet them last night. She seemed to have fun. And there were no major confrontations or home break-ins, at least none that I'm aware of."

There was silence on the other end of the line and after a second she realized why. Kat thought she was twisting the knife about her involvement in Hannah's past missteps.

"That wasn't meant as a dig," she added quickly.

"I know," Kat said, before moving on quickly. "I'm glad it went well. Hopefully it's a sign that things are changing."

"Yeah, I hope so too. She's been talking to her therapist regularly too. That may be helping."

"Good," Kat said quietly. "Every little bit helps."

Something about Kat's tone gave Jessie the odd feeling that she was holding something back.

"Is there something else?" she asked.

"No," Kat said quickly, unconvincingly. "I've just got a lot on my mind. Nothing you need to worry about. Just be careful."

"You too," Jessie said, deciding not to press. She hung up and sat quietly in the car, doing her best to push away the memory of the awkward ending to the call. Dwelling on that would only lead down a rabbit hole.

Less easy to get out of her head was the lingering feeling that she should be back in L.A., helping catch the bastard who was hunting her. She knew it wasn't a credible option right now but the guilt remained.

At least you're doing some good up here. Just keep telling yourself that.

Before she'd entirely convinced herself, Ryan got back in the car.

"What did Kat say?" he asked.

She filled him in on the dealership lead and the hostel operation. As she did, she saw a pained look come over his face. She knew what was going through his head. He was beating himself up again, thinking that if hadn't frozen outside the Santa Monica hostel where the Night Hunter murdered Alan Trembley, the killer might be in custody now, or maybe even dead.

"Hey, don't go there; it won't do you any good." she told him, and before he could protest, she switched subjects. "What did Garrett want?"

Ryan took a second to regroup before answering.

"He found Ellen Wade's phone in her car. There were some texts from her husband. They were less than loving. The words 'selfish,' 'bad mom,' and 'failure' show up a lot."

"That's interesting," Jessie said. "Has anyone officially informed him of her death yet?"

"No. Garrett offered to make the notification."

Jessie shook her head.

"I think he should come with us. Someone will need to be there for the kids. But I want us to make the notification so we can see his face when we tell him."

"Then we better hurry," Ryan said. "I don't think the rubberneckers around here know who died yet. Wade's body was bagged before it was brought up the hill. But with her car in the lot, someone is going to piece it together. We don't want them calling Gerard Wade before we see him."

"Then let's go now," Jessie said.

Ryan had put the car in "drive" before she finished the sentence.

CHAPTER TWENTY THREE

Jessie hated this part.

It sounded like Gerard Wade was a real asshole, at least according to Garrett.

"I don't think he ever hit her," the deputy told them before they left the crime scene. "But he's yelled at her more than once in public. I've seen him make both her and the kids cry."

Jessie didn't have a deep reservoir of sympathy for a man like that. Even so, telling a man that his wife had been murdered was never fun, especially when there were little children in the house.

Of course, the fact that she'd apparently died last night and he never called her in as missing was suspicious. So were the multiple texts in which he berated her for everything from not replacing the expired milk fast enough to scheduling a work call when he wanted to watch a game, which meant he had to watch the kids.

Ryan pulled into the Wade driveway and they waited for Garrett to arrive. The family home was a few streets off Central Circle Drive on a winding road called Crestridge Drive. The houses here seemed a little fancier than those close to the center of town. This one was two stories and though it was designed to look like a large log cabin, it was clear that it had been built with more contemporary materials.

Garrett pulled up behind them and they got out. The sun was shining brightly now but it didn't make the day much warmer. Jessie didn't need to justify using her beanie as a disguise. Without it, she wasn't sure she could function out here. She really had become a Southern California person since moving from New Mexico for college just over a decade earlier. These days, temperatures in the forties were cold to her. When it hit the twenties like today in Wildpines, her brain hurt. As they walked to the front door, Ryan walked Garrett through their plan.

"We want to gauge his reaction when he gets the news," he said. "One of us will tell him about Ellen. Depending on what he says or does, we may need your help with the kids. Got it?"

Garrett nodded, though he looked understandably nervous. He knocked on the door and they waited. He tried again after a minute.

"Should I ring the bell?" he finally asked.

"Let's try to avoid it if possible," Jessie said. "I'm hoping the kids are still asleep and that would definitely wake them up."

The issue was resolved when the door suddenly opened to reveal a bleary-eyed guy wearing a robe, t-shirt and sweatpants. He looked to be in his mid-thirties. His black hair was shooting everywhere and his bloodshot eyes suggested he downed more than a couple of drinks the previous night.

"What's going on, Garrett?" he asked, his voice still thick with sleep.

"Can we come in, Gerard?" Garrett replied.

Wade looked at him, then at the two strangers accompanying him, and scratched his head.

"Uh-huh," he finally said, holding the door open.

They stepped inside. Jessie noted that the interior of the place was in no way rustic. The furniture was modern, as were the appliances. A large TV was attached to one wall.

"Are Geoff and Estie still asleep?" Garrett asked.

"I assume so. Ellie usually wakes them up at seven so we've got a little time. What's this all about? Who are these people?"

"My name is Randy Hosea, Mr. Wade," Ryan said, extending his hand. "This is my colleague, Jennifer Barnes. We're in town working a case in conjunction with Garrett here. We'd like to talk to you about your wife."

"You mean talk *to* her? Is this about that attempted hack last month?" Wade asked, then went on without waiting for an answer. "She's probably in her office. She wasn't in bed when I woke up. You want me to go get her?"

Ryan glanced over at Jessie and she nodded slightly. She wanted him to deliver the news so she could focus exclusively on Wade's reaction.

"I'm sorry to have to tell you this, Mr. Wade, but your wife was found dead this morning."

The man stared at Ryan as if he'd spoken in a foreign language.

"Wait, what?" he finally asked.

"Ellen Wade was found dead in a ravine near Mile High Muscle."

Jessie studied Gerard Wade. The eyes were no longer bleary. He was fully alert. There wasn't grief on his face, just perplexed shock. Of course, there wasn't any standard reaction to getting news like this, so

Jessie wasn't inclined to draw too many conclusions. But if he felt guilty about something, it wasn't discernible from his expression.

"That's not true," he muttered slowly.

"I'm afraid it is true Mr. Wade," she told him. "Would you like to sit down?"

"Okay," he muttered, though he didn't move.

Garrett took the initiative and led them all to the living room. Once they sat down, Jessie launched in. The rawness of the moment was a double-edged sword, making it painful to discuss what happened but also allowing for more truthful responses.

"Mr. Wade," she said gently, "I apologize in advance but we need to ask you some questions which may be quite difficult to hear. Please don't take offense. It's just that we're trying to get to the bottom of this and every minute is crucial."

"Why?" he asked. "What happened?"

"Ellen was murdered," Jessie said evenly. "It appears she was killed last night while leaving the gym. Her car was still there this morning."

"No," he protested, "that can't be right. I was texting with her as she was leaving. I can show you. I even told Cal he had to go because she'd be home soon."

"Who's Cal, Mr. Wade?" she asked.

"Cal Blackwood—he's my neighbor, lives two doors down. We were watching the Ducks' hockey game. It went into overtime but I said he had to leave anyway because Ellie gets pissed when he's here late."

"What time did Cal leave?" Ryan asked casually, as if he wasn't fishing for an alibi.

"A few minutes after Ellie texted that she'd be home soon. I can check the time on my phone."

"That message was sent at 10:49," Jessie said. After checking Ellen's phone, she'd committed much of the text data to memory already.

"Okay," Wade said. "In that case, Cal probably left five minutes after that. It doesn't take long for her drive home so he would have left quick. Wait, how did you know the time?"

"We have her phone, Mr. Wade," Jessie told him, deciding it was time to get more aggressive. "We've looked at all the texts, including the one where you demanded an update from her after she'd just given you one."

"That was just to make sure she wasn't close when Cal was still here. She never even got back to me. Wait, are you saying she didn't reply because she was dead?"

His voice rose unexpectedly. It seemed that after a long stretch of just not getting it, he was finally starting to comprehend that his wife had been murdered. Part of her wanted to let him process it. But she set that part aside. She needed answers before the kids woke up, while he was still vulnerable.

"Mr. Wade, I know this is a lot to take in," Jessie said with what she hoped was firm empathy. "But right now, you need to answer our questions. Are you saying Cal can confirm your whereabouts last night?"

"Yes," he said before adding. "Are you checking my alibi?"

"I am. We're just trying to eliminate you as a suspect as fast as possible. Would you consent to providing your phone to us?"

"Why?" he asked.

"So we can verify your location last night using its GPS data," Ryan explained. "We can get a court order if we need to but that takes time. You giving it to us now allow us to move much faster. We can eliminate you quicker. It's also a show of goodwill. It indicates that you have nothing to hide."

"Should I do that, Garrett?' Wade asked turning to Deputy Hicks.

"That's not my decision to make, Gerard," Garrett said. "But if I was in your shoes, and I hadn't done anything wrong, I'd do whatever I could to help the authorities solve this fast. And eliminating you as a suspect lets them move on to the next steps."

"Okay," Wade said. "It's in the bedroom by the bed. I'll go get it."

Jessie shook her head at Garrett. She didn't want the guy touching the phone again until they looked at it.

"That's okay," Garrett said softly, "I'll get it. I know where your bedroom is."

Once he left, Jessie took advantage of the deputy's absence to pursue another line of questioning.

"Gerard," she said, using his first name for the first time in the hopes of creating a conspiratorial bond between them, "I didn't want to ask this in front of Garrett but I need to know: were you and Ellie having problems?"

To her surprise, his eyes suddenly welled up with tears. He nodded.

"Yeah," he choked out. "Things have been pretty rocky lately. I work really hard and I have a long commute but she doesn't get it. She

113

thinks that I should dive into 'family man' mode the minute I get back home. And then she goes off to the gym or to do website maintenance for a client. Plus, she was always talking about how she had to help out people in her special business group. It never ended. We've argued a lot the last few months. No one said it but to be honest, I think we're on the verge of separating."

"Why didn't you call anyone when she didn't come home last night?" Ryan asked, not letting the guy get comfortable in his self-pity. Wade shrugged.

"I had a bit to drink and I guess I just crashed before she got home. It happens sometimes. I slept right through the night until I heard you knocking. She wasn't in bed so I figured she was in her office or making breakfast. I didn't know anything was wrong until you told me."

"Daddy?"

They all turned around to see a little girl with blonde hair who looked to be about six standing at the far end of the room. She was wearing footy pajamas and holding a stuffed giraffe. The sight of her made Jessie's heart crack a little. The girl was around the same age as Jessie when her own father murdered her mother in front of her and left her to die in a freezing cabin next to the body. The similarities were unsettling.

"Hey sweetie," he said, rushing over to her and scooping her up. "Did daddy and his friends wake you up?"

"No," she said, her arms wrapped around her father but her eyes fixed on Jessie and Ryan. "I had to go potty and heard you when I came out of my room. Who are they?"

She pointed accusingly at them. Her father seemed at a loss for words. Just then, Garrett came out of the hall behind her.

"Hi Estie," he said warmly. "Do you remember me?"

"You're Deputy G-Man!" she said excitedly. "You talked to my class at school."

"That's right," he said, sounding as if his being here was the most natural thing in the world. "And I had such a fun time that I thought I'd come say hi again. If your daddy says that it's okay, I might even be willing to take you and Geoff to school this morning."

"But Mommy always does that," she said suspiciously.

"I know," Garrett replied casually. "But she can't do it today and your daddy is super busy. Do you want to ride to school in a police car?"

114

Her misgivings disappeared immediately. She broke into a smile and nodded vigorously.

"Then why don't you go get ready. We'll whip up some breakfast for you and your brother and then I'll be your chauffeur for the morning. Sound good?"

"Yes," she said, wriggling happily in her dad's arms. He put her down and she darted back down the hall. Garrett watched her go then turned to Wade.

"I thought you co..... e some time to wrap your head around this," he said as he walked over to Ryan and handed him Wade's cell phone. "We may be able to keep Ellie's identity as the victim quiet for a few more hours. That'll give you a chance to work this through for yourself and get things in order before explaining it to the kids. It will also give them a little extra time to enjoy being children before everything crashes down around them. I'd suggest you pick them up before lunch though. By then, word will have spread."

"Okay," Wade said, though he didn't seem to have gotten all of that. Garrett looked over at Jessie and Ryan to make sure he'd acted properly. Both nodded that he had.

"Is it okay if Wade takes a shower and gets dressed now?" he asked. "I can make the kids some breakfast, drop them off at school, and then have him meet me at the station to give a formal statement."

"That sounds good," Ryan said. "We'll leave you to it while we follow up on some other leads."

They let themselves out and were halfway down the driveway to the car when Jessie finally spoke.

"Exactly what leads were you thinking we should follow up on?" she asked. "I think that between Wade's hockey buddy alibi and his phone GPS, we both doubt he's going to end up being our guy."

"I agree. That's why I was actually hoping you might have a suggestion," he replied, sounding as defeated as she felt.

She didn't have any that she was immediately excited about. But considering they had only hours before the case was taken from them and their true identities were potentially revealed, she decided to grasp at the most obvious straw.

"We *do* know of one connection among all three of these women: they were each members of the Wildpines Business Association. And we know that the husband of the woman who started the group doesn't want us accessing their website's chat forum. I say we start there."

115

She could tell he thought it was a long shot too, but considering that he didn't have any better ideas, he wisely kept his mouth shut.

CHAPTER TWENTY FOUR

The more Jessie studied the WBA website, the more frustrated she got. They were getting nowhere.

She and Ryan were sitting at the breakfast table in Rich McClane's cabin, both with laptops open. Hannah was in her room, passing the time by watching episodes of *The Office* on her phone. She had asked if she could go to the Elevated Grounds coffeehouse again later to meet with her new friends and Jessie had agreed. After what felt like hours but was really only forty-five minutes, she looked up from her computer screen.

"This is a waste of time," she said. "Until we get the DNA on that strand of hair or the warrant allowing us to look at the website's chat section, we're just blindly throwing darts. There's no way to know the relationships among these people just from reviewing their websites."

"I've been going back through articles in the local paper, *The Wildpines Gazette*, hoping to uncover something juicy," Ryan said.

"And?"

"Nothing much. It's a weekly paper funded by the very businesses it covers. Not surprisingly, most of the articles are fawning. Even the ones that hint at problems are intentionally bland. Maybe the WBA shouldn't be our focus. After all, all the victims are attractive women of similar ages. Maybe the killer just goes for that type."

"I don't think so," Jessie said, surprised at her own certainty. "I can't explain why but I'm sure this business group is the key to these murders. This is a small town but there have to be dozens of women in their thirties nearby. Why these three? Two were blonde and one was a brunette. Only one has kids. Each of them was married but since Sarah Ripley wasn't even a local, people might not even know she had a husband. The one thing we know for sure that all these women have in common is that they're female small business owners of a certain age. I wouldn't be surprised if the killer is somehow using the site to select his victims. Maybe they all wronged him or her in some way."

"But how could we ever know that?" Ryan asked. "Even Garrett, with all his local knowledge, isn't going to be privy to the internal battles of an insular business-centric group."

Jessie sat thinking quietly for a moment. Ryan was right. Garret wouldn't be of much use on this. They might have better luck randomly talking to WBA members in the hopes that one of them revealed some long-simmering dispute unknown to the general public. She scanned the alphabetical list of businesses on the list in the hope that one might jump out at her. She got to the end and sighed. None were obvious contenders. It was a crapshoot.

She stood up to stretch and to give Ryan a kiss on the cheek. As she did, she glanced at his screen, which still had *The Wildpines Gazette* site up. She glanced back at her own screen, which had the last few alphabetical member business listings. Then it clicked for her.

"I know who we should talk to," she said.

"Who's that?"

"Someone we should have already considered after what you said earlier. How about a business owner who is a member of the WBA, uses Ellen Wade's website design services and covers the Wildpines business community, even in a toadying manner. Who's the Editor-In-Chief of *The Wildpines Gazette*?"

Ryan clicked on the masthead link.

"Her name's Lorraine Porter," he said, looking up expectantly. Jessie smiled back.

"Let's go say hi."

*

For an ostensible journalist, Lorraine Porter didn't come across as especially curious. In fact, Jessie thought she seemed allergic to probing questions.

Porter's uneasiness was exacerbated by her physical discomfort. A large woman in her late forties with graying hair and weathered skin that suggested she'd lived most of her life in the harsh mountain weather, she shifted back and forth in her rolling chair. Her constant movement was making Jessie borderline seasick.

"Let's try this again—" she said before Porter interrupted.

"I don't understand what the big deal is," the woman said, her already loud voice booming through the tiny *Gazette* newsroom. Her office was walled off from the rest of the three-person staff but it was clear the others could hear every word. "Unless you think the WBA is a secret front for a drug cartel or something, I'm not sure what you're driving at."

118

Jessie had to be careful how she proceeded. She and Ryan were hamstrung by twin concerns. They didn't want to get too specific about why they were asking these questions. It seemed unwise to come out and say they were investigating three murders when only Clarice Kipling's death—and not the manner of it—was public knowledge.

Equally unwise would be pushing too hard, which might compromise their false identities. The last thing they needed was for Porter's reportorial instincts to kick in because she was curious about why two out-of-town investigators were looking into a local business group. So she tried to play the classified card.

"Ms. Porter, we're not at liberty to reveal the nature of our investigation at this time. But if you're forthcoming with us, we might be able to return the favor, perhaps with an exclusive down the line."

"That's a lovely offer, Ms. Barnes," Porter said, lowering her voice for the first time. "But here's the truth. We are a hyper-local paper. We cover lost hikers, forest fire outbreaks, and local school sports. When it comes to Wildpines shops, unless there was a break-in or someone goes out of business, we're essentially a press release machine. We're here to promote the town, not denigrate it. We're certainly not looking to treat the inner workings of a local business association like it's the Watergate scandal. As far as I'm concerned, it's just a standard local organization, nothing more."

"Really?" Ryan pressed. "Wasn't the person who started it brutally murdered four nights ago?" He managed to give the impression that he genuinely didn't know the answer to that.

"Why do you assume that had something to do with the WBA?" Porter asked, her eyes narrowing. "Does this have anything to do with the body that was found by the Brightside Market this morning? Or the mysterious unpleasantness up on Rockview Drive on Tuesday night that I can't get Garrett Hicks to tell me anything about?"

Jessie felt her chest tighten suddenly. These were questions they didn't need Porter asking when they only had hours left before the whole world knew about the murders. Right now, they still had the advantage of relative freedom to move about and pursue leads. If the local newspaper editor started poking around, they wouldn't even have that.

"I thought the *Gazette* was just a press release machine," she shot back, hoping to distract the woman by baiting her. "Are you suddenly finding your journalistic integrity?"

"I—," Porter started to say. But Jessie sensed she had her on the defensive and plowed ahead.

"What about the chat forum on the WBA website? Are you on it?"

"No," Porter admitted, her face turning pink. "The forum is members only. You have to be invited and I wasn't."

"That doesn't bother you?" Jessie pressed, happy to have moved the conversation away from unidentified murder victims. "Don't you wonder what benefits they get from being in the members-only chat forum that you don't?"

"It never occurred to me," Porter said unconvincingly.

"Seriously?" Ryan asked incredulously. "I'm sorry but I have to ask: what does this group actually do? I mean, you already have a chamber of commerce. How does the WBA benefit members in any way the chamber doesn't?"

"I'm not sure that it does, Mr. Hosea," Porter replied, seeming to have found her bearings again. "But that's not really the point. *The Gazette*—which means me—wants to be supportive of local businesses. The WBA may not do much. I guess it's more of a mutual admiration society. But what's wrong with that? Besides, if I had joined, people in town would ask why. I don't need that. I really don't think it's much more complicated than that."

Jessie disagreed but it was clear that they weren't going to get any more out of the woman, at least not without risking the investigation or their cover stories. As if the universe had decided it agreed with her, a text came in to both her and Ryan at the same time. It was from Rich McClane and it got straight to the point.

Your warrant was approved.

Jessie and Ryan looked at each other. Both stood up.

"Thanks for your time," Ryan said brusquely as they headed for the door. "We'll be in touch if we have additional questions."

Porter looked like she had a few of her own but they were out the door before she could ask any. They were already leaving the *Gazette* newsroom, bundling up against the mid-morning cold, when a second text from Rich came through.

You have permission to access the website chat room. Garret will meet you at Martin Kimble's place with a hard copy. Move fast. Things are getting hairy around here.

CHAPTER TWENTY FIVE

The Night Hunter sat patiently in his booth, staring out the diner window at the hostel across the street.

At times like this it was hard to fight off the giddiness. But he knew that the sight of an excitable old man would be more memorable to future witnesses than a weary one, so he maintained the façade of an elderly gentleman sipping coffee while he read the paper and occasionally looked out the window at passers-by.

On the inside it was a much different story. After over a week without any success, he finally had cause for hope. He had started to wonder whether his used car ploy would ever pay off—in fact, he'd almost forgotten about it altogether— but now it seemed like it finally might.

Weeks ago, he'd bought a used Ford Tempo he never intended to take ownership of. The purchase was one of several potential fail-safe methods to help him get to Jessie Hunt if she decided to go to ground. None of the others had panned out but this one had promise.

He'd placed a tiny camera under the eaves of a storage shack across from where the 1988 Tempo sat beside a nearly-as-old Honda Civic. It was motion-activated and since few customers were interested in those cars, there wasn't much motion most days.

Still, he checked the footage every evening just in case and last night he hit pay dirt. Jessie's private investigator friend, Katherine Gentry, had found the Tempo. And later that night, much to his delight, she'd put the pieces together and returned to look at the Civic. He'd nearly giggled out loud as he watched her take notice of the "crumpled up" piece of paper on the floor of the backseat. He got an adrenaline shot when he watched her immediately pull out her phone and make a call. At that point, he had to stop watching. After all, he had work to do.

Finally, after over a week of frustration, of total silence in which he could find neither hide nor hair of Jessie, her paramour Ryan Hernandez or her half-sister, Hannah Dorsey, there was renewed hope that he could track them down.

It was that potential that made him drive to Pasadena in the middle of the night to set everything up. He wanted to watch the upcoming show, of course. But more importantly, he needed to set everything up for the real performance, the one that would get him what he needed: access to Jessie.

And the most delicious part of the whole thing was that if his plan worked out, it would be Katherine Gentry, Jessie's loyal, brave, quick-witted best friend who inadvertently led him to her.

As the waitress passed by, he felt another giggle coming on and coughed softly to hide it. She didn't even look at him.

CHAPTER TWENTY SIX

Hannah started to worry that he was bailing on her.

Chris and the others were supposed to meet her at Elevated Grounds on their lunch break. But just after Jessie and Ryan dropped her off at the coffeehouse on the way to *The Wildpines Gazette* office, he texted: *Delayed a bit. Instructor droning on. Can you wait?*

She said that she could and decided to window shop for a bit. This time she walked in the opposite direction from where she'd gone yesterday, to the largest building in town, a three-story, all-wood, outdoor shopping plaza that had everything from a retro arcade to a blown-glass gallery.

She stopped into an artisanal soap shop on the third floor called Sense of Scents. The place was surprisingly crowded for midday on a weekday. It only took a few seconds to understand why. There was a photo of a woman attached to a corkboard on the wall. Below the picture was message that read: *Clarice, you were a good boss and a great friend. You'll be missed. Always in our hearts, The SOS Team.*

This was the store of one of the murdered women Jessie and Ryan were investigating. She briefly considered leaving out of a sense of respect. But then a stronger feeling took hold of her: morbid curiosity.

She knew that Dr. Lemmon wouldn't approve but she stuck around, enjoying watching the staff and patrons play-act at sorrow over the loss of someone that seemed, based on everything she'd heard, like a bit of a pill. In one corner, a female employee was hugging an older woman, who was dabbing at her eye with a tissue.

Hannah wandered closer, hoping to pick up their conversation, but they were whispering too quietly to be heard. Frustrated and slightly ashamed, she moved over to the citrus soap section and started smelling different bars.

She tried to remember what Dr. Lemmon had said in their video chat last night; it was normal to have the impulse to pursue the adrenaline highs. The key was deciding whether the high she was after was healthy or self-destructive, and if it was the latter, to stop herself from acting on it.

Lemmon reminded her that last night, she'd confronted a creep who was borderline stalking her. She hadn't initiated the incident and she'd taken action with the safety of a large group around. For a more traditional person, it was a bold, high-risk move. But for Hannah, it was actually far more restrained than her past responses to similar situations.

Lemmon wasn't happy that she had Chris push her to create a physical moment, or that she then lied about it to everyone there, but the doctor was pleased that she was at least honest about it in their conversation. And she was especially proud that Hannah had backed out of going to the second bar with her new friends. That was the epitome of stopping herself from making a self-destructive choice. When she hung up, Hannah felt good about that choice, like she'd turned a questionable situation into a positive one.

She'd didn't want to undermine all that one day later. And yet, as she looked around the bustling shop, she recognized the familiar urge growing in her belly. Every employee was engaged with a customer. There were no obvious cameras in the store, nor any signs saying recording was taking place. The soaps didn't have security stickers and the front door wasn't equipped with the technology to detect them anyway. She could drop a bar of Mandarin Musk into her pocket and walk out without anyone being the wiser.

Without even thinking about it, she picked up the soap and slid into her interior coat pocket. After pretending to peruse a few hemp lotions, she moved toward the door. As she reached for the handle, her phone buzzed. She looked down. It was a text from Chris: *Just left the Conservatory. See you in five.*

She stood in front of the door, thoughts bouncing around her mind. Was this a sign; the universe trying to give her one last chance to stop before she made a mistake? She glanced back at the table with the citrus soaps and an embarrassing thought occurred to her. She didn't even like mandarin. The Luscious Lemon bar had appealed to her much more and yet she'd left it alone. Had she left it on the table because taking that one would be an affront to the efforts of Dr. Janice Lemmon? Was she a shoplifter with a conscience?

Someone opened the door from the outside and she stepped to the right to let them in. Glancing behind her, Hannah saw that the only employee with a clear view of her was busy lighting a candle for a customer. Quickly and smoothly, she pulled the Mandarin Musk bar of soap out of her pocket and placed it on the shelf closest to her. Then she walked outside and moved toward the stairs, never looking back.

As she darted across the street to the coffeehouse, she tried to put the whole incident behind her. She didn't want to think about why she had backslid right after a moment of success. She didn't want to wonder if she would ever truly move past this.

She arrived at Elevated Grounds just as the Conservatory bus pulled up outside. Chris, Patrice, Carlos, and Melina hopped out. They all greeted her with hugs. Patrice and Melina even kissed her on both cheeks. Chris did not, though he watched the exchanges with interest.

"Did you hear the news?" Patrice asked as they all walked inside.

Hannah shook her head. That could mean anything. If it was related to the murder of the mother of two young kids, she had. But she didn't want to tip her hand so she feigned ignorance.

"No, I'm kind of out of the news loop up here. What happened?"

"Gunnar Quaid, the guy you called out last night, got arrested!"

"When?" Hannah demanded. "For what?"

"That's a bit of an overstatement, Patrice," Chris said, smiling as if he was used to drama from his friend. "He wasn't formally arrested. Apparently after he got kicked out of Wildyology, he went down to a bar called Wild Things where he promptly harassed some gal who slapped him and called the cops."

"Yeah," Melina added. "Deputy Hicks—we all call him Garrett— came down and threw him in the station lockup for the night. He said that he'd heard about what happened at Wildyology and that if there was one more incident like that, he was going to officially charge him and send him down to the Southwest Detention Center in Murrietta to face the folks there. I hear that place is hardcore. Supposedly Gunnar was crying when he got dragged out."

"Do you know what time that happened?" Hannah asked, trying to remember when she overheard Jessie and Ryan saying the woman was killed last night.

"I'm not sure," Patrice said, "but I don't think it was that long after your little adventure. Why?"

"No reason," Hannah said quickly. "But it's nice to know someone around here in law enforcement gives a damn."

They reached the front of the line and everyone turned their attention to the server. As Melina gave her order, Hannah's thoughts drifted off. She had wondered if a sketchy guy like Gunnar might be the killer Jessie and Ryan were looking for, if he was even on their radar.

Should she mention that he was locked up at the time the third woman was killed or would they have already figured that out? If she said anything, her confrontation with the guy would inevitably come up. That would almost certainly lead to Jessie questioning her judgment and end the chances of any future hangouts with these people.

"You're up," Chris said, snapping her back into the moment.

As she looked at the menu, Hannah came to a decision about Gunnar: she was keeping her mouth shut.

CHAPTER TWENTY SEVEN

Deputy Garrett Hicks was waiting outside his car when Jessie and Ryan arrived at Martin Kimble's house.

"Does Kimble know about the warrant?" Ryan asked as they joined him.

"No," Garrett said, handing over the hard copy of the warrant, "I didn't want to give him a heads up."

"Good call," Ryan said as he walked quickly to the door. "Kimble may claim he doesn't know anything about the site but that doesn't mean he doesn't know how to wipe it."

Jessie noticed that when he moved with purpose, Ryan's limp was barely noticeable.

"Are you sure he's even home?" she asked Garrett.

"That's his car," the deputy said, pointing at a pickup at the edge of the driveway. "Martin does most of his field work when the weather is better. In the winter he works from home a lot, writing ecological reports for the Forest Service."

Ryan knocked on the door urgently. It didn't take long for Kimble to answer.

"What is it now?" he demanded angrily. "This is bordering on harassment."

Ryan showed him the warrant.

"This gives us legal authority to review the WBA website chat room comments. You're required to give us the administrator log-in information. If you object, you'll be arrested for obstruction of justice and we'll get the data anyway, so I recommend you cooperate."

For half a second, Kimble looked like he might actually object but then his expression changed to resignation.

"I'll get the log-in," he said dejectedly before walking over to a cabinet and pulling out a file. He handed it over.

Jessie sat down at Clarice Kimble's desk. By the time she'd booted up the woman's computer, Ryan had the log-in ready. She punched it in as the administrator. As it loaded, Ryan pulled out the laptop he'd brought along. He logged in as a member and the two of them scrolled through the comments. Garrett stood nearby and kept an eye on Kimble, who sat forlornly on the couch.

It didn't take long to understand why the man had been so reticent to hand over the log-in info. There were a variety of subject categories with bland names like "startups, "support," and "teambuilding." But at the very end of the list was one called "communication" that seemed to need a secondary log-in.

"What's this?" Jessie asked Kimble.

He walked over and looked at the screen. She could tell she'd found the very thing he was hoping she'd miss.

"Just another chat category," he said unconvincingly.

"One that requires an additional password?" Jessie asked. She was skeptical.

"That category doesn't show up on my member screen at all," Ryan noted.

"Mr. Kimble, up until now you've just been difficult," Jessie said deliberately, "But we're entering criminal territory here. Give me the log-in for the "communication" category now."

Kimble sighed heavily, then returned to the cabinet and pulled out another file labeled "long term records." He handed over the second to last page, an old phone bill summary. It had a Post-It attached with some unintelligible words scrawled on it.

"What does it say?" Jessie demanded impatiently.

"SpecialFriends4Ever—all one word."

Without comment, Jessie typed it in and waited for the page to load. At first she didn't understand what she was looking at. The most recent exchange began "My place tomorrow. Usual time." The response said simply "confirm." The exchange prior to that started with the line "Have to postpone until Fri. His mtg. was delayed a day." The response was succinct, "OK, ☹."

But it all became more clear a few seconds later when she read the next exchange . It began with the message "dtf 2nite @ your place?" The answer was definitive. "Y. She has PTA @ 7. Come at 7:30. Watch for her car."

Jessie looked over at Kimble, whose face turned red. He averted his eyes. His reaction confirmed what she suspected: this wasn't a chat room at all. It appeared to be a matchmaking service for locals who wanted to have flings and it seemed that Clarice Kimble ran the whole thing.

"So if I understand this correctly," she said to Kimble, trying not to let her excitement at the discovery overpower her, "This whole WBA group is just a front for people to have affairs?"

"No," Kimble insisted haughtily. "The group is real and it helps people. This is just an additional feature for those who are interested, a discreet way for folks to get the pleasure they can't get at home."

"But I thought you said you and Clarice were swingers," Ryan reminded him.

"We are," Kimble said, as if he was talking to a slow child, "but not everyone around here is on board with that kind of activity. Sometimes one partner wants to swing and the other doesn't. They might even consider doing so cheating. In those cases, Clarice provided a way for the interested party to get the satisfaction they needed without upsetting their significant other."

"Did she take a fee?" Jessie asked expectantly.

"There is a small membership fee to join the WBA. Those invited to become members of the overall chat forum don't pay extra."

Jessie thought he was being too cute by half and she was losing patience with him.

"Mr. Kimble, you said they don't get charged to be in the 'overall' chat forum but what about to join the specific 'communication' forum?"

Kimble hesitated before answering. "She may have charged a small fee for maintenance, so that participants could interact in a safe, private manner."

"How much was the maintenance fee?" Ryan asked.

"$250 a month."

"So people basically paid $3000 a year to be in her adultery club?" Jessie clarified.

"I wouldn't use that term," Kimble huffed.

"I'll bet," Jessie shot back. "I'm not a huge fan of it either. How about we just call it the 'Special Friends Forum' from now on? Would you prefer that euphemism?"

Kimble didn't respond and instead looked away petulantly. They left him to stew in his self-righteousness as they pored over the details of the forum. Kimble was nothing if not thorough. Because all of the "get-togethers," as she called them, had to be scheduled through the site to ensure privacy, she had a complete record of every member interaction.

129

That meant she could keep tabs on all their activities. That included everything from direct messages they exchanged with other interested members to the dates, times, locations, and even quantity of those get-togethers. No one could balk because, with calls and texts too risky, this was the only way to ensure their communications were secure.

And just as Jessie had suspected, all three murder victims were right in the thick of it. Of course, Clarice ran the whole thing, though she didn't seem to have partaken of the festivities. Apparently she was satisfied with swinging. But there was Ellen Wade. Her profile listed dozens of meet ups with the same two or three partners. They always took place during the same window of time when she supposedly went to Mile High Muscle. Jessie suspected that on the nights that she didn't legitimately go to the club, she was getting another kind of workout.

The rendezvous were almost always at either her partner's place or at the Riggs Mountain Resort off Highway 243. That made sense. Jessie recalled Rich McClane saying that the motel was struggling and would likely give them a reduced rate if they stayed there. She could imagine that if things were that bad, they might turn a blind eye to someone who wanted to pay an hourly rate.

Sarah Ripley was listed too but had only had a few get-togethers, less than a half dozen, almost all at her home. In fact she had one scheduled for the night she died, though it appeared that her partner for the evening, someone charmingly named Dutch Dalton, sent a message cancelling just before their appointed meeting time, 10 p.m.

"I can tell you why Dutch cancelled," said Garrett, who saw the message she was reviewing. "He was at a Town Council meeting until pretty late on Tuesday. I remember because I had to testify at around 9:30. When I left, it was after ten and he was still there. It might have looked bad for him to cut out early for a late-night hookup."

"Great," Ryan said, frustrated, "one more quality suspect eliminated."

Jessie closed her eyes and took a deep breath. There was a ton of useful information here, but it would take time to go through it all and establish the links among the women and which ones actually mattered. Unfortunately, time was something they were fast running out of. She stood up and whispered in Ryan's ear.

"Let's go back to the cabin to review this stuff."

He nodded and whispered back.

"If we had Jamil Winslow available to cull through all this data, I'm sure he'd uncover the key connection among the victims fast. But without his tech wizardry, we're going to have to do it the old school way."

"Right," Jessie agreed, "And don't forget that there's a Sheriff in Riverside with an itchy media trigger finger. We may not have long to do it."

CHAPTER TWENTY EIGHT

Kat tried to hide her disappointment.

She wasn't doing a great job but it was better than Jamil could muster. He looked like his dog had run away. As they stood outside the Pasadena Hostel alongside Detective Jim Nettles, all three wondered what had gone wrong.

Only a couple of hours ago, they thought they'd hit pay dirt. From Central Station, they watched on hidden cameras as the undercover officers posing as Canadian student backpackers checked in at the hostel and did casual but thorough interviews and searches. But no one at the hostel—employees or guests—had any recollection of someone matching the Night Hunter's description ever staying there. No one recognized the composite photos or drawings they passed around.

When that effort was unsuccessful, the full search team on standby was sent in do a more painstaking walk-through of the place, but they also found nothing. Jamil had already searched camera footage from right around the hostel going back weeks and didn't find anyone even close to matching the man.

Eventually they all left. But Kat wasn't satisfied. Despite Decker's reluctance to waste more resources, she'd convinced him to let her and Nettles do one last assessment of the area now that it had been cleared as safe. She played up the angle that they might pick up on stuff that officers less familiar with the case wouldn't. It worked.

Jamil—clearly burned out on staring at street view camera footage—had begged to come. She took pity on him and pressured Nettles to do the same. But now that they were here, it seemed that the forty-five minute drive from downtown L.A. to Pasadena had been for naught. They hadn't come across any earth-shattering clues. It was a bust.

Nettles and Jamil walked across the street to grab drinks from a corner store. Kat decided to stay put and sat down on a bench in front of the hostel, resting her head in her hands. She went over everything again, wondering what she'd missed. It couldn't have been a coincidence that the crumpled paper in the car next to the one bought by the Night Hunter had the address of a hostel, when that was exactly the kind of place where he'd been staying.

But the lead was a dead end. Of course, it was possible that the man realized he'd lost the paper with the address and simply decided not to risk staying here, no matter how unlikely it was that he'd be discovered. He'd repeatedly proven how scrupulous he was in his planning. He probably had a dozen other lodging options at his disposal.

She sat up and looked to see if Jamil and Nettles were on their way back yet but they were still in line to pay for the drinks. Trying to clear her head, she looked absent-mindedly at the adjoining buildings on the block. They all had the same Old Town Pasadena architectural style, with lots of red and brown brick structures built in the 1920s. She could even see historical marker plaques near the doors of a few.

The building at the corner of the block had a plaque, which was probably the only reason it hadn't been torn down. With its puckered roof and boarded up windows and front door, it gave the impression that it was on the verge of collapsing all by itself.

Looking at the sign, it appeared that the building used to be a medical supply store, though some of the letters had faded to the point that she couldn't make out the name of the place. She squinted at the sign, trying to make it out, and was about to give up when an odd sensation that she couldn't quite explain fluttered in her chest.

She stood up and walked across the street. As she did, some of the letters became easier to discern. What had originally looked like "land Hu Medica upply" became something else entirely: "Garland Hunt Medical Supply." She gasped involuntarily.

"What's up?" someone called out.

She looked over to see Nettles and Jamil standing in the middle of the street, holding their drinks and looking at her curiously. She motioned for them to come over and pointed at the sign. Jamil looked at it and them at her.

"We should call it in," he said immediately.

"Why?" Nettles asked. "I don't get it."

"Hold off on the call, Jamil," Kat said. "We need to know what we're dealing with before we have everyone come out here again."

"What *are* we dealing with?" Nettled asked, frustrated. She turned to him, surprised that he hadn't put it together yet.

"You don't think it's a little suspicious that the business across the street from where we hoped to find the Night Hunter has both the first

133

name of his long-time nemesis and the last name of the woman he's hunting?"

Nettles' face flushed.

"When you put it that way," he admitted, "it kind of does. So why don't you want to call it in?"

"I do," she insisted. "But my credibility with Decker is already shaky after the hostel search came up empty. I don't want him to think of me as Chicken Little. Let's check it out first."

"I'm not sure that's a great idea," Jamil cautioned. "Remember what happened to Trembley. He was lured into that hostel and the Night Hunter got the jump on him."

"That's why we're going to be extra cautious," Kat countered. "Nettles and I will go in together with weapons drawn. Meanwhile you'll stay out here and be our eyes. Warn us if anyone tries to enter the building. And don't let anyone approach you, no matter how innocent they look. It might seem crazy for him to show up here when everyone's looking for him, but this guy *is* crazy."

Jamil still looked reticent but Nettles was fully on board. Since the front door was boarded up with planks of plywood, they decided to enter through the back alley. Even in the middle of a chilly but sunny day, walking along the narrow pathway was unsettling.

Kat couldn't help but remember Andy Robinson's warning about the Night Hunter the previous night: "He is ten steps ahead of you. He will manipulate you, without you ever knowing it, to get to her. He may have already laid the trap."

Was this that trap? Was she doing exactly what he wanted? She knew it was possible but wasn't sure what choice she had. She couldn't ignore such a promising lead, though the primitive, fear-based part of her brain was screaming that she should.

When they got to the door marked "GHMS," Nettles silently noted that it looked like it had been jimmied open recently. Using hand gestures, Kat indicated that she'd pull it open and he should be ready to shoot if anything jumped out at them. He nodded.

She yanked the door open and Nettles squared up. But nobody leapt out at them. He stepped inside and she quickly followed, leaving the door wide open. Between the open door, the holes in the roof, and the gaps between the plywood boards over the windows, more than enough light streamed in to give them a solid view of the place.

The interior of the building had been largely stripped clean. There was one shelving unit along the back wall and a reception desk that appeared to be bolted to the floor. But other than that, there was little in the place other than strewn about trash, a few empty paint cans, and a couple of plastic painting tarps.

Even though it would be virtually impossible for anyone to surprise them considering there were no places to hide, they moved through the space carefully. Kat's eyes darted back and forth quickly as she looked for anything out of the ordinary.

After several fruitless minutes, she was about to call this search a bust too when she noticed several thick streams of dark liquid leaking out from one of the tarps. She pulled out her flashlight and pointed it in that direction. It looked red. Nettles saw what she was doing and walked over. She indicated for him to pull the tarp away and aimed her gun at whatever was underneath. He ripped the plastic sheet back.

Kat gulped hard, fighting a sudden wave of nausea, as she tried to make sense of what she saw lying on the ground. It appeared to be a human being, or at least segments of him. The figure was male, probably in his fifties, and from the look of his clothes, most likely homeless. He still had the basic components of a person but they had been cut into sections. His arms, legs, and head had been neatly separated from his torso and set an inch apart from it, so that he looked more like a marionette than a man.

This wasn't the Night Hunter's typical M.O. but Kat had no doubt that this was his work and that it was recent. The blood wasn't dry yet and the smell was strong. She guessed that this had been done in the last few hours.

Even as she took in the horror before her, Kat knew the man was still playing his cruel games. Somehow, he knew she'd discovered the address crumpled up in the Honda Civic and that she would be coming to this place. He'd left this body as a calling card and a taunt, to let her, and by extension Jessie, know that he wasn't done; that he could do these things right under their noses and not get caught.

"This was him," she told Nettles. "Call it in."

He nodded and went back outside, clearly not wanting to spend one more second in this place than he had to. But Kat stuck around and continued to walk around the nearly empty space. The Night Hunter may have thought he couldn't be caught but she wondered if that was so.

This murder was a major undertaking and it would have had to happen on short notice. Jessie discovered the note in the Civic around 10:45 last night. Decker had people surveilling the Pasadena hostel across the street by 3 a.m. That left barely over four hours for an elderly man to organize his tools, get to Pasadena, select a victim, somehow get him in the abandoned building, incapacitate him, dismember him, and get out, all before the cops arrived. It was a daunting, time-sensitive task and even someone as experienced as the Night Hunter might have made a mistake. And if he did, they would find it.

She pulled out her phone. In general, she preferred not to bother Jessie with every peak and valley in the investigation. But this was different. It was huge. She deserved to know.

CHAPTER TWENTY NINE

Jessie's phone rang, startling her.

She'd been sitting at the breakfast room table in the cabin, so focused on finding useful connections from the WBA website's Special Friends Forum, that she'd lost track of much else. From his surprised expression, it was clear that Ryan had been in the same headspace. She looked at the screen. It was Richard McClane.

"Hi Rich," she said, putting him on speaker, "good news or bad?"

"A little good but mostly bad," he said, launching in without offering a choice as to which they wanted first. "I'm pushing forensics hard on that strand of hair you found on Ellen Wade's body. I have one tech I trust implicitly and she said they're very close. She also promised to update me directly the second they have anything on it. I'll pass that straight on to you."

"If that's the bad news, I can't wait to hear the good news," Ryan said wryly.

"Unfortunately, that's as good as the news gets," Rich said, not playing along. "The reason I have to depend on that one loyal tech is because I've been largely cut out of the loop. Sheriff Kazansky is pissed in general and especially with me. He's taking over. He's just assigned his detectives and they're a pair of lackeys—their names are Mitchell and Caster. Don't expect them to be forces for good."

"When are they coming?" Jessie asked.

"Kazansky has scheduled a press conference for an hour from now. He'll want them there, standing behind him like good soldiers. They'll leave for Wildpines as soon as he's done. That gives you about two hours, maybe three tops before the town will be overrun with Riverside County Sheriff's Department people. And I guarantee they'll know who you are. So if you don't have this squared away by then, I recommend you beg off. You're welcome to stay in the cabin, but you'll probably want to make yourselves scarce otherwise."

The idea of bailing when they seemed to finally be making progress was inconceivable to Jessie, though she knew he had a point.

"Great," Ryan said, sounding equally frustrated by the suggestion. "No pressure there."

137

"Does that mean that you don't anticipate solving three murders in the next three hours?" McClane asked, his arch tone suggested he expected no such thing.

"We've actually had a few breakthroughs," Jessie told him. "That warrant for the WBA website was a big help. It turns out the site was a front for an infidelity club forum run by Clarice Kimble. Both Ellen Wade and Sarah Ripley were members. We're certain that the forum is somehow connected to the killings."

"That sounds promising," McClane said.

"You'd think," Ryan replied. "But we've been here in your cabin, banging our heads against the wall trying to find the relevant connection. So far, we've come up empty. From everything we've looked at, there are no shared romances among the women. No spouses were involved or seemed to know anything about it. We can't find any angry or inflammatory messages. There's nothing that clearly shows that this forum was the motivation for the murders. But there's too much here for it to just be a coincidence. The answer is somewhere in this site data. We just have to find it."

"Well, do it quick," McClane said. "Time is your enemy now."

He hung up, leaving Jessie and Ryan staring helplessly at each other.

"What next?" he asked. "Just keep plugging away and hope something pops?"

"I don't know that we have any other choice," Jessie said. "We don't just have to worry about Kazansky's people big-footing us. This killer has struck on three out of the last four nights. I'm worried that no amount of police presence is going to stop another attack tonight. We have to keep pushing."

She had just returned her attention to the laptop screen when her phone rang again. This time it was Kat. She answered and hit the speaker button once more.

"Jessie?" Kat said with unexpected urgency.

"Hey. What's wrong?"

"He struck again," Kat said, getting straight to the point.

"At the hostel in Pasadena?"

"No. That place was clean. We found a body in an abandoned building across the street. It was a rush job. He didn't have time to do his typical skinning routine so he made do by cutting the guy into pieces."

Jessie saw Ryan's head drop. She knew what he was thinking: that another person was dead because of his inaction just over a week ago.

"How did you know to look there?" she asked, hoping to steer the conversation away from the details of the victim's death.

"The building was a vacant medical supply store called 'Garland Hunt Medical Supply.'"

There was a long silence as both she and Ryan processed what that meant.

"You were right," Jessie finally said. "He planned the whole thing—the uncollected Ford Tempo, the crumbled piece of paper in the Honda Civic with the address for the hostel. He somehow knew it would be found and that someone would notice the medical supply place."

"But why?" Kat asked. "Is this just his way of saying that even with a manhunt under way, he can kill someone? We already know that. What purpose does this serve?"

"Maybe he just felt the itch," Ryan said, finally looking up again. "Maybe he knows the dragnet is closing in and he just wants to do as much damage as possible in the interim."

Jessie didn't buy it. There was a reason the Night Hunter took such a risk. But since she didn't want to kick Ryan when he was down, she said nothing. Kat filled in the gap of silence.

"The Crime Scene Unit is on the way right now. We're hoping that because he was in such a hurry, maybe he screwed up, left a print, DNA, something."

"Maybe," Jessie replied, "but don't hold your breath."

"Believe me, I'm not," Kat said. "How are you guys holding up?"

"We're muddling through," Jessie said. "Hannah's actually thriving, even though we've been here less than a day."

"Do I hear a 'but' in there?" Kat asked.

"But," Ryan volunteered. "This case we're helping out on is about to blow up. Unless we can solve it in the next couple of hours, it's going to be taken over by another department. Plus the place will be swarming with media. To keep from being recognized, we'll have to hole up again. It'll essentially be like living in an unofficial safe house."

"I'm sorry," Kat said.

"You don't have anything to be sorry for. I'm the reason we're in this situation," Ryan said, standing up. "I'm going outside to get some air."

Jessie waited until he had left the room to speak.

"Thanks for the update," she said, not commenting on Ryan's words. Neither did Kat.

"Not a problem," she replied. "I'll let you know if CSU turns up anything."

Jessie's phone buzzed. Rich McClane was calling back.

"Please do," she said hurriedly. "Sorry to cut this short but I've got another call. Talk later."

She switched lines.

"Tell me something good," she pleaded.

"Okay," Rich replied. "The techs finished the analysis on the strand of hair. They found something."

CHAPTER THIRTY

Ryan felt like crap.

As he sat on the wagon wheel bench across the snowy yard from Rich's cabin, he did his best to fight off the growing certainty that every life the Night Hunter had claimed since last Tuesday was his fault and that he would never be able to atone for his failures.

In the days since he froze up outside that hostel and watched the killer slip away into a crowd, two people had been murdered. First their elderly neighbor, Delia Morris, and now some random man in Pasadena. The fact that he had been physically limited and couldn't have chased after the Night Hunter was no defense. He knew he could have shot the man if he'd kept his wits about him. But he had panicked.

The front door opened and Jessie stepped out, looking around for him.

"Here," he called out and waited as she traipsed across the expansive yard through the thick drifts of snow. While he waited, he let his hand press on the spot where he was keeping the engagement ring in his jacket pocket.

It felt strange against his hip. He wondered if that was a sign that he wasn't supposed to have it; that he hadn't truly earned it. How could he ask Jessie to spend the rest of her life with him when he wasn't sure a life with him was something worth having?

"How are you doing?" she asked him through panting breaths as she plopped down beside him. "Still blaming yourself for another man's sins?"

"No," he told her, "Just for my own."

She looked over at him and smiled. He knew something good had happened.

"Well, far be it from me to interrupt the daily Hernandez emotional self-flagellation session, but maybe you could push pause for a few minutes to help me solve this case?"

"What have you got?" he asked, ignoring everything but the case part.

"Rich McClane got back to me about the strand of hair," she said excitedly. "He said the analysis was a rush job. But here's what they

141

know for sure: the hair is human, female, and likely belongs to someone of Asian heritage. I thought we could revisit the list of WBA business owners and maybe use some inappropriately broad stereotypes to see if we can find a match. How does that sound?"

"I'm in."

*

Ryan's enthusiasm was short-lived.

What started out so promisingly had turned into a slog. After a half hour of poring over the websites of every WBA member, looking at names, photos, and personal narratives to find a possible match, they'd come up empty.

"I know this is a small town," he said in frustration, "but how is it possible that there's not a single clearly Asian female business owner here? What are the odds?"

"I'll admit that I expected at least a few hits. Maybe we're missing something?" Jessie said, trying to maintain a positive tone.

"Or maybe we're not missing anything at all," Ryan countered. "It could just be that Ellen Wade bumped into someone yesterday who had no connection to the WBA and a piece of her hair ended up on her coat."

"That's certainly possible," Jessie conceded. "But with the blustery wind yesterday, one would think the hair would have blown off unless it got on her coat close to when she died."

Ryan closed his eyes and rubbed his temples. He felt like they were so close to cracking this. But close wouldn't do them, or a future victim, much good.

"How much longer do we have?' he asked, opening his eyes again.

"It's 12:30 now," Jessie said. "Based on what Rich told us, we have until between 2 p.m. and 3 p.m. At this point, I'm wondering if we should just go back to Lorraine Porter at *The Wildpines Gazette* and ask her for a list of Asian residents in Wildpines. As long as we're alienating everyone in this town, why not go all out?"

Now it was her turn to rub her temples.

"I don't think that's the solution," he said.

"I know Ryan," she replied. "I already feel gross about what we've done so far. I'm just employing a bit of desperation-infused sarcasm into our already tense situation."

He knew she wasn't serious but something she said did resonate with him.

"You know what? Maybe we *are* missing something. We're obviously not going to knock on the doors of everyone of Asian heritage in Wildpines. But maybe we don't have to."

"What do you mean?" Jessie asked, looking up.

"If we're right that our killer has something against certain WBA members, especially ones in the Special Friends Forum, maybe we shouldn't be looking for someone who's a member, but someone who got kicked out. Can we search the site for women who were members until say, six months ago?"

Jessie's fingers were already flying across the keyboard before he finished talking. It only took a few seconds to tell she'd hit pay dirt. She looked up at him with twinkly eyes.

"You're not going to believe this."

"What?" he demanded.

"Three months ago, a small jewelry store called Leia's Charms went out of business, at which time the owner was ousted from the WBA. Her name is Leia Choi. She designed a lot of her own stuff. Guess who did her website?"

"Ellen Wade?" Ryan said.

"That's correct. And guess who recently put down a deposit on the rental space where the jewelry store was?"

"Sarah Ripley?"

"Again, correct," Jessie replied. "I don't find any references to her being in the Special Friends Forum though."

"Yeah, but I could easily see Clarice Kimble purging her from the system as an extra 'screw you.' She seems like the type."

"Very possible," Jessie agreed. "How do you feel about paying Leia a visit and seeing if she has anything to say about the people who cut her off cold turkey?"

Ryan couldn't believe that less than an hour ago, he'd been questioning not just his professional worth but his personal value as well. It was amazing how one little break in a case could change everything.

"I thought you'd never ask," he said.

CHAPTER THIRTY ONE

No one answered the door.

They'd knocked multiple times with no response. Jessie could feel the anxiety in her gut grow with each passing second.

"Don't tell me we're going to have to get a warrant?" she moaned. "It'll never be approved in time."

"If at all," Ryan added. "Now that Kazansky's running the ship, he'll probably want to review every request and I doubt he's going to approve any request that Rich McClane submits on our behalf. We're going to have to get creative."

"What do you propose?" Jessie asked as she watched her boyfriend glance around the area.

"This is a nice area," he said. "The homes are pretty far apart. I'd bet we could wander around the place without anyone even seeing us."

He was right. They'd had to drive a good five minutes out of town, along multiple, confusing, one-lane roads to get here. The houses were large and well-maintained. But more importantly for their purposes, they weren't close enough to see the other properties well. If someone was to force open a door and claim exigent circumstances, who would balk?

"Let's take a look around," Jessie said. "I thought I might have heard a cry for help inside. It's definitely worth checking out."

Ryan nodded.

"You go left. I'll go right and meet you around the back. Call me and we'll keep the line open."

Jessie put in her ear buds and dialed his number. Once it connected he put his ear buds in too and they went in opposite directions. She moved around the side of the house as stealthily as she could, keeping low as she passed under the windows. It turned out that she didn't need to jimmy open any doors. One at a side porch was already slightly ajar.

"Side door is open," she whispered, undoing the snap on her gun holster. "I'm going in."

"Hold up," Ryan insisted. "Let me come around. We'll go in together."

"Okay."

She waited, doing her best to contain her frustration. She knew he was right. Going in together was safer. But time was running short and even with his improved walking, between the icy terrain and the need to keep quiet, it would take him forever to arrive.

When he finally did, they approached the door slowly. Each of them had their guns out. Ryan pushed the door open and Jessie stepped in first. She was in some kind of mudroom. Once Ryan came inside, they moved into the house and began to search from room to room.

Several lights were still on and Jessie could hear a fire crackling nearby. She doubted Choi would leave the place in such a state for any extended period and suspected the woman was still in the home somewhere, possibly hiding.

Ryan indicated that he was going to check the back of the house. Jessie nodded and stepped into what looked like Choi's office. She walked over to the desk. It was immaculate; not a piece of paper out of place. There was a single manila folder resting on the corner of the desk. She picked it up. It was a notice of foreclosure for the very address they were at now.

She was about to put the folder back when she noticed the edge of a piece of paper sticking out from under the desk mat. Choi clearly hadn't intended it to be seen. Jessie slid it out. A single, typed page, it was addressed to Clarice Kimble and it was short and to the point:

Clarice,
I know about the "Communications." You are operating a criminal enterprise. One call could end it all for you. But $20,000 will keep your perfect life intact. It's up to you. Await further instructions.

The letter was unsigned but the writer wasn't much of a mystery. Clearly Leia Choi was a desperate woman. She'd lost her business and was on the verge of losing her home too. Had she been rebuffed in her blackmail attempt and gone to the next level? Had she decided to lash out at everyone she blamed for her life falling apart?

"Who are you?" someone said from behind her.

She turned around to find Leia Choi standing in the office doorway, less than ten feet away. The woman was tall and thin, with sharp, severe features. She wore a heavy sweater and sweatpants and her long, black hair dangled limply. She was also holding a ball-peen hammer. Jessie squared up so that the woman could see that she was armed too.

145

"Leia," she said quietly and calmly. "My name is Jennifer Barnes. I'm investigating the death of Clarice Kimble and I wanted to ask you a few questions."

She saw Leia's jaw clench up at the mention of Clarice.

"What are you doing *here*?" the woman demanded. "You're invading my home. You're holding a gun. I have no idea if you really are who you say you are."

"I'll tell you what," Jessie said, her voice even. "Put down the hammer and I'll show you my ID. Then we can have a little talk."

"I don't think so," Leia said, beginning to get agitated. "If I put this down, what's to stop you from shooting me?"

"Leia, there's nothing to stop me from shooting you right now. If that's what I wanted, I would have done it already. I just want to ask you a few questions."

She wondered where the hell Ryan was. Couldn't he hear her through the ear buds? Jessie watched Leia's eyes dart from the letter in her hand to her face and knew things were in danger of spinning out of control.

"It's not what you think," the woman pleaded.

"Then explain it to me," Jessie replied.

But instead, Leia turned and ran from the room. Jessie moved after her cautiously, unsure if she was waiting just outside the door to hit her in the head with the hammer. Once out of the office, she saw that Leia was headed for the mudroom door they'd entered through. She chased after her and was just rounding the corner to the mudroom when she heard a thud followed by multiple grunts.

She dashed to the side porch door. Sprawled out on the snowy ground were both Leia and Ryan. He'd apparently been rushing back inside when she ran out and they collided. His gun was in the snow about three feet from him. Leia, lying right beside him, was still holding the hammer. Her head swiveled back and forth between the two intruders and Jessie saw her hand clench tight around the hammer handle.

"Don't move!" Jessie yelled, her voice cutting through the snow-muffled landscape. "You hit him, I shoot you."

Leia's hand, still clutching the wooden handle, didn't move.

"Drop the hammer, Leia," she ordered, her gun pointed at the woman's chest. "We can work this out but not until you let go of the weapon. Don't make a mistake that could cost you your life."

146

Leia looked back at her with dread etched across her face and for a second, Jessie thought she was about to swing. But then, after several interminable moments, she dropped the hammer into the snow.

CHAPTER THIRTY TWO

They couldn't throw her in the cell.

Deputy Garrett Hicks already had a sketchy-looking, bearded guy—apparently a stalker-in-training— in the lock-up and Jessie and Ryan didn't think conducting their interrogation with him sitting next to her would be all that productive. So they cuffed her to the desk that Deputy Traven had occupied yesterday. Before they started, Garrett joined them in the corner.

"You really think she did this?" he asked under his breath.

"She got kicked out the WBA," Ryan told him. "She had connections to all three women and she knew about the Special Friends Forum, even if she wasn't a member. She wrote a blackmail note to Clarice Kimble. And the strand of hair we found on Ellen Wade's body is a general match for her ethnicity. We won't know for sure if it was hers until we can do a DNA test. But otherwise, she's about as close to a perfect suspect as we could hope for."

"But I've known Leia for half a dozen years," Garrett maintained. "She's high strung for sure. But I didn't think she had a violent bone in her body."

"Looks can be deceiving, Garrett," Jessie said. "Don't trust them."

"I guess so," he agreed, "Because as much of a jerk as Gerard Wade appears to be, he doesn't seem to be responsible for this."

"Why do you say that?" Jessie asked, though she wasn't surprised to hear it.

"I talked to his buddy, Cal Blackwood, the one he said he watched the hockey game with. Cal confirmed the alibi *and* that Gerard rushed him out right after Ellie texted that she was coming home. I also checked the location data on both their phones and it jibes."

"Can't say I'm surprised," Ryan said.

"You probably won't be surprised by this either," Garrett continued. "When we went to pick up the kids from school at lunchtime, there was a lot of chatter. I overheard some parents whispering about Ellie's car being in the Brightside Market parking lot. Word is starting to spread that she was the victim found in the ravine and seeing me help collect the kids won't diminish the gossip. I also heard murmurs about the 'new girl in town' going missing. They clearly mean Sarah Ripley. This whole thing is about to explode. I wouldn't be stunned if folks come into the station asking questions soon."

"Great," Ryan muttered, "just what we need—more pressure." He looked at his watch and Jessie did the same. It was 1:06 p.m. That meant they had about an hour to get a confession from Leia Choi, maybe two at the most.

"We should get started on the interrogation," Jessie said, walking over and sitting down across from the woman. With her head down and her dark hair hiding her face, she looked almost wraith-like. Ryan sat down too. Garrett lingered off to the side. Jessie looked at him and mouthed the word "Miranda."

He nodded and read her rights. "With those rights in mind, do you wish to speak to us?"

Leia didn't look up. Jessie stepped in.

"Leia," Jessie said as warmly as she could, hoping to alter the dynamic a little, "Back in your office, you said it wasn't what I thought. I want to give you a chance to explain yourself. If you aren't responsible for Clarice's death, help us understand your situation. Are you willing to speak with us to clear things up?"

Leia lifted her head. "You won't believe me."

"You don't know that," Jessie said, sensing an opening. "Are you at least willing to try?"

After a long pause, she nodded. "I guess."

"Okay," Jessie said, not wasting any time, "We're going to ask you some simple questions. The more straightforward your answers, the better it is for everyone. Why did you have that hammer?"

As much as she wanted to get to the question of Clarice Kimble's death, she couldn't start there.

"I was working outside in my studio out back," Leia said quietly. "That's where I make my jewelry. I heard some voices from the house and went to check it out. I grabbed the hammer for protection. The porch door was open wider than I left it so I went to the office, where I keep my gun. That's when I saw you."

Jessie glanced over at Ryan, who nodded. Apparently that comported with what he'd told her earlier. He'd found a shed out back that looked like a work studio. That's where he'd been when he heard the two women talking through his ear buds. He's hurried back to the house, just in time to collide with Leia on her way out the side door.

"Let's talk about the note," Jessie said.

"I didn't kill Clarice!" Leia blurted out loud enough for the bearded guy in the cell to look over.

"But you *were* blackmailing her," Ryan pressed.

"I was going to but I never got the chance. I'd been holding on to that note for weeks, debating whether to go through with it. Then she died. I was going to burn it after that because I knew if it was ever found, people would react like you are now. But part of me just couldn't get rid of it. Even though Clarice was dead—and I know this sounds terrible—I was still angry with her. If I got rid of the note, it was like saying my hurt at what she did to me wasn't valid, like I had to get rid of the feelings too. It was like I was giving up on ever getting justice."

"What does that mean?" Jessie asked. "Justice for what?"

Leia looked up at Garrett. "Ask *him*. He knows what she was like. Clarice could be…difficult. She was very fickle with her affections. If she felt you wronged her, she could be petty. And for reasons I never understood, she decided that I had wronged her. She cut me out, dumped me from the WBA, and started bad-mouthing me. She told other members that my designs were stolen from someone else, which wasn't true. She never said who or gave any proof. But it didn't matter. None of the other members wanted to cross her. They talked about me behind my back. My business dried up. Somehow even the tourists heard about me. Ellen Wade stopped doing my site. I actually went to her office yesterday afternoon and pleaded with her to reconsider; to help me at least redo the site so that I could shift my focus exclusively to online sales. But she said she couldn't risk pissing off Clarice."

Jessie thought it interesting that Leia talked about Ellen so casually, as if she was still alive.

"And Sarah Ripley took over your space," Ryan noted.

"Yeah," Leia confirmed. "But she was really sweet about it. I didn't know her very well but she came out to my place about a week ago to tell me she was getting the lease and that she hoped there were no hard feelings. She even offered to stock some of my work in a display case. We're supposed to have a meeting about it next week."

She said it as if the meeting was still on. Jessie fought the urge to look over at Ryan to gauge whether he thought her seeming ignorance about both Sarah's and Ellen's fates were believable. Personally, she couldn't decide.

"Let's talk about the blackmail note again," she said. "In it, you referenced the 'communications' part of the WBA site being a criminal enterprise. Were you part of the Special Friends Forum too?"

"What's that?" Leia asked.

"It's the forum that members used to coordinate their affairs."

Leia's eyes went wide and again Jessie couldn't be sure if she was sincerely surprised or just a great actress.

"Until you said that," she answered, "I wasn't even a hundred percent sure that's what it was. I knew Clarice and Martin were into swinging. At first I thought the group was about that. But I knew some of the people in their swinging circle weren't affiliated with the 'members only' group in the WBA so I started to get suspicious. Plus you hear things around town, that maybe it was for something more illicit. So I took a chance. I figured that if it wasn't anything illegal, she wouldn't respond. But if the 'communications' forum was something criminal, she might pay up. It was a long shot but I was desperate. I needed the money and thought this might be a way to get revenge on the person who put me in this position."

"There are lots of ways to get revenge," Ryan said skeptically.

Leia shook her head angrily.

"No," she insisted. "I was mad. But I would never kill anyone. I know it sounds weird but I've known these people forever. I still viewed them as my friends, even the ones who turned their backs on me, even Clarice."

Ryan looked at Jessie and she knew from his expression that he didn't have any more questions. His mind seemed made up. He didn't believe this woman. But Jessie wasn't so sure.

The more she thought about, the more credible it seemed that Leia was a desperate, failed blackmailer than a serial killer. The facts, particularly that she kept the blackmail note, seemed to support the former. What possible reason would Leia have for keeping it in her home if she had killed Clarice? She decided to ask a question that would go a long way to helping her ascertain the truth.

"Would you be willing to let us check the geo-location on your phone for the last week?' she asked. "It could help verify your story."

"I guess," Leia shrugged. "But I don't know how much good it would do. I live by myself and I've mostly been home all week. When I do go places, I don't always take it with me."

"It could still help," Jessie said. "We'd also like to do a DNA test on some of your hair. Are you open to that?"

151

Leia's eyes narrowed at the question.

"Why?"

"It could help eliminate you as a suspect," Jessie said, not completely lying. Of course it could also sink her.

Leia looked at Garrett again, whose face was impressively blank. When she turned back to Jessie, her response was clear even before she spoke.

"I've answered all your questions. I'm giving you my phone. But taking my hair feels like an invasion of privacy on a different level. I'm sure you can get some kind of warrant to make me give it up, but I think I'm going to say no until you do that."

Jessie decided not to push the issue. The truth was that even if Leia had agreed, they wouldn't be able to get results before Sheriff Kazansky's hand-picked detectives arrived in town and they had to drop off the radar. She stood and motioned for Ryan and Garrett to join her outside.

"You think we've got enough to charge her?" Garrett asked once they were out of earshot.

"No question," Ryan said. "Despite her explanation, she's got an obvious motive. And from the sounds of it, even once we get her GPS phone data, she won't have an alibi."

"But we don't have a murder weapon," Jessie said.

"Come on," Ryan replied, mildly irritated. "You know she could have hidden that thing anywhere. It could be sitting out in the woods, buried in a plastic bag in the snow."

"So it all comes down to the DNA on the hair," Garrett suggested.

"That might not even help," Jessie said. "If Leia really went to visit Ellen at her office yesterday, she could reasonably claim that the hair got transferred then. Maybe Ellen gave her a sympathetic hug or something."

"So what do I do?" Garret asked. "Keep her cuffed to that table until the Riverside detectives arrive?"

"Can you cut that guy in the cell loose and put her in there?" Ryan asked. "If she did do this, maybe being behind real bars for a bit will get her to reconsider whether a deal might benefit her."

"I can do that," Garrett said. "I was mostly keeping Gunnar in there to scare him straight."

"What did he do exactly?" Jessie asked, looking back through the glass at the guy slumped against the wall of the cell.

"Oh, he's a constant pain in my ass. The guy is missing the social appropriateness gene. He's got a habit of staring at teenage girls, sometime following them around town. He's never gone beyond that but you can imagine that I've gotten more than a few complaints about how uncomfortable he makes people. But he finally went too far last night and I threatened to send him down to a real jail if he didn't get his act in order."

"What did he do?" Jessie asked.

"Oh, he was creeping on some out-of-town girl last night at Wildyology and allegedly he got too close, like actual physical contact. He bumped into her. She called him out in front of everyone. Apparently it was quite a scene. The band stopped playing. She started shouting that he'd been following her around all afternoon and that he'd be suspect number one if anything happened to her."

Jessie looked over at Ryan to see if the story about a scene-embracing teenage girl at Wildyology was raising the same alarm bells for him that it was for her, but he seemed focused on Garrett's story.

"People started heckling him," the deputy continued. "He got kicked out and went to Wild Things, where he caused more trouble. That's when I got called in. So I threw him in the pokey overnight to let him know this was serious."

"How do you know he won't get worse?" Jessie asked.

"I've known the guy my whole life. He just doesn't understand that people find his behavior unsettling. He stares, oblivious to how he's perceived. Frankly, I'd be more concerned if he was stealthy about it. Still, initiating physical contact crosses the line. Between that and the subsequent harassment, I tossed him in the cell. He cried most of the night and pleaded with me not to tell his mom. She lives just up the hill in Pine Grove and he's worried that if she finds out, she'll disown him. He's that kind of guy."

"But *not* the kind of guy who might stab three thirty-something women?" Ryan asked, asking the question that had popped into Jessie's head as well.

"Considering that I once saw him bawl like a baby when one of his cousins got cut with a Swiss army knife, I'm disinclined to believe it. He hates the sight of blood. But before we found out about the female hair, I checked his whereabouts, just in case. He was on a camping trip from Friday through Monday so he wasn't even around when Clarice died. And he was behind those bars when Ellen Wade was killed. So that'd be a 'no.'"

"In that case," Ryan said. "Go ahead and put Leia Choi in the cell. We're going back to Rich's cabin to review everything. But let us know right away if it looks like she's cracking. We're running out of time."

Once Garret returned inside the station, they headed for the car.

"You're not sure," he said, reading her mind.

"She looks good on paper," Jessie admitted. "But it just doesn't feel right to me. It's too perfect, like she's being served up on a platter for us. Plus, I just can't get over why, if she killed Clarice, she'd keep that blackmail note. It's basically a confession. And if she *didn't* do this, you know we're the last stop for this train. Kazansky's lackeys will charge her no matter what, just so their boss can snag some headlines. Once they take over, the train leaves the station. And it won't stop until she goes down for this, whether she deserves it or not."

"Then we better move fast," Ryan said," Because in about an hour, maybe less, this will be out of our hands for good."

CHAPTER THIRTY THREE

It was too good to be true.

The True Grass Root, or TGR—the name the killer had taken to using on web forums—was reading the piece on *The Wildpines Gazette* website. It had everything one could hope for. In her op-ed, Lorraine Porter revealed that local loser Gunnar Quaid had just come to see her after spending the night at the Sheriff's station, where he'd watched as Leia Choi was questioned by out-of-town detectives in the murder of Clarice Kimble.

Even better, Lorraine tied Clarice's death to two other suspicious events in town in just the last thirty-six hours: the dead body found near Brightside Market and Mile High Muscle just this morning and the rumors of a body found up on Rockview Drive.

Then she posed a series of juicy questions. Were these events connected? Could Leia Choi have snapped and gone on a killing spree? And who were these out-of-town investigators? She revealed that they had questioned her just this morning, asking insulting questions about the operation of the Wildpines Business Association. She further revealed that she could find no investigators with the names Jennifer Barnes or Randy Hosea associated with the Riverside County Sheriff's Department or any other Southland law enforcement agency.

This was wonderful news. It seemed likely that Leia Choi was going to be blamed for the work of TGR. That wasn't the plan but it couldn't have gone better. Better yet, the only people who seemed interested in pursuing this were about to be run out of town with pitchforks. TGR could go back to normal, lead a regular life again, and no one would ever suspect a thing. It was a gift. And yet.

Now TGR had a taste for it. The sweet satisfaction that came from that first puncture as the knife popped through the flesh was intoxicating. Even better was the sensation as the blade sliced into human gristle like it was butter. And there might never be a better time to partake of the pleasure again.

If TGR acted quickly, as in tonight, the deed could be done and the body dumped well outside town. By the time it was discovered, there would be no way to know when she'd been killed. It could easily be attributed to Leia Choi as her last kill before capture. It was perfect actually.

And TGR could think of one last perfect victim, someone who deserved everything she had coming to her. While the WBA forum was the original source of the transgressions, the willing participants were the true filth. They were an affront to TGR's sense of decency and decorum and there was an obligation to rid the world of such whores, so that those few who behaved in an upright, moral way could thrive.

So it was settled. One more thrill. One last night of vengeance that would look like the handiwork of Leia Choi. Then a return to everyday life, living freely among the very neighbors whose lives had been forever destroyed. It was time to prepare.

CHAPTER THIRTY FOUR

For the third time in the last five minutes, Jessie looked at the clock in Rich McClane's kitchen.

It was 1:48. According to what Rich had told them, the Riverside detectives might show up in town in the next ten minutes or so. Or they could arrive an hour later. Either way, she and Ryan were basically out of time.

The chances of finding anything to exonerate Leia Choi in that window were remote. And if they were going to tell Rich and Garrett to charge her, they needed to do it ASAP. Files had to be handed over and their association with the case ended. Rich might be able to scrub their involvement but not if they were out and about in town with locals pointing them out to the new detectives.

Ryan sighed heavily and she knew what was coming.

"Why are we still doing this, Jessie?' he asked. "I know you have reservations but we haven't found anything implicating anyone other than Leia Choi. Why haven't we pulled the trigger and given the go ahead to charge her? It seems like a no-brainer at this point."

It was hard to argue with him. Everything pointed to her. They didn't have the GPS data on her phone yet, but by her own admission, it might not be exculpatory. They could get a DNA test on her hair but that wouldn't be determinative either. She couldn't hold everything up just because something didn't feel right. Ryan was right. It *was* a no-brainer. But that was the very problem.

"It's too perfect," she said, her voice rising louder than she'd intended.

"Everything okay in there?" Hannah called out from the living room.

They had picked her up from the coffeehouse on their way back from the station, where she said she'd had a great time. She even mentioned that she'd like to keep in touch with a few people she'd met once all this madness ended, especially a girl named Patrice and a boy named Chris. When she'd said the last name, Jessie noticed her face flush.

She said nothing about that, nor her suspicion that her sister's evening at Wildyology last night hadn't been quite as mellow as she'd suggested. There would be time to address that later. For now, she needed to stay focused.

"Everything's fine," she called back before fixing her gaze on Ryan and whispering intently. "It's *not* okay. Like I said back at the station, it's as if Leia is being served up on a platter for us, like someone else is using her as a patsy."

Ryan shook his head in frustration.

"We're not dealing with the Night Hunter here, Jessie. Who up here do you think is capable of that?"

Something about his words clicked for her, like a puzzle piece being snapped into place.

"I'll tell you who—someone else who knew about how the WBA Special Friends Forum really operated and didn't like it. Or maybe someone who got kicked out of the WBA, just like Leia, and decided to get revenge, or both. Either way, the real killer would want a pawn she knew could divert attention away from her."

Another thought occurred to her and she began furiously typing on her laptop keyboard.

"What is it?" Ryan asked.

"Assume for a second that Leia is innocent and the killer wanted to frame her, what would be a perfect way to do that?"

"I have a feeling you're about to tell me."

She looked at her screen and felt a surge of adrenaline. Then she turned it so he could see it too. It was the website for a company that made high-end wigs. Right at the top of the page in bold lettering was a notice stating that *"all of our wigs are made of the finest human hair sourced directly from the Southeast Asia. No synthetic materials are used in the creation of any of our products."*

"That's pretty typical," she told him. "Most hair for wigs is imported from either India or China."

"So you're saying someone could have worn the wig as a way to implicate Leia?" Ryan asked, sounding curious but unconvinced.

"That; or it could just have been a disguise. Maybe our killer is a blonde and thought wearing a wig with dark hair could better hide her identity."

"Assume for a second that I buy this," Ryan said. "That could be anyone. How can we possibly narrow it down?"

Jessie thought for a second, playing out her theory in her head before she spoke it aloud. Finally she looked over at Ryan.

"If I'm right, the hair is secondary. We should be looking at other people who got kicked out of the WBA recently and then see if that person isn't a brunette."

Ryan's expression went from skeptical to intrigued.

"Do the search," he said excitedly.

She put in the same parameters as she had during the original search that revealed Leia Choi was removed from the WBA. Within seconds she had the list. It was short.

"There are only two hits for other people removed in the last few months. One is for a guy named Sean Foley. He's a carpenter and blade smith."

"That sounds promising," Ryan said. "I bet he's got a wall of knives at his disposal."

Jessie agreed but as she studied his page, her heart sank.

"No good," she said. "It looks like he was only removed from the association because he moved. His website says that he relocated to Flagstaff, Arizona, a month ago."

"Okay," Ryan replied, clearly disappointed. "What about the other hit?"

"I've actually heard of this one," Jessie said, "Charlotte and Stanley Riggs, owners of Riggs Mountain Resort. That's one of the places Rich suggested as an alternative if we didn't like his cabin, remember?"

"Yeah," Ryan recalled. "He said they're hurting for business and would probably give us a good deal. I wonder if they're struggling because Clarice had negative things to say about them."

"Quite possibly," Jessie agreed. "It looks like they were removed as WBA members just last week. And look at this. Apparently Charlotte Riggs was a participant in the Special Friends forum."

Ryan responded excitedly. "That might explain why Ellen Wade used the motel for some of her get-togethers. If they were all in the know, it would be a safe place to hook up. Now that I think about, I feel like I remember seeing that Sarah Ripley's first dalliance was there too, before she started using her house exclusively?"

"That's right," Jessie confirmed. "But it looks like the Riggs Resort fell out of favor on that front as well. I don't see any hookups there lately. And there's more: just two days after the business was removed from the WBA site, Charlotte's credentials for the Special Friends

Forum were revoked as well. That was last Friday, two days before the first murder, more than enough time to buy a wig."

Ryan smiled. He was clearly on board now.

"That's a pretty good dual motive for murder," he said. "First her business takes a hit. Then Clarice Kimble bars her from the town's exclusive cheating club, one that she knows both Sarah Ripley and Ellen Wade are members of. What color is her hair?"

Jessie pulled up the "about us" page from the Riggs resort website. It showed a couple in their forties. The husband, Stanley was red-cheeked, schlubby, and balding. He was also a good two inches shorter than his wife. Charlotte was skinny, with pinched features. It was clear that she'd once been attractive but that the years of working a demanding job in a harsh environment had worn her down. Notably, she had light brown hair.

"No wonder she was looking elsewhere," Ryan said. "Stanley isn't going to get mistaken for McDreamy anytime soon."

"Real nice," Jessie said reprovingly. "Maybe he's got a great sense of humor. Anyway, that doesn't matter. We have an address. We have a suspect. We have her hair color. And we still have at least a few minutes until those Riverside detectives are supposed to show up. Let's make the most of them."

CHAPTER THIRTY FIVE

They were just pulling off Central Circle Drive onto Highway 243 when Jessie got hold of Garret Hicks. She put him on speaker and started asking questions the second he picked up.

"Garrett, what do you know about Charlotte Riggs?"

To his credit, there was only the briefest, stunned pause before he replied.

"Not much to tell. She's lived here as long as I can remember. She's quiet, keeps to herself, very churchy. I know she doesn't think much of her husband. She seems to roll her eyes every time he speaks. Why?"

"We're headed out to question her," Jessie told him. "It looks like she was part of the Special Friends Forum until recently, when her membership was revoked. Does she have any history of violence?"

"None that I'm aware of," he said. "You guys want me to meet you out there?"

Jessie looked over at Ryan. He shook his head.

"If you come," he said, "who's going to run interference if those detectives from Riverside show up?"

"I was actually about to call you about that," Garrett replied. "I just heard from Detective Mitchell. Apparently he and Detective Caster stopped for lunch in Banning. They're just heading up the mountain now. He wanted to 'coordinate,' which basically meant he wanted me to clear a section of the station for their exclusive use. I think they're going to be bummed when they discover there's only one section. But that's not the point. For your purposes, the important thing is that they'll be rolling in here in about a half hour."

"Good to know," Ryan said. "That might be enough time to determine if Charlotte Riggs is our killer and bring her in before those guys arrive."

"I'm afraid I have some bad news too," Garrett added reluctantly.

"What?" Jessie asked, sensing that he was underplaying it.

"After I let Gunnar Quaid go, he went straight to Lorraine Porter at *The Gazette* and told her everything he saw and heard at the station. She just posted a piece on the website listing Leia Choi as the prime suspect in Clarice Kimble's death. She also tied the killing to the other women, though she hedged just enough to protect herself."

"Oh God," Ryan moaned. "We're going to have a panic on our hands."

"It gets worse," Garrett said. "She said you questioned her about the WBA and that she can't find any record of investigators with your names. I'm not sure Charlotte Riggs, or anyone else for that matter, is going to be keen to talk to you from here on out. And as long as we're on the topic, I know I'm not supposed to ask any questions, but should I be asking you guys some questions?"

"Best not," Ryan told him emphatically. "This is one of those times where you just have to trust that your boss is making the best decision for you."

Jessie agreed wholeheartedly but her attention was focused elsewhere. If someone decided to follow up on Charlotte's article, their cover story could fall apart real quick. The idea was enough to make her heart beat a little faster.

"How long ago was the piece posted?" Jessie asked.

"Twenty minutes."

"Maybe she hasn't seen it yet," Jessie said hopefully.

"It's possible," Garrett said. "I don't get the sense that she's the type to refresh the local news obsessively. So are you sure you don't want me there?"

"We've changed our minds," she said after getting thumbs up from Ryan. "You can come."

"Okay. I just need to reach out to Pete Traven and have him take over here at the station, to keep an eye on Leia. He's just up at Rusker Park making sure no one's illegally parked at the trailheads. I'll join you in just a few."

"Thanks, Garrett," Jessie said. "And can you call Rich McClane too and give him a heads up? I'd do it myself but we're pulling up to the Riggs place right now."

"Will do," he promised.

After they hung up, Ryan parked in one of the three spots in front of the resort. The term was generous. The Riggs Mountain Resort looked more like a dilapidated, fleabag motel than an exclusive retreat. The paint was peeling of the exterior walls. The light in front of the office flickered restlessly. There were countless missing shingles and the ones that clung to the roof looked battered. Jessie thought that if the whole

162

motel was picked up and dumped in a dark corner of downtown L.A., it wouldn't look out of place.

"How do we want to play this?" she asked once Ryan turned off the car.

"Let's start with the WBA," he suggested. "That way we don't set her off with questions about the murders right away. Besides, the article said that's what we were questioning Lorraine about. If she read it, we could tell her we're just doing our due diligence."

"Sounds good," Jessie said, getting out. She was about to zip up her jacket but decided against it. It was just after 2 p.m. and the sun was shining overhead. She guessed that the temperature was a balmy forty.

A bell tinkled as they entered the office. The inside was no more impressive than the exterior. The decor appeared to be a good thirty years old, with wallpaper that was clinging to the drywall for dear life. The carpet looked like it hadn't been cleaned this century. The computer monitor on the counter was the size of a carry-on suitcase. She was amazed that it was usable at all. A small man that she immediately recognized as Stanley Riggs stepped through a dusty curtain and plastered on a fake smile.

"Welcome," he said with all the chipperness he could muster. "Do you have a reservation?"

"I'm afraid we don't," Jessie said, easing into the conversation.

"That's all right," Riggs replied. "Luckily you're here midweek and we have a couple of vacancies. How many nights were you looking to stay?"

"Actually, we're not looking for a room," she said gently, hoping to let him down easy. It didn't work. He looked crestfallen. Even his pink cheeks seemed to slump along with the rest of him. He tried to recover, casually patting down the few hairs that remained on his head.

"Why are you here then?" he asked, for the first time showing any sign of suspicion.

"We were hoping to talk to your wife, Mr. Riggs," Ryan said. "Is she available?"

Riggs now looked overtly mistrustful.

"No. Why? What's this all about? Who are you?"

"I'm sorry, Mr. Riggs," Ryan said, pulling out his fake ID, "We should have introduced ourselves initially. We're investigators helping out local law enforcement on a case. I'm Randy Hosea. This is my partner, Jennifer Barnes. Where is your wife?"

163

For a second Riggs looked like he might balk, but then thought better of it, apparently deciding it wasn't worth the hassle.

"She went to Hemet on a supply run last night. She decided to stay overnight because she was worried about the weather. I expect her back in a few hours. What case are you talking about and what does it have to do with Charlotte?"

Jessie saw that he was getting agitated and tried to ease the tension.

"It's related to the Wildpines Business Association, Mr. Riggs," she said. "We've discovered some questionable activity on the part of the architect of the group and we're talking to past and present members to get a better picture. You and your wife were members until recently, correct?"

"Yes," Riggs said. "Until just last week, when Clarice—God rest her soul—ousted us. I still don't have any idea why. Is this related to her passing?"

"We don't know yet," Ryan said reassuringly. "Right now, we're just gathering information."

"Okay," Riggs said slowly. He obviously knew they were holding back. "Can *I* answer any questions for you?"

Jessie glanced at Ryan. There didn't seem to be any way to question the man without suggesting that his wife was cheating on him, which wasn't an appealing option. She could tell that Ryan felt the same way. But they were out of time and manners weren't currently a priority. Maybe the guy might inadvertently know something that could be useful. She was about to dive in when she had another thought.

"You know, Mr. Riggs," she said warmly, "Maybe my partner could ask you a few things. But to be honest with you, my stomach is giving me a little trouble. I really have to use the restroom. May I borrow yours?"

"Of course," he said, "It's through the curtain, last door down the hall on your left."

"Thank you so much," she said, and then turned to Ryan, willing him with her eyes to understand what she was planning to do. "Randy, maybe Mr. Riggs can give us some basics on what he knows about the group while I'm indisposed."

His expression told her immediately that he did understand. She should never have doubted it.

"No problem," he said. "Take your time."

She nodded her thanks, moved behind the counter and pushed through the dusty curtain into the hallway behind. Maybe Charlotte

Riggs wasn't around but that didn't mean there wasn't potentially useful evidence here that might prove her guilt.

She knew that she was risking any future prosecution if she found something incriminating. But there wasn't time to sweet talk Stanley Riggs into letting her look around. There wasn't time to get a warrant. There just wasn't time.

She moved as fast as she could. The hallway was musty and dimly lit. Behind her, she could hear Ryan asking Riggs when they first opened the Resort, doing whatever he could to stall. She poked her head into the first room on the right.

It was sparsely decorated with a single bed and a dresser and a vanity. Stepping inside, she opened the closet to find several dresses but no wigs anywhere in sight. None of Stanley Riggs' clothes were hanging up. Apparently he was relegated to using the dresser drawers. She opened them to check, just in case. But there was nothing shocking there, just t-shirts, sweats, socks, and some bras and panties.

She moved onto the next room on the right. It also had a single bed and a dresser. There was a hunting magazine on the bed and a photo of Ted Nugent on the wall. Suddenly she felt desperately sorry for Stanley Riggs. It seemed that he and his wife had separate bedrooms. She wondered if Charlotte used one of the guest rooms for her hookups.

She quickly checked his closet but found only jeans, sweaters, and a couple of jackets. She was about to close it when she noticed a little slit of light piercing through the back wall of the closet. Looking closer, she saw that there was a thin gap between the boards of the wall. Her fingers suddenly trembling, she reached out and managed to grab the edges of one plank. It easily came loose. In the narrow space behind the plank was a metal pole with a mannequin head on it. Resting atop the head was a wig with long black hair.

CHAPTER THIRTY SIX

Jessie stifled a gasp as the truth hit her: the wig wasn't Charlotte's. It was Stanley's!

A shot of adrenaline cascaded through her system as a series of rolling realizations overwhelmed her. Stanley Riggs was short and slight and if disguised with a wig, could be easily misidentified as a woman at first. But he was still strong enough to drag Ellen Wade across a large, icy parking lot.

Suddenly it all made sense. In the wake of their business being dropped from the WBA for no apparent reason, Stanley must have gotten suspicious. Trying to figure it out, he likely went on Charlotte's laptop and discovered her involvement in, and subsequent removal from the Special Friends Forum.

It must have been a shock to simultaneously learn that his wife was part of a club that organized cheating for its members *and* that her participation may have somehow led to his business falling apart. She could only imagine the sense of emasculation and betrayal he must have felt.

In his rage, he would have wanted to punish his wife. But knowing that wasn't possible—that it would cast immediate suspicion on him—he decided to punish the woman who made Charlotte's cheating possible, Clarice Kimble. And when he realized that at least two other women in the group had used his motel as a rendezvous spot, he decided to punish them too. She wondered whether he'd always intended to frame Leia Choi by wearing the wig or if that had just been a happy accident.

Then something else occurred to her. Maybe Stanley had originally decided he couldn't kill his wife. But what if he'd since changed his mind? What if he realized that by murdering her in the same way as the other victims, her death might be viewed as just one of the many victims of a deranged serial killer? What proof was there that Charlotte had actually gone to Hemet last night on a supply run as he claimed?

She heard Ryan's phone ring from down the hall. He answered and though she couldn't make out everything he said, she was pretty sure she heard the name "Rich." She decided to head back out to the office.

166

He was in the dark about the situation and that made him vulnerable. She needed to decide whether to subtly alert him to the situation or simply pull her gun and order Riggs to the ground.

She stepped out into the hall. Her mouth was dry and she could feel sweat dripping down her back. She started to tiptoe back toward the office. Suddenly she felt an arm wrap around her neck and yank her back into the bedroom. Her throat closed up as a forearm and bicep clamped together powerfully on the sides of her neck. She felt the panic rise in her chest and tried to yell out, but there was only a raspy squeak.

Though she couldn't see behind her, she knew who it was. Stanley Riggs was shockingly strong for such a small man. Trying to keep the fear that was enveloping her from taking over, she reached down and unholstered her gun. She was just lifting it up when Riggs slammed his free hand down on hers, knocking the weapon to the ground. It slid on the floor and disappeared under the bed.

Riggs yanked her sideways and through watery eyes, she saw him close and lock the door with a deadbolt. To her horror she saw something she'd missed earlier. The door had a second lock, a sliding metal security bar, which he pushed into place. She realized that even if Ryan was at full strength, it would be nearly impossible for him knock the door open with brute force, at least not in time to do her much good. Jessie could feel her strength fading as Riggs tightened his arm around her neck. She knew that in another few seconds she'd be unconscious, unable to protect herself.

There was a sudden banging on the door behind them. Riggs was startled and for the briefest of moments, his grip on her loosened. It wasn't enough to break free but she was able to get a half gasp of air. With renewed hope and a surge of energy, she did the only thing she could think of. She raised her right foot high in the air and slammed it down hard on the top of Riggs' right foot.

She heard him grunt and felt his arm loosen again as he bent over slightly. It still wasn't enough to get away but she hadn't expected that. She only wanted to shock him long enough to try what she did next. Reaching up with her left hand, she made a fist with her thumb extended outward and jabbed it hard behind her in what she hoped was the general direction of his eye.

It must have worked because she heard him howl in pain. The sound mixed with the banging on the door and Ryan yelling something unintelligible from the other side. She ignored it, instead jabbing her bent right arm back, slamming her elbow into Riggs' ribcage.

167

His grip on her neck loosened enough for her to rip free. But he managed to grab her by the shoulders as she pulled away. Gripping them tight, he swung her violently in the direction of the closet. Her head and shoulder slammed into its back wall and she slumped to the ground. The mannequin stand toppled over from its closet hiding spot, landing on the floor beside her. The wig came off the head and rested limply on the carpet like a dead animal.

Riggs stomped toward her, blood coming from his left eye. The pain of the collision was immediately overtaken by the dread that rose up within her as he approached. With her ears ringing and her vision slightly fuzzy, she tried to get to her feet, but her legs were wobbly. She felt Riggs grab her by the jacket and start to yank her up. Grasping for anything, her hand brushed the mannequin pole and she latched onto it.

As she was ripped upward, she swung the pole toward Riggs' head. She didn't see it make contact but she felt it and heard it. There was a loud thwack and her attacker immediately let go. The mannequin pole flew out of her hands and, still unsteady on her feet, she stumbled forward past him. She collapsed on the ground, where she rolled over onto her back.

Stanley Riggs was standing at the closet door, clutching his chin, which was bleeding profusely. He looked disoriented for a moment but then his one good eye fixed on Jessie. He smiled, oblivious to the blood dripping down his neck onto his button down shirt. He reached up to the closet shelf, grabbed something from under a folded blanket, and pulled it out. It was a butcher knife.

In the distance she could hear Ryan shouting her name over and over again as he slammed his body uselessly against the thick, wooden door. Yet somehow the much quieter voice of Stanley Riggs cut through the noise.

"Time for you to join the other bitches," he growled as he stumbled towards her.

Jessie gulped hard and scooted backward on her butt toward the door. There was no way she could get to her gun under the bed. The mannequin pole was halfway across the bedroom. Her back bumped into the wall next to the door. There was nowhere else to go. Riggs was only steps away.

"What did you do with Charlotte!" she suddenly screamed, not even sure why. All she knew was that the only weapon she had left was her words.

Riggs stopped moving and revealed his toothy, bloody grin.

168

"The same thing I'm going to do to you. The same thing that should be done with all you whores."

A desperate idea came into her head and she went with it. If it didn't work, there wasn't much to lose.

"You can't keep your woman so you have to kill them all? Is that it?' she spat as venomously as she could.

"Not all of them," he announced proudly, "Just the ones who deserve it, like you."

His face a hateful grimace, Riggs looked torn between wanting to taunt her more or just slice her up. But she couldn't risk waiting any longer. She wasn't sure this would work but she was out of options and time.

"Ryan?" she shouted. "You hear where his voice is coming from?"

"Yeah!" he called back.

Jessie saw Stanley Riggs' nasty, contorted smirk suddenly twist into a frown as his eyes went wide.

"Shoot!" she screamed and dove to the right, as far away from the door as she could get.

Riggs took a step toward her but before he could take a second one, a barrage of shots tore through the wooden door. Jessie couldn't tell how many hit him, but he was thrown immediately backward and crumpled to the floor. He gasped loudly as his right hand tried to maintain its grip on the butcher knife. After a few seconds, it loosened and the knife slipped from his fingers and onto the floor.

"Jessie!" Ryan shouted. "Are you okay?"

"Give me a second," she yelled back as she pushed herself upright again into a seated position. She shoved the security bar back to its original spot. After that, with great effort, she rolled over, got to her knees and reached up to unlock the deadbolt. Then she slumped back down again and faced Riggs.

His breathing was more labored now, with one long, slow raspy breath followed by a short, sudden inhalation. The pattern repeated a second time. And then, without warning, it stopped completely.

"The door's open," she muttered.

169

CHAPTER THIRTY SEVEN

They didn't have much time.

Jessie gave Ryan the basics of what had just happened as he checked her for concussion or other injuries. When he was satisfied that the damage was limited to bruising on her neck, he carried her out to the office. He was just placing her down on the ratty loveseat by the front door when Garrett walked in.

"What the—?" the deputy began.

Ryan cut him off. "I can't explain it all right now but we caught the killer and we need your help to make it stick."

Garrett was briefly stunned into silence before he regrouped.

"Could you explain a little more please?"

Jessie felt like she could speak now and did her best to catch him up.

"Stanley Riggs committed these murders," she said hoarsely. "He's lying dead in his bedroom where Ry…Randy shot him after he attacked me. I don't have it all figured out yet but I think he discovered that Charlotte was part of the Special Friends Forum. He didn't think he could go after her so he took his anger out on anyone else he could tie to the group. But I do think he eventually killed his wife too. He basically admitted as much to me. You'll need to start a search for her body."

She swung her legs off the loveseat and slowly sat up.

"What are you doing?" Garrett demanded. "You should stay lying down. You look like hell."

"What time is it?" she asked.

"2:12," he answered.

"Then I don't have time to lie down. Those detectives will be rolling into town in the next fifteen minutes and we need to get our stories straight before then."

"Why can't the truth be our story?" he wanted to know.

Jessie wished it was as simple as that. There was no way they could tell the Riverside detectives everything without putting themselves in danger from the Night Hunter. But maybe they could tell Garrett. She looked over at Ryan, who shrugged.

"It's your call," he told her.

"He deserves to know," she replied before turning back to Garrett. "I know Rich McClane told you not to ask questions. Hell, even he doesn't know the whole truth. But no one can know we're involved. It would put our lives at risk."

"How?"

"Garrett, this is a lot to take in. But my name's not really Jennifer Barnes. It's Jessie Hunt. I'm a criminal profiler with the LAPD. And Randy Hosea there is actually Ryan Hernandez, an LAPD detective. We're up here, away from Los Angeles, because a serial killer called the Night Hunter has been trying to kill us, along with my little sister. He's very old but he's also brilliant. He uses experience and deception to murder his victims. And he's got a vendetta against me. We hoped that by coming to Wildpines for a while and maintaining a low profile, we would stay off his radar. Our captain thought we could help his old friend Rich out on this case without attracting much attention. But that obviously didn't pan out."

Garrett looked like his brain was about to explode but she didn't have time to bring him along slowly so she pushed on.

"So, if word gets out that the two of us were involved in solving these murders, the Night Hunter will be able to track us again. And he's good enough to find us. That's why *you* have to be the one who solved this case. *You* have to have killed Riggs when you came here to question him and he attacked you."

Garrett shook his head vehemently.

"Even if I said yes, there's no way it would work. You guys were all over town in the last twenty-four hours. Lots of people saw you. This motel has your prints. It was Rand...Ryan's weapon that shot him. That will all come out."

Now it was Ryan's turn to shake his head as he pulled out his gun.

"This isn't my service weapon. It's personal and untraceable. It's yours now. No one will give you a hard time for using an unlicensed gun to take a down a guy who killed four women. Make sure to wipe down the mannequin pole and the bedroom locks for prints. Those are the only things Jessie touched. In addition to the gun, I touched the bedroom and front door handles so get those too. For everything else, Rich McClane will help you. He can massage the paperwork and deal with unwanted questions. We wore heavy jackets and beanies everywhere we went. No one got a clean look at our faces the whole time we were here. And unless Wildpines has invested in a bunch of security cameras, none of which I saw, we won't be ID'd by facial recognition tech."

"Someone will figure it out," Garrett insisted. "Even if those Riverside detectives are as thick as Rich says, they're not going to believe that two ghosts conducted a bunch of interrogations and then disappeared into the mist. They'll figure out what happened eventually."

"Maybe," Jessie conceded, "but not right away. You'll be giving us time to come up with a plan. We just need a day or two to find somewhere safe to go. No one knows we're staying at Rich's cabin so unless those detectives are geniuses, figure it out, and raid the place before then, we should be okay. And if the story does eventually fall apart, we'll take the heat. In the end, everyone will know that you put yourself on the line to save us from a vicious killer. And that won't go unappreciated, not by us and not by the Los Angeles Police Department."

Garrett stood there, his brow furrowed, deep in thought. Jessie didn't want to rush him but every second he waited was one that put them in greater danger. Still, this was his choice and he deserved to make it without any more pressure from them.

"You better get going," he finally said. "You don't want to be anywhere near here when those guys arrive."

"Thanks, Garrett," Jessie said. "You don't know how much this means to us."

"Don't get all mushy," he replied, his face flushing. "Just get going and remember to park your car in Rich's garage. You don't need anyone who might be searching the area to run the plates."

"Will do, sir," Ryan promised, helping Jessie to her feet.

Garret wasn't done.

"And call me from your car on the way back to the cabin. I need you to walk me through what happened in detail so I can tell these guys exactly what it is that *I* did here."

He held the door open and they hurried out as fast as they could. It was 2:17. They had to completely disappear in the next ten minutes.

172

CHAPTER THIRTY EIGHT

They kept the curtains pulled shut.

It was probably overkill but it was getting dark and they didn't want anyone driving by to wonder why the lights were on at Rich McClane's place when he was in town doing sheriff stuff.

Because a trip to the store was out of the question, they made do with leftovers. Hannah put together an impressive duck stew but Jessie's throat was really sore so she stuck to instant oatmeal. As she swallowed small bites, she thought back over the last few hours.

They had spent most of the afternoon going over the case, trying to piece together what had happened so that Garrett could better explain how *he* came to suspect Stanley Riggs. As they reviewed the communications in the Special Friends Forum with the benefit of hindsight, several things became apparent.

First, Charlotte Riggs had multiple affairs. Second, she clearly didn't have much concern that her husband would find out because she made her login information for the forum autofill. It must have driven Stanley crazy to discover what she'd been doing right under his nose all this time. Learning that she couldn't even be bothered to hide it well would have added insult to injury.

Third, it was now much clearer why Stanley had used the wig. The forum chats were littered with Charlotte's derogatory comments about his appearance: his height, his apple-red complexion, his sad, remaining flyaway hairs.

He must have known that there was no way he could have gotten close to any of his victims if they knew who he was. So he used his small frame as a weapon, likely drawing them in by disguising himself as another woman in some kind of distress. With long black hair and all bundled up, none of them would have realized it was him until it was too late.

Finally, with time to read the forum messages more closely without time constraints, it became clear why Clarice Kimble had cut Charlotte out of both the WBA and the Special Friends Forum. The messages between the two of them were cryptic but it seemed almost certain that

Charlotte had propositioned Martin Kimble at some point very recently. The phrases "off limits," "over the line" and "my MK" were all used.

They texted all of these details to Garrett. He must have been incredibly busy because he only responded once, to let them know Charlotte Riggs' body was discovered wrapped up in a pickup truck behind the motel. He said that she was probably dead less than an hour when the sheriffs found her. It looked like Riggs was about to dump her somewhere when Jessie and Ryan showed up.

Jessie followed up by asking if their cover story was holding but he didn't reply so she tried Rich McClane. He didn't text back, instead calling a minute later.

"Sorry," he told them. "I had to find somewhere private. There aren't many places like that around here right now. Between law enforcement and crime scene folks, there are probably two dozen representatives of the Riverside County Sheriff's Department on site, and that includes the honorable Sheriff Nicholas Kazanky himself. I'd say there are about half that many reporters here too."

"So are they buying Garrett's story?" Ryan asked.

"So far, so good," Rich replied. "Kazansky swooped right in and took credit for the whole thing. He praised Deputy Garrett Hicks as the epitome of what the department is all about. That means he's invested now. Anything that doesn't fit neatly into his narrative of events will not see the light of day. He'll make certain of that."

"How do you know?" Jessie asked.

"Because it's already happening," he replied. "A few local residents came by the station earlier mentioning some mystery investigators. But Kazansky doesn't want any part of it. He's dismissed them out of hand. I don't know how he plans to deal with the issue long-term. But he clearly doesn't want any flies in his glory ointment and in my experience he's pretty good at swatting away those flies."

Ryan laughed bitterly.

"Never have I been so hopeful that an unscrupulous, narcissistic law enforcement professional would succeed in his scumbaggery," he said, speaking Jessie's thoughts aloud.

"I spoke to a far more principled cop a little earlier," Rich said. "Decker filled me in on the exact particulars of your situation back in L.A. Under the circumstances, he thought I should have the full picture. Do you know what you plan to do next? Of course, you're more than welcome to stay at the cabin as long as you like."

174

"We appreciate that, Rich," Jessie said. "I think we're just going to stay here overnight. The marshals are allowing that but they'll be here first thing in the morning to pick us up. Then it's back to safe house living until the madman hunting us is caught or killed."

"I understand," he replied. "Well, while you're here, let me know if you need anything. I know you can't go running out for any food or toiletries so I'm happy to bring stuff to you when I get a free moment."

*

It turned out they didn't need anything. The cabin was fully stocked on toiletries and Hannah managed to be her typically creative gastronomic savant. Even though Jessie hadn't felt up to partaking, she thought the duck stew smelled great as she slurped up the last of her cereal.

After dinner, as Hannah washed the dishes, she mentioned that the Wildpines Arts Conservatory had a summer session that included a program on Indigenous Culture and Cuisine.

"You guys think that I might be able to go?" she asked, "that is, assuming this whole 'elderly serial killer' thing gets resolved?"

"Is that something that really interests you?" Jessie asked.

"Sure. If I ever have a normal life again, it's the sort of thing I'd absolutely be into. It might help me decide if culinary school is really what I want to do after graduation. Besides, I like it up here. I can think more clearly. I can breathe. And the people are nice too. I've already made few friends here. Both Patrice and Chris said they could help expedite my application."

"If things go back to normal, we can talk about it," Jessie said.

She again noticed her sister blush at the mention of the name Chris. Again she said nothing. Nor did she mention what Garrett had told them about last night's incident with Gunnar Quaid at Wildyology.

Initially, she was upset that Hannah hadn't mentioned it. But upon further reflection, she understood. Had she said anything, Jessie had to admit she would have said no to any future outings. And from what she could tell, this incident wasn't her sister's fault.

This Gunnar creep had been following her around earlier in the day and initiated physical contact at the restaurant. Hannah was only protecting herself by making a scene, bringing attention to the threat she was facing. And as promised, she'd stayed at Wildyology until she was ready to be picked up, just as Jessie had asked her too. Calling her

175

out didn't seem productive. After all, as their shared therapist had told her on more than one occasion: to rebuild trust, at some point you have to give a person the benefit of the doubt.

After dinner, while Ryan and Hannah had some ice cream, she stepped outside to get a little air. The cold stung her already sensitive throat but she ignored it as she trudged over to the wagon wheel bench where she'd found Ryan mentally beating himself up earlier in the day.

As she slogged through the calf-high snow she looked up. It was completely dark now and there wasn't a cloud in the clear night sky, only countless shiny stars, almost none of which she could have seen back in L.A. By the time she reached the bench, she was panting and she could feel beads of sweat running down her back.

She sat down and sighed heavily, watching her breath appear briefly before fading into the darkness. She couldn't help but think that, even though they were only getting two nights up here, it had been worth it just to get away. Like Hannah had said, she could breathe here.

She pulled out her phone, curious to check what the rental rates were on cabins in the area. She immediately noticed multiple missed calls from Kat. In that moment, she felt as if an invisible vice was squeezing her chest. She checked and saw that the phone had accidentally been turned to silent.

Ignoring the sense of dread that suddenly consumed her, she was just starting to call her friend back when the phone rang. She looked down and saw that it was Kat. The invisible vice spread its grip down to her stomach as she answered.

"Hey," she said, struggling to keep her tone level.

"Jessie," Kat said, her voice tight with anxiety. "We've got a problem."

CHAPTER THIRTY NINE

Jessie mentally ordered herself to stay calm.

"What's wrong?" she asked.

"I'm at Garland Hunt Medical Supply. You were right. The crime scene team didn't find anything. No prints, no DNA. But something felt off. The Night Hunter wouldn't have sent us on that sick treasure hunt for no reason. And then I started wondering how he could have known I found the crumpled note in the Toyota Civic in that used car lot. I figured he had to have set up some kind of camera to keep an eye on the place. That got me thinking that maybe he did that here too. So I asked Jamil to do another check. He just finished. There are no cameras but he found something else."

"What?" Jessie asked, though she already knew the answer.

"There are multiple listening devices hidden throughout the building," Kat told her. "Jamil's still looking but so far he's found three, including one close to where I stood when I was talking to you. Jamil says they're extremely sophisticated, sensitive enough to pick up the other end of the conversation, even if you weren't on speaker. So the Night Hunter probably heard our entire conversation. The problem is, I don't remember exactly what we said."

The pit in Jessie's stomach now seemed to swallow her entire body.

"I do," she managed to whisper. "We talked about helping out on a case that that was about to blow up and get major media attention."

"Oh, that's not so bad," Kat said relieved. "That could be any case. He'd have a half dozen to choose from. How would he possibly know which one you meant?"

"What's the biggest case you've heard about in the last twelve hours?" Jessie asked.

"There's always something," Kat replied. "Actually the one that got the most attention today wasn't even here. It was some quadruple murder up in the San Bernardino Mount—."

She stopped mid-word. Her subsequent gulp was audible.

"If you know about it, he knows about it," Jessie said under her breath. "How long ago did you first learn about the story?"

"Let me check," Kat said. After a few seconds she replied. "I got an alert on my phone. That was at 3:31 p.m. That's barely over four hours ago. How long does it take to get there?"

"Even with traffic, probably not four hours. I've got to go."

"Should I call anyone?" Kat asked quickly.

"Call everyone," she said and hung up.

She stood up, unsure what to do next. Part of her wanted to just scream for Ryan and Hannah to come out on the porch now. But there was no way to know for certain if the Night Hunter was already here and she couldn't risk tipping him off if he was.

She sat back down and forced herself to think. He had to know they were in Wildpines. It would be foolish to assume otherwise. But even as small as the town was, it was paranoia to think he could know about Rich's cabin. Or was it?

The man knew about Decker. That meant he could probably discover the relationship between him and Rich McClane. And if he found that, it wouldn't hard to search for McClane's link to the town and learn that he owned a cabin here. Even if he didn't make that connection yet, he'd know to tail Rich, in the hopes of getting him alone and forcing information out of him.

Trying to act casual, she pulled off her gloves and texted Rich: *The Night Hunter knows we're in Wildpines. He may be here now. He probably knows that you know Decker. That puts you in danger. Have Garrett watch your back.*

She was about to add the line, "send the cavalry" but then stopped. If the Night Hunter *was* here at the cabin, he might already have Ryan and Hannah incapacitated. If he heard sirens coming, it was possible that he might run, but she doubted it. After coming so close to killing her, Ryan, and Hannah just a week ago, it was unthinkable that he would back out now. If he came all the way up here, he was committed. He wanted to finish the job. He'd kill them and face capture before he'd run.

She sent the text without the request for help, then briefly considered texting Ryan or Hannah to warn them. But that led to the same concern. If the Night Hunter was already in the cabin with control of Ryan and Hannah, *he'd* be the one to see the text. He'd know she knew and he might just kill them.

The only advantage she had at this moment was that he didn't know that she suspected he was here now. Her seeming ignorance of the

178

situation was her disguise. Until she knew her family was safe, she had to maintain the illusion.

Jessie put her phone back on silent, stood up again, and walked toward the cabin. As she moved, she stuffed her gloves in a pocket, unzipped her jacket and surreptitiously released the clasp on her gun holster. She swallowed hard, though her mouth was dry from the cold and the apprehension. Her legs felt wobbly and she knew it wasn't just because of the deep snow.

She walked slowly, listening for any unusual sound or voice. But the snow deadened everything, a natural silencer. She got to the porch and stood there for a moment, pretending to catch her breath. She couldn't see any movement inside through the window. She opened the door, looking around while trying not to seem like she was looking around. Nothing appeared out of place. She took off the jacket and hung it on the rack by the front door, which she then locked.

As she stepped from the hall into the living room, she saw that the TV was on, though the volume was low. The large lamp in the corner of the room was off so the TV offered the only source of light in the room. Ryan was slumped on the couch. She couldn't tell if he was sleeping, unconscious, or worse. She inhaled deeply, prepared to call out to him, but forced herself not to. Hannah was nowhere to be found.

She wandered nonchalantly into the living room, pretending not to notice Ryan's status as she looked at the screen.

"What are you watching?" she asked casually.

He startled awake, his eyes cloudy with sleep.

"Sorry, he mumbled. "I guess I drifted off. *Inception* was on."

"That's a good one," Jessie said, hiding her relief that he was alive as she moved over behind him, "maybe we should see if Hannah wants to watch too. Do you know where she is?"

"I think she's in her room," he said, sitting up straight with a perplexed look and rubbing his face. She knew why. They had just watched the same movie a few days ago on the safe house couch. He continued, "But she—."

Before he could finish, she leaned over the couch, wrapped her arms around his neck, and gave him a kiss on the lips. Holding him tight so his body wouldn't move suddenly, she whispered "Don't react. He's here."

Impressively, Ryan gave no indication that he'd heard her. Instead he called out to the other room.

179

"Hey Hannah, come in here for a minute," he said. "We want to show you something cool."

"Can it wait?" came the annoyed reply. "I'm FaceTiming someone." Jessie had never been so happy to get an irritated response from her sister.

"Just come out for a minute," Jessie insisted. "I promise you can go right back. We just want you to check this out."

After a long pause that made Jessie worry that something had happened, they heard her say, "Hold on; I'm coming."

Hannah trudged out of her room and joined them, standing at the entrance to the room.

"Come over here and look at this," Jessie said, pointing at the TV. "You've never seen this movie."

Hannah looked at the screen, and then stared at her sister incredulously. She started to say something but Jessie spoke first.

"You really should check it out," she said with a fake smile plastered across her face. "It's very cool. The whole premise is that people can sneak into your dreams, into your world without you knowing. You can't be sure if the reality around you is what you think it is."

Hannah studied Jessie's unblinking eyes and her forced grin. For another second she seemed confused. And then, all at once, she didn't.

"Sounds cool," she said, before slowly walking over and sitting down next to Ryan.

"Why don't you guys get under the blankets and I'll be right back," Jessie said, handing Ryan the thick cover resting on the arm of the couch. "I think the fire needs stoking."

She walked over to the fireplace, knelt down, and began poking at the logs, sending sparks everywhere as she tried to think. If the Night Hunter hadn't already gotten to Ryan and Hannah, then maybe he wasn't in the house. Maybe he *had* gotten stuck in traffic and wasn't even in town yet. She wanted to believe it. But she couldn't. She had to proceed as if he'd already set his plan in motion.

After having thoroughly battered the logs, she left the poker tip lying among the embers and stood upright again, looking around the room. He was here, somewhere in this house. He could have attacked when Jessie was outside but he hadn't; because that wasn't his plan. He wanted this to last. He wanted to savor it.

If she was going to beat him, she had to change the dynamic. She had to convince him to play by her rules, not his. And as counterintuitive as it was, the best way to do that was to let him know she was in on the game. Ignoring the thumping of her heart, she cleared her throat and spoke.

"Are you going to hide all night?" she called out loud enough that her voice echoed throughout the house, "or are you going to show yourself so we can finish this thing like equals? Don't you want to know once and for all if I'm better than Garland? Or are you too scared to find out?"

CHAPTER FORTY

Ryan and Hannah both gasped, shocked at her decision. There were several seconds of silence before she heard a static-y, crackling sound. It was coming from the back of the cabin. She peered down the dark hall in that direction. Suddenly a voice cut the through the static.

"Haven't you ever heard of foreplay, Jessie?" a familiar voice asked playfully.

She turned on the hall light. In the distance she saw a small device on the floor just inside the wooden back door, which had a window up top and a small doggy door at the base. The device looked like the receiver unit of a baby monitor. The Night Hunter must have placed it there.

"When you say that," she yelled down the hall, hoping her voice sounded more confident than she felt, "it makes me think that in addition to your inability to appreciate the value of human life, you're probably not great boyfriend material either."

There was another long silence. When he finally responded, the Night Hunter sounded less amused.

"There's no point in stalling with pathetic attempts to goad me, Jessie. No one can help you anymore. Not the LAPD. Not your private eye friend, your bleating sister, or your cowardly, enfeebled boyfriend. You're finally going to learn what you're made of. Did Garland Moses train you well enough? Are you his equal or just a sad facsimile of the original? I know that question has been eating at you ever since he died. Now you can find out once and for all. But for that to happen, you have to do as I say."

"Why would I do that?" she demanded.

Without warning, something slammed up against the back door window. It took a second to process that it was a person, an older woman with curly gray hair. Her glasses made a clinking sound as her face was smushed up against the glass. There was a gag in her mouth. Behind her, with a gun to her head, was the Night Hunter.

"Because if you don't," he said, his already cold voice made almost otherworldly by the buzz of the baby monitor, "this lovely old lady's brains are going to end up all over the back porch. Do you understand?"

Jessie, her blood running cold, nodded that she did.

"Good. So here's what's going to happen. You're going to toss your gun into the kitchen; same with your phone. Your sister and boyfriend will follow suit. Then you will come open this door and return to where you're standing now. If you do anything else, this woman dies. If either Ryan or Hannah moves from the couch, this woman dies. If anyone makes a sudden move, this woman dies. Got it?"

"Got it," Jessie said. She didn't have much choice so she slid her gun and phone into the other room. Ryan and Hannah did the same with their phones.

"Your gun too, Detective Hernandez."

"I don't have it," Ryan yelled back. "It was taken after it was used to stop a killer earlier this afternoon."

"Ah yes, that story about the brave, local yokel deputy seemed too good to be true to me," the Night Hunter said. "Still, if I find that you're lying, this woman...well, you get the idea. Now come here and unlock and open the door, Jessie."

She walked slowly toward him, trying to think of a way out of this. Nothing came to mind. As she approached the window, she saw the terrified look in the older woman's face. Her glasses, whose frames had little flowers on them, fogged up with her own panicked breath. Jessie feared she might have a heart attack before he got a chance to shoot her. She opened the door and took a step back.

"Now facing me, walk backward to where you were before," the Night Hunter said, shoving the older woman into the house and placing the baby monitor transmitter on the floor next to the receiver.

As she took small slow, backward steps, Jessie got a good look at him for the first time. Until now, she'd seen him mostly in fuzzy surveillance camera screenshots and composite drawings. She had glimpsed him once in person, the night he murdered and scalped a neighbor and used her hair as a disguise to get into her house.

Physically, he was unimposing. He was clearly well into his seventies and he moved like it, shuffling more than walking, and with a pronounced limp. Jessie gathered it was a result of falling from Garland Moses' two-story apartment balcony during their altercation all those years ago. He wore glasses and his gray hair was neatly parted to the side and appeared to be held down by a thick hair cream. His face was wrinkled and his back was hunched. Other than an angry, horizontal scar that cut almost four inches across his forehead, he looked like any other, frail elderly man. But as broken as his body seemed, his eyes were alive with energy.

She could see the glee in them. He'd been waiting for this for months, possibly longer. And yet, she doubted this moment was just about her. Yes, he wanted to test Garland Moses' protégé. But this was about more than that.

Over twenty years ago, Garland had nearly caught him and almost killed him. Though he survived their encounter, the Night Hunter was forced into hiding, injured and unable to resume his murderous vocation for fear of re-igniting the interest of multiple law enforcement agencies. She suspected he always harbored the desire to come for Garland, to pay him back. But when Garland was murdered by Jessie's ex-husband, he was deprived of that payback.

This was the closest he would ever get. By not just killing Jessie, but besting her too, he believed he would finally get vengeance on her mentor. He could snuff out the person that Garland thought worthy of teaching, the woman who could take his place. She wondered if she could use that belief against him.

"It feels weird to call you Night Hunter," she said as conversationally as she could. "Is there a name I can use? I mean, we'll learn it eventually, when the forensic people work over your corpse. But until then, what should I call you?"

He laughed with malevolent sincerity.

"I love your confidence, Jessie," he said. "Unfortunately, should the day ever come when my body is tested, it will be very disappointing. My fingerprints have been burned off. All my teeth have been replaced. Most of my crimes took place before DNA testing was in regular use and even back in the old days, I was very careful. I'm not dead yet but I'm already a ghost. Nonetheless, a name seems appropriate in such an informal setting. So you can call me Wally."

"Okay, Wally," Jessie said, now back in the living room. "So how do you see this playing out?"

Wally came out of the hall into the living room and Jessie saw him eyeing Hannah and Ryan to make sure they weren't hiding anything. She heard Hannah gasp slightly when she saw the old man and his equally elderly hostage but she wasn't sure why.

"Stand up," he instructed both of them. "All of you turn around and lift your shirts above your waist. Jessie and Detective Hernandez, do the same with your pant legs. I hope you're not hiding any surprises attached to your ankle."

They did as he said. When he was satisfied, Wally turned his attention back to Jessie and picked up like they'd never been interrupted.

"How do I see this playing out? That's an excellent question. Unfortunately, despite all my machinations, my plans were complicated by your notorious Southern California traffic. You can understand how excited I was when I learned that despite being in hiding, you were involved in some case that was about to break in the media. When I heard about the Wildpines murder spree, it wasn't hard to confirm it was you. Your Captain Decker went to the police academy with Undersheriff McClane, who has a cabin here. Any doubt I had was erased when I looked at the local paper's website with its story referencing two mysterious investigators—a man and a woman—interrogating locals. So I hopped right in the car. Little did I know that leaving mid-afternoon on a Wednesday, a 110 mile trip would take three and a half hours."

"Yeah, the traffic's a real bitch, Wally," Jessie said, hoping to throw him off his rhythm. She'd noticed that as he spoke, his words came faster and his eyes got more frenzied. She needed to cool him off before he got out of control.

"Indeed," Wally said, taking a breath and gathering himself again. "You can imagine how difficult it was once I got here. Police were everywhere. I knew I needed someone in my possession that would help you make good decisions. Luckily, I came across this lovely lady closing up her shop. What's your name again, dear?"

He pulled the gag out of her mouth violently and tossed it to the floor.

"Maude," the woman croaked, fighting back tears. Behind her, Jessie heard Hannah inhale deeply a second time and realized that somehow, her sister must know this woman.

"That's right," Wally said. "So I followed Maude home and 'convinced' her to join me on my little jaunt over here. Let me assure you that it was not fun. We had to wait until dark to trudge a quarter mile through the woods to get to your back door. At our age, that's no easy feat."

"You're a very impressive person," Jessie said, deadpan.

"Thank you for that," he replied, amused at her sarcasm. "All that is to say, I haven't really had my normal amount of time to envision how

185

this would all play out. No syringes with paralytic agents. No X-Acto knives. I had to leave all that in the car; too cumbersome, very disappointing. But I do have the gun. I do have Maude. And I do have the three of you. So that should suffice."

"Really?" Jessie said mockingly, furiously trying to come up with some kind of edge as she bantered with the madman, "after all your hard work, your years of meticulous planning, your signature kills with machetes and tiny knives that sliced flesh up into ribbons, you're going to take out your nemesis with a gun? How prosaic."

"Isn't it though?" he replied, refusing to be baited. "Regrettably, my options are limited. I don't know how long it will be before your friends in the Marshal Service arrive to take you back into the bosom of their protective custody. So time is of the essence."

"They're not coming until the morning," Jessie told him. "If you let the others go, you can have all the time in the world you want with me."

Wally's smile evaporated.

"Please don't insult me," he said, his voice tight with barely controlled fury. "We were having so much fun up until now. Even if I believed you, even if I consented to your request, your unstable sister and crippled boyfriend would rush to enlist the aid of Barney Fife and the gang. By even suggesting such a thing, you embarrass yourself."

Jessie could sense the situation deteriorating. She turned to look at Ryan and Hannah, neither of whom had said a word. She understood why. There was no way of knowing what might set this man off. But it was clear to her that something had to change. She'd stalled as long as she could but it was getting them nowhere. Wally was losing patience. They needed to change the dynamic fast, before he lost interest in ridiculing them and moved on to more drastic measures.

As she stared at the most important people in her life, something Wally had just said lingered in her brain. It gave her an idea, one that was probably unwise. But at this point, there were no wise moves left, just reckless ones. The only question was how she could let them know what she wanted to do without tipping the Night Hunter off. She decided to go big.

"I'm sorry," she said turning back to him and pretending not to be sickened by the words she was about to say. "I shouldn't have insulted you. As much as I'm appalled by what you've done, the profiler part of me can't help but admire and respect you. The craft you put into your kills is impressive, if grotesque. And as much as it saddened me, the way you took out Detective Trembley was a marvel to behold. I know it had an impact on Ryan, which is what turned him into a quivering mess."

As she said it, she turned back to Ryan, staring at him, willing him to understand. At first he looked hurt, but as she bore into him with her eyes, he seemed to get that she wasn't insulting him. She was sending him a message.

"And Hannah here," she continued, "you're right about her too. She was always a bit off. But since you sliced up that girl who shared her initials, she's really lost it. She gets hysterical at the drop of a hat. I'm not sure any amount of therapy will help."

Hannah too had a brief moment of upset before Jessie saw something click behind her eyes. Then the slightest hint of smile passed across her sister's lips before she opened her mouth and screamed.

CHAPTER FORTY ONE

The wail echoed through the room. Before anyone could say a word, it was followed by a torrent of shrieking verbal attacks.

"You bitch! After everything I've been through, you say that? What kind of sister are you? We're about to die and this is how you choose to end it? Haven't I been through enough?"

She took a step toward Jessie but Ryan grabbed her, holding her back. As he did, he stumbled and yelped in pain, grabbing his leg. Hannah turned her fury on him.

"*Now* you do something?" she spat at him. "You'll hold back a teenage girl but where were you when Trembley needed your help? Frozen in fear in your car, that's where!"

"Don't," Ryan said, wincing in pain as he channeled both physical and psychic wounds. "It was one moment of indecision. It shouldn't define my whole life. I don't deserve that."

Jessie turned back to the Night Hunter, who seemed equally perplexed and exhilarated by their mutual breakdowns. Under normal circumstances, Jessie might have hoped that her sister's screams would be heard by neighbors. But the cabin was too isolated for that. It was clear that the Night Hunter had made the same calculation.

"Please," she pleaded with him, "They've been through enough. Do what you want with me but don't bring them into this. That doesn't punish Garland."

"Yeah," Hannah agreed. "Let me take the old lady home. I was in her shop yesterday. She almost had a heart attack when some pushy customers came in. She can't handle this. I'm surprised she hasn't keeled over already."

Jessie glanced at Maude, who did seem white and clammy.

"Oh God, she's right. Look at her," she insisted. "You had her marching through the snow and now you've got a gun to her head. At least let me help her lie her down by the fire. You can still aim that thing at me."

Wally seemed to hesitate briefly. She knew it must be difficult for him to hold her up and keep the gun trained on the rest of them. But then his expression hardened.

"If she dies, she dies," he said coldly. "Not really my concern."

It seemed that hearing those words sent Maude over the edge. Jessie watched with horror as the woman's eyes rolled back in her head and her body went limp. She collapsed, her body ripping free of Wally's grip and slumping down in front of the fire. His eyes never left Jessie, nor did his gun.

"Fine," he said with a nasty smirk. "I guess I'll let her lie down."

Jessie looked at Maude, crumpled and contorted, then back at Wally.

"Please, just let me help her lie flat so she's not all twisted up like that."

She didn't wait for an answer, sliding over to the older woman and gently rolling her over onto her back next to the fire. The two of them were only feet from where Wally stood. He was close enough to press his gun to her head if chose to.

Once she had the older woman settled, she looked over at Hannah and Ryan and arched her eyebrows expectantly before returning her attention to Maude, who was mumbling softly, seemingly regaining consciousness. She rested her hand on the woman's forehead, as if trying to gauge her temperature.

"I've lost interest in these little games," Wally said. "It's not what I wanted, but I think I'll have to content myself by watching blood pour out of your brains one by one. Jessie, I think you should be the one to decide. Who dies first: your boyfriend or your sister?"

Jessie looked up at him. He was focused on the others, his gun pointed midway between them. She turned to the two people she loved most in the world. They were both staring back at her. She knew that this almost certainly wouldn't work; that she had likely lost this long, deadly game with the Night Hunter. But she had to try.

Praying they would understand, she nodded ever so slightly, letting them know it was go time. Neither responded but the look in their eyes told her everything she needed to know: they got it.

"Him first!" Hannah yelled, pointing at Ryan. "What good is he anyway? He'll always be a shell of who he was. Put him out of his misery."

The words seemed to hit Ryan like a punch as he doubled over, gagging loudly. Out of the corner of her eye, Jessie saw Wally's attention hone in on the movement. Without looking down, she reached out and seized the handle of the fireplace poker she knew was only inches from Maude's forehead.

189

In one swift motion, she swung it toward Wally's right hand, the one holding the gun. But he was ready for her. Wally took a step back and the poker passed through the empty air where he'd stood only a second earlier. His mouth curled into a twisted smile as the poker made contact with the floor, echoing throughout the house.

But in his spiteful joy, Wally missed something. His attention was so focused on Jessie's unsuccessful attack that he failed to notice the other one. By the time he saw Ryan leaping at him, using legs that suddenly seemed to be working just fine, it was too late to aim his gun. They collided and Wally landed hard on his back with Ryan on top of him. His gun slid off down the hallway. There was a loud thump as the older man's head hit the hardwood floor.

Jessie scurried over and, while Ryan rolled the man onto his back, used the gag that he'd shoved in Maude's mouth as a makeshift handcuff, tying his wrists together. Then she rolled him onto his back again. He stared up at her with slightly dazed eyes. She wasn't sure if he was concussed or just stunned by the turn of events.

"You're under arrest Wally," she said quietly.

As she said the words, the gravity of the moment threatened to overwhelm her. Only seconds earlier, there seemed to be no hope. The three of them, along with Maude, were pawns in a cruel game that was certain to end in all their deaths.

But now they were safe. The Night Hunter was in custody, no longer a threat to them or anyone else. A rolling wave of relief cascaded through her entire body.

Ryan sat Wally up and dragged him over to the hallway wall, where the older man slumped heavily. He was breathing hard and looked like he might be on the verge of his own heart attack. The thought made Jessie look over at Maude. Hannah had already gone to her side and was stroking her hair, whispering something in the woman's ear that she couldn't hear. She turned back to Ryan.

"You should get your phone," she told him. "We need an ambulance here ASAP."

Ryan nodded and pushed himself upright. As he walked into the kitchen, Jessie noticed that his "limp" had almost completely disappeared. Glancing back at her sister, she saw that her tears had also left as quickly as they had arrived. Both of them had played their parts—souls too damaged to be threats—well, at least well enough to distract Wally.

190

The Night Hunter, who hadn't spoken since the chaos erupted, cleared his throat.

"You didn't beat me," he muttered bitterly.

She couldn't help but snort.

"Your current predicament would seem to suggest otherwise, Wally."

"Sure," he said, grinning nastily. There was blood on his teeth. "But you couldn't do it on your own. Garland Moses was all by himself and he came within seconds of taking me down. Only a loose sewer grate saved me. It took three of you to do it. I guess we know the answer to that question eating at you since your husband murdered your mentor—you're not his equal."

Jessie stared at him impassively, surprised at how little his words affected her.

"Wally," she said, "You're right about one thing. I'm not Garland's equal, not even close. He was the greatest criminal profiler of the last quarter century. I'd have to be pretty arrogant to think I was better than him. I was just honored that he considered me worthy of his time. But that's the only thing you're right about."

"Oh really?" he said, trying to look uninterested and failing.

"Really. First of all, the man who killed him wasn't my husband. He was my *ex*-husband, and he's currently in the ground, where I put him. Secondly, the reason I beat you was because I *wasn't* all by myself, like Garland was. I was with my family. My family, who made you think that they were weak when they were strong, who stuck with me when things were at their worst, who had my back no matter what, because that's what family does. But you wouldn't understand that, Wally. You may be a genius, but when it comes to people, you're actually pretty stupid."

The old man stared at her and, for what she suspected was the first time in years, he seemed speechless. But of course, it didn't last long.

"Tell that to Alan Trembley," he said, his voice dripping with acid, his eyes gleaming with hatred. "Tell it to your kindly old neighbor Delia Morris and her cute, little dog, Grant. Tell it to Jenavieve Holt and Jared Hartung and Hallie Douglas and the party streamer strands I made from their skin. Tell it to—."

A gunshot interrupted his words. His body slammed back against the wall, suspended there for what seemed like forever before sliding to the floor, leaving a red stain on the wall behind him. Blood poured from his chest as he tried to speak. His lips moved but no words came out, only one rough sigh before his eyes lost their ecstatic fury and went blank.

Jessie turned to see where the shot had come from. Hannah looked back at her and placed Wally's gun on the floor beside her.

"Shut up," she muttered under her breath.

"What did you do?" Jessie demanded in horror.

Hannah looked in her eyes. Her face was surprisingly serene.

"You heard him," she said softly, her voice full of quiet confidence. "He wasn't sorry. He was proud of himself. And if he was arrested, if he was convicted, he'd still be a threat. Sure, they'd probably never let him out. But he'd infect someone else, someone who might continue his dirty work when they got released. He was too dangerous to let live. So I ended him."

Jessie, filled with despair, could only stare at her sister, speechless.

CHAPTER FORTY TWO

Jessie removed the gag before the cops arrived.

When the Riverside County Coroner took the Night Hunter's body away, his hands were at his sides, as if they had been that way when he died. Jessie didn't tell Maude what to say, but after the woman got some oxygen she felt well enough to give a statement. Without prodding, she specifically mentioned that Hannah had shot Wally in self-defense. No one seemed inclined to doubt her.

Jessie wasn't sure how to feel about that. She could barely process that her sister had just shot an unarmed, handcuffed man. Yes, he was a brutal serial killer. But despite what Hannah claimed, he was no longer a threat to them. There was no way she felt up to untangling all the thorny questions of conscience right now, so she set them aside in a corner of her mind to deal with later.

Luckily there was other stuff to keep her busy. Rich McClane had selected one of the other Riverside detectives, a woman named Matilda Broughton whom he held in high regard, to question them about the events of the last few days. She was diminutive and squat, with short black hair and a calm, unfussy demeanor that Jessie admired.

Broughton got the surprise of her life when she was not only informed that the man being carted away was an infamous serial killer, but that the people she was questioning had actually solved the Stanley Riggs case too.

Garrett confirmed it all, explaining that he'd temporarily taken credit at their insistence to protect their identities from the very serial killer who came after them mere hours later. Though her head looked like it might spontaneously combust, Broughton managed to keep a straight face and take copious notes. Jessie felt bad for her. She wasn't going to be sleeping at all tonight.

"How's Sheriff Kazansky going to react to all these revelations?" Ryan asked Rich McClane once Broughton stepped out.

"Don't worry about that," Rich replied. "I'll just suggest that he take credit for it. He can tell the press that this was part of a secret strategy to protect fellow law enforcement officers from another jurisdiction; that he actually intended the whole thing as a trap to capture the Night Hunter, a trap that worked. Trust me, he'll love it."

With that issue seemingly resolved, Jessie consented to let the EMTs re-check her neck. As they wrapped up, a black SUV arrived at Rich's cabin. Their old buddies, U.S. Marshals Sam Mason and Tommy Anderson, emerged and helped them relocate from what was a crime scene to a different cottage.

It was a courtesy that they had even come. The threat that had brought them here was gone. They could have told everyone to hop in the car and leave right then, but they took pity on the haggard crew and let them stay overnight to get some sleep. Still, until they were safely returned to L.A. tomorrow, their supervisor and Jessie's one-time guardian angel, U.S. Marshal Patrick Murphy, had instructed the men not to leave Jessie alone.

When she finally managed to drift off to sleep, it was well after 3 a.m. She slept fitfully, dreaming of giraffes running in the snow and somewhere behind them, a hunter.

*

Jessie awoke with a start.

Based on the angle of the light streaming through the blinds, she knew she'd slept late. When she checked her phone she saw that it was 10:24. Ryan wasn't in bed. She was surprised that a Marshal hadn't already rapped on her door, telling her it was time get moving.

She skipped the shower and got dressed quickly. When she walked out to the living room, she found Sam Mason on the couch, looking at his phone.

"Where's Ryan?" she asked.

"Went for a walk."

"And Hannah?"

"Still sleeping," he replied, "Or at least pretending to. She hasn't come out of her room yet."

"What about Tommy?"

"He got the short straw and had exterior duty," Sam said. "He spent the night in the SUV."

Filled with guilt, Jessie decided that even though she was no chef and it likely wouldn't be up to her sister's standards, she'd try to make some breakfast. She searched the cupboards and found some instant

194

coffee and pancake mix. There were some eggs and bacon strips in the fridge. Everything smelled fine so she got started.

There was enough for everyone, so after she plated everything, she told Sam to grab a seat and went out to the SUV to let Tommy know too.

"Thanks," he said, looking exactly like a man who'd spent all night in a car.

"Sure. Do you know which way Ryan went?"

"Just up the hill behind the house," he said, pointing. "He's that speck over there. I told him that if he couldn't see the SUV, then I couldn't see him, so he's being a good boy and sticking close."

"Okay, I'll text him that food's on," she said, pulling out her phone. Before she could start, it rang. Kat was calling.

"I have to take this," she said. "Can you let Ryan know about breakfast?"

"Sure," Tommy said, pulling out his own phone as he walked to the cottage. "And just so you know, Murph said he wants us to pull out no later than noon. Now that your protectee status has changed, he can't get approval for us stay with you past 3 p.m."

"Understood," Jessie said, then answered the phone. "Hey Kat, what's up?"

"Hi, I didn't want to bother you last night during all the craziness but I thought I should check in. How're you guys doing?"

"Better than this time yesterday," Jessie assured her. "Though there's probably going to be a tough road ahead."

"What do you mean?" Kat asked.

Jessie sighed. She didn't want to get into the details of how she, Hannah, and Ryan had used each other's weak spots as tools to trick the Night Hunter.

"I'll explain more later. For now, let's just say that in order to stop this guy, we kind of had to tear each other apart a little. There are some open relationship wounds that still have to heal. But we'll get there. How are things back in the big city?"

"Also good. I stopped by Central Station earlier this morning. Captain Decker is in a good mood. He said that with the Night Hunter case resolved, Homicide Special Section is getting plaudits from everyone. Good stories on the news, relief among residents. He said headquarters is even talking about bumping up the HSS budget."

"Wow, forty-eight hours ago the unit was at death's door." Jessie noted.

"I guess that's what happens when two of its members catch a serial killer that prospective officers study at the police academy."

Jessie knew what she wanted to say next but suddenly found it hard to get the words out.

"Is everything okay?" Kat asked after a few seconds.

"Yeah. I just wanted you to know that we wouldn't have caught him if it wasn't for you. If you hadn't sensed something was off and told Jamil to check that vacant building again, I'm not sure we'd be talking now."

"I doubt that," Kat said, embarrassed. "You guys are pretty good at what you do."

"We are," Jessie agreed, "But we let our guard down last night. Your warning saved us."

"I'm happy to help," Kat said simply.

"You know," Jessie continued, fighting back the tears starting to well up, "I wanted to have this big talk with you, to go over what happened with Hannah and clear the air. It was so important to me. I wanted you to ask for my forgiveness so that I could look you in the face and decide if you deserved it. But I don't want to do that anymore. I think I'm just going to forgive you right now and ask if you'd be my best friend again. How would you feel about that?"

There was a brief pause on the other end of the line and Jessie knew that Kat was trying to keep control too.

"I'd feel pretty good about it," she finally said.

"Bygones?" Jessie asked.

"Bygones," Kat said and they were both quiet for a bit. When Kat spoke again, Jessie sensed immediately that something was different. "There's another thing."

"What is it?"

She got the same odd feeling that had overcome her yesterday morning when Kat called her at the Ellen Wade crime scene. She *had* been holding something back.

"I hate to tell you this when you've been through so much already. But I promised there'd be no more secrets between us, so as much as you deserve a break, you also deserve to know: Andrea Robinson called me the other day."

A pit formed in Jessie's stomach. It had been a while since she'd last heard that name. Most recently it was when Andy had tried to kill herself after Jessie wouldn't visit her at the psychiatric prison where she was being held.

"Okay," Jessie said warily. "Why?"

"She said that the Night Hunter would manipulate me to get to you. She warned me that if I wasn't careful, I would put you in danger."

"Well, she was off on that one," Jessie said. "Like I told you, you're the one who warned us."

"Eventually, yes," Kat conceded. "But he *did* manipulate me. I read that crumpled note in the used car at that dealership, just like he wanted. I went to that vacant building in Pasadena and called you, which led him to find out where you were. Robinson was right. I don't know how, but she predicted all of it."

"So what are you saying?" Jessie asked, "That I should ask Decker to let her join HSS?"

"No Jessie," Kat said, not amused. "I'm saying that a fabulously wealthy, mentally unstable murderer who once tried to kill you is thinking about you a lot. I'm saying that you should be careful."

CHAPTER FORTY THREE

"Morning sunshine!"

Startled, Jessie turned around to see that Ryan had made it down the hill. She waved to him and spoke quietly into the phone.

"I hear you, Kat. But Ryan is coming over and I don't want him to have to deal with this right now. Talk later, okay?"

"Okay. Take care," Kat replied and hung up.

Jessie put her phone away and told herself to smile so that Ryan wouldn't be suspicious.

"Morning yourself, early riser," she said. "Are you an aspiring mountain climber now?"

He laughed at the idea.

"Are you kidding?" he said. "That hill wiped me out. I'm just glad there was snow to break my fall if my legs gave out."

"They seemed to operate pretty well last night when you tackled that bastard."

"I got lucky," he said dismissively.

"You don't do lucky, Ryan Hernandez," she said, giving him a kiss.

"I got lucky when I met you," he countered.

She blushed despite herself. As much as she loved what he said, she was equally relieved. Either he wasn't holding her "quivering mess after Trembley was killed" comment against her or he was an incredible actor. Either way, she was happy to play along.

"Listen to you, all romantic first thing in the morning."

"It's almost eleven," he pointed out.

"Being less romantic now," she noted.

"Sorry," he said. "I actually did see something romantic earlier. Did you notice the fountain in the yard over there?"

Jessie looked where he was pointing. There was indeed a small fountain with some kind of sculpture in the center of it, though she couldn't see it clearly.

"What is it?" she asked.

"Check it out," he said, taking her hand and leading her through the snow. As they walked over, she looked over at him.

"Are we going to talk about it?"

"About what," he asked nervously.

"About how my sister gunned down an unarmed man last night," she replied, surprised that didn't know what she referencing immediately.

"Oh right, of course. I guess I just hoped we could put that discussion off for a little while. It seems like it might be a long one."

"Yeah," she agreed, "And we probably don't want to have that discussion with two U.S. marshals nearby. I guess we can hold off until we get back."

"Sounds good," Ryan said, relieved. "For now let's put that out of heads and focus on the pretty fountain."

When they got closer, she saw what was in the middle of it—a small sculpture in the classical Greek style. A naked man and woman were entwined with arms wrapped around each other. It was hard to discern where one body ended and the other began.

"This town is full of surprises," she said.

It really is," he agreed, before his smile turned into a frown. "What's that?"

He pointed to what looked like a small, plastic grocery bag at the base of the fountain. Bending down carefully, he picked it up. There was something in it.

"Be careful," Jessie warned, suddenly on edge. "We can't be sure Wally didn't leave that as some last-ditch measure to take us out."

"You think he left a bomb in a plastic bag by a fountain?" Ryan asked skeptically.

"I wouldn't put it past him."

"I guess we're about to find out," he replied untying the bag and reaching in.

"Ryan!" she said urgently, dismayed at how careless he was being.

Oblivious, he grabbed hold of something and pulled it out. When he opened his hand, she realized what it was: a small, black ring box. Just as she was processing that fact, he bent down on one knee, his leg sinking into the snow.

"What the—?" she began. She didn't even know how to finish the sentence. Her throat went dry and her heart threatened to pound out of her chest.

"Jessie Hunt," he said, looking up into her eyes, "Since the first moment I saw you in Professor Hosta's criminology class, I couldn't take my eyes off you. Over the years, we've been partners, friends, and then, to my great joy, something much more. Nothing would make me happier than being your husband. I want to wake up every morning with you beside me. I want to grow old with you. I want us to go from comparing scars to comparing wrinkles. Jessie, will you marry me?"

NOW AVAILABLE!

THE PERFECT IMAGE
(A Jessie Hunt Psychological Suspense Thriller—Book Sixteen)

"A masterpiece of thriller and mystery. Blake Pierce did a magnificent job developing characters with a psychological side so well described that we feel inside their minds, follow their fears and cheer for their success. Full of twists, this book will keep you awake until the turn of the last page."
--Books and Movie Reviews, Roberto Mattos (re *Once Gone*)

THE PERFECT IMAGE is book #16 in a new psychological suspense series by bestselling author Blake Pierce, which begins with *The Perfect Wife*, a #1 bestseller (and free download) with over 5,000 five-star ratings and 900 five-star reviews.

In a high-end Los Angeles suburb, wealthy wives are being found dead in their luxurious homes, with seemingly no connection. As Jessie plunges deeper into their exclusive world of clubs, lunches, vacations and every possible perk, she quickly realizes that appearances are not what they seem in their silver-spooned world—and that a killer is actively hunting amongst them.

A fast-paced psychological suspense thriller with unforgettable characters and heart-pounding suspense, THE JESSIE HUNT series is a riveting new series that will leave you turning pages late into the night.

Books #17 (THE PERFECT VEIL) and #18 (THE PERFECT INDISCRECTION) and #19 (THE PERFECT RUMOR) will be available soon.

Blake Pierce

Blake Pierce is the USA Today bestselling author of the RILEY PAGE mystery series, which includes seventeen books. Blake Pierce is also the author of the MACKENZIE WHITE mystery series, comprising fourteen books; of the AVERY BLACK mystery series, comprising six books; of the KERI LOCKE mystery series, comprising five books; of the MAKING OF RILEY PAIGE mystery series, comprising six books; of the KATE WISE mystery series, comprising seven books; of the CHLOE FINE psychological suspense mystery, comprising six books; of the JESSE HUNT psychological suspense thriller series, comprising nineteen books; of the AU PAIR psychological suspense thriller series, comprising three books; of the ZOE PRIME mystery series, comprising six books; of the ADELE SHARP mystery series, comprising thirteen books, of the EUROPEAN VOYAGE cozy mystery series, comprising six books (and counting); of the new LAURA FROST FBI suspense thriller, comprising four books (and counting); of the new ELLA DARK FBI suspense thriller, comprising six books (and counting); of the A YEAR IN EUROPE cozy mystery series, comprising nine books, of the AVA GOLD mystery series, comprising three books (and counting); and of the RACHEL GIFT mystery series, comprising three books (and counting).

An avid reader and lifelong fan of the mystery and thriller genres, Blake loves to hear from you, so please feel free to visit www.blakepierceauthor.com to learn more and stay in touch.

BOOKS BY BLAKE PIERCE

RACHEL GIFT MYSTERY SERIES
HER LAST WISH (Book #1)
HER LAST CHANCE (Book #2)
HER LAST HOPE (Book #3)

AVA GOLD MYSTERY SERIES
CITY OF PREY (Book #1)
CITY OF FEAR (Book #2)
CITY OF BONES (Book #3)

A YEAR IN EUROPE
A MURDER IN PARIS (Book #1)
DEATH IN FLORENCE (Book #2)
VENGEANCE IN VIENNA (Book #3)
A FATALITY IN SPAIN (Book #4)
SCANDAL IN LONDON (Book #5)
AN IMPOSTOR IN DUBLIN (Book #6)
SEDUCTION IN BORDEAUX (Book #7)
JEALOUSY IN SWITZERLAND (Book #8)
A DEBACLE IN PRAGUE (Book #9)

ELLA DARK FBI SUSPENSE THRILLER
GIRL, ALONE (Book #1)
GIRL, TAKEN (Book #2)
GIRL, HUNTED (Book #3)
GIRL, SILENCED (Book #4)
GIRL, VANISHED (Book 5)
GIRL ERASED (Book #6)

LAURA FROST FBI SUSPENSE THRILLER
ALREADY GONE (Book #1)
ALREADY SEEN (Book #2)
ALREADY TRAPPED (Book #3)
ALREADY MISSING (Book #4)

EUROPEAN VOYAGE COZY MYSTERY SERIES
MURDER (AND BAKLAVA) (Book #1)
DEATH (AND APPLE STRUDEL) (Book #2)

CRIME (AND LAGER) (Book #3)
MISFORTUNE (AND GOUDA) (Book #4)
CALAMITY (AND A DANISH) (Book #5)
MAYHEM (AND HERRING) (Book #6)

ADELE SHARP MYSTERY SERIES
LEFT TO DIE (Book #1)
LEFT TO RUN (Book #2)
LEFT TO HIDE (Book #3)
LEFT TO KILL (Book #4)
LEFT TO MURDER (Book #5)
LEFT TO ENVY (Book #6)
LEFT TO LAPSE (Book #7)
LEFT TO VANISH (Book #8)
LEFT TO HUNT (Book #9)
LEFT TO FEAR (Book #10)
LEFT TO PREY (Book #11)
LEFT TO LURE (Book #12)
LEFT TO CRAVE (Book #13)

THE AU PAIR SERIES
ALMOST GONE (Book#1)
ALMOST LOST (Book #2)
ALMOST DEAD (Book #3)

ZOE PRIME MYSTERY SERIES
FACE OF DEATH (Book#1)
FACE OF MURDER (Book #2)
FACE OF FEAR (Book #3)
FACE OF MADNESS (Book #4)
FACE OF FURY (Book #5)
FACE OF DARKNESS (Book #6)

A JESSIE HUNT PSYCHOLOGICAL SUSPENSE SERIES
THE PERFECT WIFE (Book #1)
THE PERFECT BLOCK (Book #2)
THE PERFECT HOUSE (Book #3)
THE PERFECT SMILE (Book #4)
THE PERFECT LIE (Book #5)
THE PERFECT LOOK (Book #6)

THE PERFECT AFFAIR (Book #7)
THE PERFECT ALIBI (Book #8)
THE PERFECT NEIGHBOR (Book #9)
THE PERFECT DISGUISE (Book #10)
THE PERFECT SECRET (Book #11)
THE PERFECT FAÇADE (Book #12)
THE PERFECT IMPRESSION (Book #13)
THE PERFECT DECEIT (Book #14)
THE PERFECT MISTRESS (Book #15)
THE PERFECT IMAGE (Book #16)
THE PERFECT VEIL (Book #17)
THE PERFECT INDISCRETION (Book #18)
THE PERFECT RUMOR (Book #19)

CHLOE FINE PSYCHOLOGICAL SUSPENSE SERIES
NEXT DOOR (Book #1)
A NEIGHBOR'S LIE (Book #2)
CUL DE SAC (Book #3)
SILENT NEIGHBOR (Book #4)
HOMECOMING (Book #5)
TINTED WINDOWS (Book #6)

KATE WISE MYSTERY SERIES
IF SHE KNEW (Book #1)
IF SHE SAW (Book #2)
IF SHE RAN (Book #3)
IF SHE HID (Book #4)
IF SHE FLED (Book #5)
IF SHE FEARED (Book #6)
IF SHE HEARD (Book #7)

THE MAKING OF RILEY PAIGE SERIES
WATCHING (Book #1)
WAITING (Book #2)
LURING (Book #3)
TAKING (Book #4)
STALKING (Book #5)
KILLING (Book #6)

RILEY PAIGE MYSTERY SERIES

ONCE GONE (Book #1)
ONCE TAKEN (Book #2)
ONCE CRAVED (Book #3)
ONCE LURED (Book #4)
ONCE HUNTED (Book #5)
ONCE PINED (Book #6)
ONCE FORSAKEN (Book #7)
ONCE COLD (Book #8)
ONCE STALKED (Book #9)
ONCE LOST (Book #10)
ONCE BURIED (Book #11)
ONCE BOUND (Book #12)
ONCE TRAPPED (Book #13)
ONCE DORMANT (Book #14)
ONCE SHUNNED (Book #15)
ONCE MISSED (Book #16)
ONCE CHOSEN (Book #17)

MACKENZIE WHITE MYSTERY SERIES
BEFORE HE KILLS (Book #1)
BEFORE HE SEES (Book #2)
BEFORE HE COVETS (Book #3)
BEFORE HE TAKES (Book #4)
BEFORE HE NEEDS (Book #5)
BEFORE HE FEELS (Book #6)
BEFORE HE SINS (Book #7)
BEFORE HE HUNTS (Book #8)
BEFORE HE PREYS (Book #9)
BEFORE HE LONGS (Book #10)
BEFORE HE LAPSES (Book #11)
BEFORE HE ENVIES (Book #12)
BEFORE HE STALKS (Book #13)
BEFORE HE HARMS (Book #14)

AVERY BLACK MYSTERY SERIES
CAUSE TO KILL (Book #1)
CAUSE TO RUN (Book #2)
CAUSE TO HIDE (Book #3)
CAUSE TO FEAR (Book #4)
CAUSE TO SAVE (Book #5)

CAUSE TO DREAD (Book #6)

KERI LOCKE MYSTERY SERIES
A TRACE OF DEATH (Book #1)
A TRACE OF MURDER (Book #2)
A TRACE OF VICE (Book #3)
A TRACE OF CRIME (Book #4)
A TRACE OF HOPE (Book #5)

CPSIA information can be obtained
at www.ICGtesting.com
Printed in the USA
LVHW111156160821
695402LV00001B/56